30 Days Lost

By

Haris Khan

Copyright © 2022 by – Haris Khan – All Rights Reserved.

It is not legal to reproduce, duplicate, or transmit any part of this document in either electronic means or printed format. Recording of this publication is strictly prohibited.

Table of Contents

Part 1..1

    Chapter 1: Nothing Special 1

    Chapter 2: Fight for Survival 27

    Chapter 3: The Dream...48

    Chapter 4: The Heist 66

    Chapter 5: The Footage 77

    Chapter 6: The Briefcase...100

    Chapter 7: Back to School 118

    Chapter 8: The Speech 133

Part 2..146

    Chapter 9: What Happens Next................................146

    Chapter 10: The Final Test.......................................150

    Chapter 11: Sanctuary 166

    Chapter 12: The Message...184

    Chapter 13: New World Order..................................199

    Chapter 14: The Alignment of Fates 218

    Chapter 15: The Mind Emporium 241

    Epilogue: 14 Days Later...269

Part 1

Chapter 1: Nothing Special

Boring would be an understatement. The lesson had been going on for an hour and I wanted to stick pins in my ears. I hated Economics, wished I had never chosen it as an A-Level. First thing on a Monday too, Sheesh. Mr Griffin was blabbing on about Aggregate Demand. I honestly could not care less. Who needs Economics? Just print more money and tell nobody about it. Problem solved. At that moment, my eyelids started to feel heavy. They were being pulled close by an indescribable fatigue.

It was at that moment that a crash could be heard, awakening me from my slumber. Within the blink of an eye, the entire set had clambered to the window to see what had happened. Gaping through the glass, I could make out a colossal, well-built man who appeared to be at least 7 foot. His head was bald and shining, and he wore dark sunglasses covering his eyes. His arms were built like tree trunks with his hands being the literal definition of power. My jaw dropped when I saw that clasped in his hands was the neck of Johnny the Groundskeeper.

The Stranger was squeezing the life out of Johnny using all his strength. All of a sudden, he reached into his pocket and pulled out a silver hilt that gleamed in the sunlight, intricate with buttons and shapes of all sizes. With a flick of his chunky finger, the Stranger pressed a button on the hilt which whirred and suddenly a burst of flames erupted out. The 10-foot flame ripped through Johnny's body, instantly disintegrating him. The man instantaneously glowed before meta morphing into a pile of ash. His skull fell from his singed body and plummeted to the earth. The Stranger stepped on the skull and crushed it under is supreme might. He then whipped off his sunglasses and tore off his face as if it were a piece of paper, revealing a cybernetic monstrosity. His laser eyes pointed like daggers and his teeth were razors. There was an android in my school!

With a mechanical whir, he turned his head and looked at me, dead in the eyes, through the window. The sheer fear I felt made me feel lifeless. The whole class started screaming while the school alarms blared out. The machine was still looking at me, staring into my soul, ready to slaughter me and devour my organs. With a sonic pound, it blasted off the floor and into my direction. The glass between us rippled and shattered into tiny diamonds before scattering around the room. Out of nowhere, the machine's metal fist connected with my cheekbone, sending shockwaves through my body. He sent me flying across the room until my body slammed against the whiteboard. In a frenzy, the machine started throwing punches at all the members of my class. Pupils were flying all over the room while Mr Griffin was hiding under his desk, pupils wide, and sweat dripping.

Once again, the machine ignited the hilt and hell was let loose. The fire blazed and started melting the desks. The flame burnt through the wall and into the adjacent classroom. I knew that this would be the end for me as clearly I stood no chance against this machine. But then neither did anyone else. If anyone could save the day, it would have to be me. Frantically, I felt around for any sort of weapon that could be used. *Pencil, no. Ruler, no. Chair?* I grabbed hold of a chair before charging forward and smacking it into the machine's head. It was briefly knocked down only for it to jump back onto its feet with inhuman precision. I kept on hitting it with the chair, again and again and again. However, it was not long before the leg on the chair snapped off. This was futile.

With the machine momentarily knocked down, I looked for any other sort of weapon. And that was when it hit me. Within the burnt hole in the wall, were several exposed wires. I seized a bunch of them and shoved them into the machine's eye socket. For a brief moment, that felt like an eternity, nothing happened. But out of nowhere, the machine's eyes got brighter and brighter. It started to make cackling noises and smoke burst from its head while it frantically rushed around. Its head spun continuously while sparks of light burst out. The Android walked around with its legs like that of a baby walking for the first time. Its steps were random as it headed for the window. Before long, it completely stopped moving, the whirring stopped and it just stood there. The machine fell flat, toppling over the window ledge, falling down to a concrete demise.

The class looked around. There was an awkward second of realisation as to what I had just done. The silence broke into thunderous applause as I had saved the school. It was all me. The class surrounded me and started cheering.

"Jason, Jason, Jason!" My name was chanted through the halls.

"Jason, Jason, Jason!" my name echoed through the school. I was a hero and would be remembered forever. My portrait would be kept next to the headmaster's desk in his office. My name would be engraved on a bench and even the new teaching block would be named after me. When people thought of 'The Queen's School', they would think of me, Jason Clyde, the boy who saved the lives of thousands.

"Jason, Jason, Jason!" The chants were getting louder and louder, somewhat intimidating with a hint of aggressiveness.

"JASON!"

The sound of Mr Griffin's voice yanked me out of my moment of glory. I looked around, and the room was back to normal. The Aggregate Demand Diagrams were still on the board. Everyone was seated and the robot was nowhere to be seen. I glanced at the clock and it read 09:05. Only 5 minutes of the two-hour lesson had passed.

"Nice of you to join us again," Mr Griffin said restlessly.

I was planted back into my normal, boring, dull, miserable, unfair life and so looked out the window, hoping with every cell of my body that an evil robot would show up. Just imagine.

My story began about 2 months ago, Monday October 7th, 2019. I had just finished my first full month of Sixth Form at 'The Queen's School' in London. It is a posh private school with magnificent buildings, huge sports fields and even a state-of-the-art concert hall. However, the problem with going to such a good school is that everyone was so clever. Too clever in fact. Queen's boys were all high-flying students. The majority of them being the children of CEOs of big companies. They would spend all their holidays going on exotic holidays such as safaris, scuba diving and skiing. Skiing was by far the most popular holiday from Queen's pupils. I'd never been skiing and if somebody asked why not, it was simply due to the fact that I did not want to break a bone. Definitely not because my parents were not well off enough to afford it. Every term, there was at least one boy on crutches or with a sling. You did not even have to ask about the cause of injury, as you knew it was from skiing. There was also the occasional rugby injury amongst pupils.

Skiing, the world's biggest killer of rich boys. It was either that or drug abuse. Queen's boys were so intelligent when it came to drugs that they know the best hiding spots on the school site. You wouldn't expect well off kids to be so naughty, but you would be surprised. Most kids used their parents' money to buy themself some top of the range cocaine. They also had very expensive vapes so whenever you would enter the boys' changing room, there would be an expectation to be smothered by the combined smell of deodorant and cherry flavoured vape.

Queen's boys would act as if the world revolved around them. If they would ever cross the road at a green light, they would blame it on the driver if anyone crashed into them. But the thing is, Queen's boys would never cross roads nor would they even walk anywhere. They either had a chauffeur driving them everywhere or they would take a taxi. I remember taking the bus with one of my friends once. It was his first ever time taking one and so tried to pay the bus fare using a £50 pound note. When the driver said no, he then offered to PayPal him money directly into his bank account. The situation could not have been more awkward.

The thing is, it can be nice to have rich friends. Whenever I went to a restaurant with a friend, I would always pick the most expensive meal because I knew that my one of my friends would pay for me. But that was only when I went out with a friend, which is very rare. *I wonder why?* There was this one time where I was invited to my friend's local country club to have 'supper'. (There are 5 meals a day for Queen's kids. There is breakfast, then there is the 'late morning refreshment'. Next there is luncheon. A drop of Afternoon tea is next, and the day finishes with supper).

The country club was full of 50-year-old pale white men all dressed in white. I, on the other hand was wearing a school shirt (The nicest thing in my cupboard). We had English breakfast tea along with French toast for starters. For the main course, we had Mediterranean Shrimp Kabobs which was interesting to say the least. And for dessert, a slice of Madeira cake. When I say slice, I mean a slither at best. It appears the richer you get, the smaller the portion sizes are. With a £20 note at McDonald's I can get about six Big Macs. In the rich world, I can get a vegan beetroot breaded burger with crusted sweet potato for the same £20. And that would be if I was lucky. The food would all be organic, of course. But this is all besides the point as I just wanted to explain the kind of people that I went to school with.

Back to the present. Economics, 9:05am, Monday, bored as hell. There are seven of us in our set. There's me, Jason, legendary outlaw, ladies' man and all-round great guy. Moving on, we have the genius of the class, Raj. He is my closest friend and the boy is literally a walking calculator. When he was not in school, he would either be reading textbooks or taking part in maths Olympiads. I am pretty sure he was so clever that the school would pay him to attend. He once scored 190 in an online IQ test. But then again, you can never really trust online tests.

Next, we have Haresh Reeshvam. He was the class clown and the kind of guy who pretended to be dumb but was secretly a genius. His Dad was the founder of the internationally famous cleaning brand 'Easy Peasy Reeshy Cleany'. Honestly Haresh was so rich that I was surprised that he even needed to attend school. Just by inheriting his dad's company, he would be set for life.

Boris Brown was the literal definition of public-school boy. He was a tall, 6-foot, boy and the son of wealthy parents. He had a chauffeur that drove him to and from school every day in a Bentley. He was almost always late to every lesson mainly due to the fact that he would buy coffee from the Sixth Form Café. You would be hard pressed to ever find Boris without a cup of coffee in hand. Also do not get me started on the state of his hair. For someone so rich, you would think he could afford a decent trim.

Wilfred Campbell was the 'gadget guy' of the set. He always had the latest iPhone, iPad, Apple Watch. At this rate, he might as well have sold his soul to Apple. He used his smartwatch to cheat in every test and got away with it. Mainly because Mr Griffin did not know what a smart watch was.

Yaseen Hussain was the nicest guy I know. His smile was a permanent feature to his face. He had a calm, stoic attitude which I admired. He also looked way too old for school with his large masculine jaw along with his 5 o'clock shadow. Whenever I tried growing out my facial hair, I just end up with a few strands of uneven fluff.

Frank Clifford was the son of the Prime Minister, Ted Clifford. Yes, you heard me correctly. The son of the Prime Minister went to Queen's and was in my class. His dad was the CEO of an energy company before he went into politics. Frank's dad wanted him to be home-schooled, but the boy said that he wanted to be 'among the people'. Frank mainly came into school to socialise and play rugby, the two things that he was decent at. He would break as many school rules as he desired knowing that the school did not have the guts to complain to his father. Which was true.

So that was my Economics class. As you can see, they were all pretty interesting characters. Do not get me started on the people that were in my other subject classes or we could be here all day. Now you are probably wondering what I was doing in such a rich school. My parents were not rich. Mum was a teacher and Dad was an accountant. The wealth all came from my older brother Julian, who was a world-famous brain surgeon. He was constantly travelling the world, making breakthroughs in science. He opted to pay for my school education so that I could become more like him.

Julian went to 'The Queen's School' several years ago with a full scholarship. He then went on to become the lead actor in the School Play, the top school musician and even went on to become Head Boy. On his last year of school, he was given an unconditional offer from Oxford to study Medicine there. He completed the entire course, with a first, in only two years and then after that went on to do big things. And meanwhile, little old me was being overshadowed by his great success. People at school did not know me as Jason. They knew me as Julian's younger, inferior brother. It was a shame that nobody could see me for who I truly was.

"Okay, the lesson is over now. Remember to bring in your homework for this Thursday's lesson." Mr Griffin mumbled.

Now was my chance, I paced out of the classroom and breathed in the fresh air. Freedom never felt so good.

"Jason, are you okay?" spoke a gentle voice.

I spun around only to see Yaseen.

"Why are you asking?" I replied.

"Nothing, it's just that you seemed a bit out of it today. Is everything okay at home?" This guy was too nice.

"Thank you for caring, I really appreciate it. Everything at home is fine, it's just that I do not think that school is cut out for me. These last few days have been so boring." Yaseen's attention had gone to his watch.

"I'm so sorry Jason, I have got Chemistry now. See you at lunch."

And with that, Yaseen briskly walked to his next lesson. He had a thing for being late. For him, being on time was just as bad as being late.

What lesson do I have now? I thought to myself, awkwardly feeling around for my timetable in my pocket, I slowly discovered what time it was.

It was 'Free Period Time'.

Or 'Study Period Time', as the would school call it. There was no way I was doing any work, especially not Mr Griffin's homework. Didn't he realise that I had a full schedule? When I was not saving the world from Android from the future, I liked to have some time for recreational activities.

Whilst on my way to the Sixth Form Centre, I could make out a shadowed figure coming towards me. He was tall with dark curly hair and stubble was beginning to spout from his chin. It was my form tutor, Mr Grove.

"Hi Jason, I hear you have a Study Period." he said in his thick yet soft voice. "Do you have a moment to come to my classroom? I have something to discuss with you."

"Erm, Yeah sure. I will be right there". I assumed that this was regarding my upcoming Nobel Prize nomination or something of that importance. Nobody interrupted my busy schedule without a solid reason.

Mr Grove's classroom was relatively small, fitting about 10 people maximum. French cinema posters were plastered across the wall. To my right there was a large verb conjugation table. Mr Grove sat in front of me at his desk where there was a computer and a multitude of sheets sprawled in all directions. I could make out a vocab test with a mark of 20/20. Mr Grove had stuck on a bright illuminous sticker. The word 'Bravo' was written in bold. However, on the bottom of the page, there was a large coffee mug stain. From its smudging it was clear that the teacher had tried to wipe it away but had only made it worse.

The chairs at the school were so uncomfortable. You would think that a school with so much money could invest into more luxurious chairs. The more comfortable they were, the more we would focus meaning that we would get better grades. That would boost the school's morale resulting in more parents sending their children to Queen's. That was some A* evaluation right there. My point was that the chair that I was planted in was like sitting on sandpaper. Any attempt of cushioning had completely withered away. It was so hard to listen to Mr Grove when all I could think about was by posterior and whether or not I would be able to walk after this meeting.

"Jason, I have had the personal pleasure of being your tutor for all these years. I knew your brother before you, and you have shown greater initiative than him. The energy you have taken into your lessons is admirable. Every term you ace your tests clearly demonstrating that you are on top of your game. I honestly think that this school is not good enough for you. Mr Ford, our headmaster and I have had a long discussion about what to do about you because we want what is best for you. And so, we have decided to let you go. You are too clever for school and so no longer need to attend considering you have learnt everything already. I believe this is goodbye. Today will be your last day of school."

No Nobel Prize? That's a shame, I honestly deserve that but I'll take a 2 year study leave instead. I thought to myself, reminiscing a perfect timeline. Of course Mr Grove did not say any of that. The only time he had ever complimented me was when I went up from a C+ to a B- in Physics.

"Jason," he paused for a moment. I could tell he was thinking of the politest way of telling me off.

"Jason, I admire your effort this term. Your attendance has been perfect." Of course he would mention the one thing I was not in control of. Mum would kill me if I even took half a day off school. If I was ever sick, she would just push me out the house and claim that my vomiting would just be the result of a bad night.

"Jason, we need to talk about your grades." *Oh Boy, this is bad.* Mr Grove had said my name three times in the last ten seconds. My grades honestly could not be that bad. Mr Griffin probably gave me a B and I should have got an A in Maths. Maths was my strongest subject and Physics was just Maths in disguise, so that should be an easy A.

"Here they are." Mr Grove handed over a small A5 sheet of paper.

MATHS B

PHYSICS B

ECONOMICS C

What!? Economics C. Mr Griffin is so stupid. Nobody gives the great Jason a C. What had I done to deserve a C? It was at that moment that I realised that I should have just dropped out of school and pursued my dreams. I should have just gone home to look for a spider and get it to bite me, becoming a superhero and enjoying the rest of my life. And now it was time to prepare for what came next, the speech from Mr Grove and the inevitable speech from my parents. The speech where they all would say that I would never live up to Julian.

"I know this may come as a shock Jason, despite your hard work. You are a good person at heart and you have been trying, but these grades are really not acceptable at this school. I have been informed to have a chat with your parents about this. Ever since Sixth Form has begun, your grades have been dropping." A trickle of sweat rolled down from his forehead. Mr Grove's eyes were flickering from side to side, unable to make eye contact with me. My bad grades looked bad on his reputation. Every teacher wanted to have a tutee like Raj. In fact, Raj's tutor, Mr Olson, just got promoted to Head of Maths. *I wonder why.*

"Mr Griffin even emailed me this morning to tell me that you fell asleep in his lesson. He seems rather unsettled by your recent behaviour and said that in your most recent essay you scored 9/25. You seriously need to pull your act together Jason. You know Julian-"

Urgh, he said the J-word. Why did everything have to come back to him? His tremendous shadow had ruined my life. You know it was unfair to compare the two of us because my parents invested everything into him. All their money, time, even their love. I decided to just stare at the ground and face the music. *Hey, there seems to be an interesting stone on the ground. I should analyse that for the next 5 minutes.*

The stone and I bonded quite a lot over those 5 minutes. He was telling me that he got deported from the school grounds and had been separated from the rest of his family after some Year 9 pupil kicked him into this classroom. He had been through quite a lot and I felt sorry for him.

"Jason, are you listening?" The voice of Mr Grove pulled me out of my heart to heart. Or heart to stone.

"Yessir," I murmured, straightening my back.

"Well then, I have said my part. Make sure you work extra hard this next term. Your teachers will be giving you predicted A-Level grades at the end of the academic year."

Before exiting the classroom, I bent down and grabbed the stone. He felt light in my hands but was rough and jagged after years of abuse. Mr Grove looked at me, puzzled. I gingerly carried my new friend over to the gravel bed and reunited him with his family. The stone saluted to me before rolling off to be with his species. It was such a beautiful sight to behold that a tear came to my eye. I then glanced to my watch. It was 10:40 and so I still had 20 more minutes of my free period.

The Queen's School Sixth Form Centre, you will never find a more wretched hive of scum and villainy. *Sorry, I can't help it with the Star Wars reference.* There were five sections to the centre. By the entrance we had the office filled with the teachers including the Head of Sixth Form, Mr Gideon. We then had the first area by the windows. The further you went into the centre, the more 'cool' you were. The nerds were at the front, the ones who were socially inept and just went on their phones all day. Teachers' pets, nerds and geeks, could all be found here. Behind the sofas you had the main area where you could find the Sixth Form Café. This was where the majority of people would hang out. By the café, you would always find Boris topping up his coffee. You would go to the main section if you wanted some real friends and wanted a good laugh.

The back area was where you would find the coolest people. These were the people who would just lounge around all day and would never work. At the very back you would find the bathrooms / changing rooms where the coolest people stay, i.e., where all the drugs were taken, and the vapes were vaped. Teachers would not dare to step foot within the toilets.

I stepped foot into the building and was overwhelmed by the noise. Even during free periods, the place was heaving. To my right were the sofas where Raj looked up from his phone and nodded at me. The nerds were all on their phones, as usual, with headphones in. The time had come for me to ascend the social hierarchy and so I walked forward instead of turning right. The time had come for me to claim my spot amongst the cool people. Not the very cool or coolest, just cool. Baby steps. As Neil Armstrong said, 'One small step for man, one giant leap for mankind'.

Each step felt like I was being pulled back. I felt the force of Raj and the others pulling me back with all their strength. They needed my friendship but I had to move on and so trudged through the thick mud with extreme weather raging overhead. I was on a treadmill with the wind slapping me backwards. Nature had turned against me but the war was not yet over. Using the last of my will power, I took one final step into the cool area. *Good job Jason, Phase 1 is now complete.* A bunch of cool kids halted their conversation and looked up at me. I had not spoken to these guys for the last three years. They were probably talking about football. What was I going to say? *Erm, yes well.* My brain cells had decided to go for their lunch break. I suddenly knew what to do; go to the toilet. I briskly paced off to the bathroom where a new plan would be constructed.

Upon entering the bathroom, I was smothered by the stench of fruit. Wilfred was sitting down, vaping. His mouth was like the exhaust of a car from the sheer quantity of fumes coming out. I burst into a toilet cubicle and locked the door. It was time to make a plan B. I needed to become cool quick, so maybe if I asked Wilfred for some vape it would make me feel cooler. Actually I would rather not get suspended. When one of the coolest kids vape, they would get away with it, but if I were to, then it would be an instant suspension. It was almost as if being cool gave you total immunity from breaking the school rules. Upon exiting, I decided that it would probably be best to do Mr Griffin's homework. The sense of defeat was overwhelming, but my studies did have to take priority else the Grove would strike back.

Break time at Queen's usually consisted of everyone getting into their friendship groups, standing up and chatting. Even though the entire Sixth Form Centre was littered with seats of all kind, Queen's pupils preferred to stand. I had never understood why. Amongst my group of friends, we had the following:

Raj, who you knew about. Tim was my childhood friend. We had known each other for about 10 years now. Lewis was always on his phone but would always randomly put it away to ask deep questions or to input his controversial opinion on a topic. There were some other people in the friendship group who had not spoken a word all term and so I did not know their names. How did they even make friends with us?

While Lewis was going on about whether or not a straw had two holes, I could make out a boy approaching the door to the building. He was struggling along and clinging onto his crutches for dear life. It was my friend, Bruce. His arms were skinny and wobbled on top of the crutches like the legs of a baby deer learning to walk. His legs on the other hand were giant and built like engines. I swiftly swung open the doors to let Bruce inside. He hobbled on into the room, smiling at me as he went past.

"Bruce, what happened to you?" I asked.

"Rugby," he moaned. Bruce was the nerdiest of the nerds of our group. He was a huge Doctor Who fan and had probably seen every episode multiple times. When he spoke, he would always reference obscure books and TV shows that nobody had ever watched or heard about. Bruce was also a very tall person, 6 foot 2. He once tried out for the school rugby team and the school liked his performance. He now played in the First Team for rugby alongside the other cool kids such as Frank, Boris, Wilfred and Haresh. Ever since he got into the team, he had been skipping comic conventions to go to the gym. He even shaved his head at one point to fit in with them. That did not go well for him as the school suspended him for 'looking too threatening'. Those were the school's words, not mine.

"You've got a lot of nerve showing up here!" Came a voice, booming from across the hall. It cut through all the conversations of everybody, slicing through the entire year. I spun round to see Frank storming across the sixth form centre. He looked like a tiger, ready for bloodshed. He pointed his finger at Bruce and yelled:

"We lost that match because of you!" Frank's fists were clenched and his veins were popping in his forehead. Even though Frank was the most powerful person in the school and the most wealthy, he still dressed as if he was off the streets. His shirt was untucked and his tie was loosened to the point where it could just slip off. Frank had the power to get away with anything he wanted which was why he would break all the uniform rules. His hair was shaven to a number 3. As with Bruce, the school was usually very strict about having hair too short, but when it concerned Frank, the rules would no longer exist.

"I am sorry, it was not my fault," Bruce squealed, gesturing to the cast on his leg. Frank stormed up to Bruce and yanked his crutch away from him. Instantly, the boy fell forward and smacked his face onto the floor. I rushed down to Bruce and tried to pull him up as his nose was oozing out blood. Enraged, I stood up and stared at Frank. So far, today had been a really bad day and thus I would have gladly taken it out on someone.

"You can't just do that to someone," I cried.

"Out of the way, nerd!" yelled Frank. *Just some generic bully dialogue.* I refused to walk away since it was time that Frank had learnt his lesson. He could not just get away with constantly abusing his power and not facing the consequences of his actions.

"Leave them Frank," replied Haresh. "He is not worth our time." Frank was now a raging bull who was preparing to charge. With one hand, he clutched the crutch he had stolen. He began to charge towards me and thrusted the pole into my stomach. A sharp pain burst through me straight away, knocking me back. For a moment, I felt dazed and confused but then my senses returned to me and so stood my ground. I seized the crutch out of his left hand and prepared for my counterattack which was cut short by a right jab to the nose. I pulled back in disarray and fell to the ground, dripping blood. It was no use, Frank had won. The bully looked down on me while Bruce lay there unconscious. Now a swarm of pupils had surrounded us completely, shocked at the spectacle.

"Stop that right now!" The voice of Mr Gideon, the head of Sixth Form, boomed from across the corridor. The crowd of pupils split like the Red Sea to let him walk through.

"Frank, I have had enough of this behaviour from you. This is the end!" The teacher gazed at me and then to the crippled Bruce on the ground. "You are suspended for the rest of this week".

"No, Father will not allow that," Frank growled. "He can have this entire school converted into a car park if he wants and can even turn all you teachers into dustbin workers."

"I have your father on the phone now, Frank," Mr Gideon uttered calmly. He passed on his phone to Frank. For a brief moment, there was complete silence. Frank had a distraught look on his face. Some muffled noises could be heard through the phone. After returning the phone back to Mr Gideon, he turned his back and ran out through the doors leaving no trace. Frank was gone.

After Luke Skywalker blew up the Death Star, there was a huge ceremony where he was given a medal for his heroism. Now when I had saved someone, my reward was simply a trip to the school nurse. And my medal was an icepack on my head.

"Bruce is okay, he just needs some rest. In case you are wondering," spoke the School Nurse. "Should I put some television on for you". The perks of going to such a rich school.

"Yes please," I exclaimed. She switched on the TV which was relatively small yet sufficient. The local news was playing.

"And now we go live to Downing Street where the Prime Minister Theodore Clifford shall speak". *Not another Clifford.* The screen changed to the front of 10 Downing Street. The house looked as normal and in front of it stood Frank's Dad. He stood on a podium with a microphone in front of him. Ted Clifford was immaculately dressed. He wore a black 3-piece suit and had a blue tie. His brown hair with streaks of grey was neatly combed to the right and was shining from an overdose of gel. He was relatively chubby with traces of a double chin as well as his jacket being barely able to button up. The smile on his face however was permanent, with large wrinkles on his cheeks from all his facial expressions. He began to speak in his deep, powerful voice.

"Here in the UK we face a housing crisis unlike any other. I have taken upon it myself to eliminate this crisis. That is why I am announcing our new Housing Scheme. We will be building new houses starting today. Our latest, state of the art technology will allow us to build new housing blocks within weeks". However, when he had finished talking, he was instantly bombarded by questions.

"Mr Clifford" a voice came. "You promised to build 100,000 new homes by 2018, why are you only starting now?"

The politician ran his hand through his hair before saying, "I have taken that time to carefully plan out this new scheme and I can assure that the target will be reached by 2020". Once again, more questions flew in at him.

"Sir, what is your response to the rising house prices? How can graduates move into houses when buildings are so costly? Will this new scheme lower prices?"

"That is the aim" the man said confidently, gazing at his watch. "We also have great mortgage schemes within this country with low interest rates that make buying houses so much easier."

When he finished there was a huge bombardment of more questions. The British public was getting more and more impatient, getting louder and louder.

"Mr Clifford, how will the housing crisis be affected by Brexit?"

"Brexit will only make things better for this country" he stated simply.

After speaking, the questions kept on coming in, yet the Prime Minister whispered something to an official behind his back. The man gently escorted Ted to the side before taking to the podium.

"Mr Clifford will be taking no further questions". The news flash soon ended and returned to the studio.

"Just another day of politics in Britain", the reporter laughed nervously.

Ted Clifford was always an ambitious person yet he was unpopular with the general public. He was elected in 2010 and somehow was re-elected in 2015 where he made several large pledges. However, since then, unemployment has only risen in the country and homelessness has gone haywire. However, I did respect the politician. If only Frank could have been more like his father. The boy should have felt disgraced at his behaviour and so I wondered what his father had told him on the phone. I had never seen Frank look so upset. *Oh well*. All that mattered now was for Bruce and I to recover swiftly. My friend still had a broken leg to overthrow.

After an hour, the school Nurse dismissed me. My stomach still ached from the encounter but I did not want to miss any more lessons. Upon entering my Maths lesson, I was surprised by the lack of recognition considering I had just stood up to the school bully. Nobody seemed to care. The teacher, Ms Dawson, had not even noticed that I missed half the lesson. She sat on her computer typing away. My Maths teacher had short black hair and always seemed to wear black. She was about 5 months pregnant with her third child and so was due to go on maternity leave soon. On her desk was her mug which had a picture of her and her baby girls. The mug stated, 'BEST MUM EVER'.

The teacher had made the classroom look as interesting as possible, but with Maths that can be tricky. The room was mainly made up of whiteboards which were polished to perfection. Whenever Dawson wrote on them, she would spend 5 minutes rubbing it out and then spraying the board before cleaning it meticulously. Whilst it was a waste of time, it was impressive having mirror-like whiteboards. The whiteboards were on all walls so whenever she taught us something, I would get a full neck workout looking left and right. The room also contained posters of all sorts. There was one which portrayed the Mobius loop. I had always looked at that one with utter disbelief and confusion as to how it worked. There were also some poorly made posters from her year 7s, discussing shapes.

The class was just doing textbook questions as usual. Her lessons always felt like a sweatshop with everyone aimlessly working with no light at the end of tunnel. The entire class had their heads looking down whilst they worked. Question after question, sum after sum. The only noise you could hear would be the sound of numbers being punched into a calculator. I simply sat down in my seat, next to Yaseen and prepared for the task ahead.

"Everything okay Jason?" He whispered in his soft and golden voice.

"Yeah, stomach feels a bit rough but it's getting there." I replied.

"Good to hear, mate," he smiled. "It was really brave what you did back there. Frank should not be able to treat everyone so badly and simply get away with it."

"Straight facts," I exclaimed. Yaseen was a great guy, always so calm and kind. The rest of the lesson went on for a while. We spent the whole time doing textbook questions on logarithms. Pretty standard stuff.

Lunch was after Maths. I had Pasta with Tomato sauce, the go-to meal. The lunch hall was rather big with eons of seats and it was always completely crowded. We sat on these huge benches that stretched on for miles. Whilst uncomfortable, they could seat many. It was like being in a prison canteen with long rows of people. One row per year in fact. I found myself sat next to Lewis and Raj. We mainly ate in silence, and then briefly spoke about the advantages of a PS4 over an Xbox One. Pretty standard chit chat. And the food, well it was as bland as ever.

The rest of the day passed by quite quickly. Now it was 4 o'clock and so I could finally go home. Freedom at last.

At the school gates, I felt a great sense of relief. One day down, hundreds more to go. One day less of this hell hole. However, the moment before freedom could be awarded to me, the school bells began to ring like that of a church. The second that the clock would strike 4, small people would erupt out of classrooms, flocking the streets as if it were a parade. I would have to be careful not to be knocked down and taken out like Mufasa. Since the majority of the swarm was made up of Year 7s, my head stuck out the top. Going back against the crowd would be an impossible task and so forgetting a book would be detrimental. At one point, the school tried to have staggered endings for all the years to prevent one giant mass but soon their plans fell apart as the school buses would be forced to wait even longer. And do not get me started on the public buses. The empty buses would be completely raided by Queen's boys like some sort of mutiny. The trick to avoiding all of this would be to leave school one minute early. However, it was harder said than done as my teachers would almost always overrun.

I stood at the bus stop amongst an army of angsty teenagers and small children. There were a few members of the public truly horrified by our masses. In the distance, I saw a cherry red bus slowly drift towards our location. The bus driver had a look of sheer terror as he saw dozens of children prepare for the fight of their lives. The second the doors flipped open, a swarm of zombies burst in, pushing and shoving one another, desperate for some flesh. After pushing my way past some children and before jumping onto the bus, the doors slammed closed, right in front of me, sealing me off from joy. The bus driver shook his head solemnly before accelerating off into the sunset. The bus was full. *Typical.* After several more attempts, I was able to escape the cursed realm of Queen's.

I used to live on a quiet road relatively far from school. Only the rich people lived near the school as the houses were very expensive. Upon arriving to my dwelling, I gently knocked on the door. Yet before my hand had even left the wooden surface, I was hauled into the house by a strong hand. My Mum grabbed me and pulled me into a big hug. Within the blink of an eye, our hug was cut short and she started inspecting me. She looked up my nose to see if it was okay, aware of the dried-up blood.

"I can't believe you got into a fight" she cried. Of course the school had to tell her. She was the one person I did not want finding out. "I have already drafted a complaint to the school, now tell me who did this to you."

"Erm well that is the problem," I said. After a brief pause, I muttered a single word; "Frank". The word, heavy on my tongue. When she heard that, her face tensed and any hint of colour abandoned her.

"I'll go and delete that email," she murmured.

This was the problem with Frank. Everyone was scared of him. It was a miracle that Mr Gideon actually told him off. Usually the Prime Minister was never there to tell off his son, so he got away with whatever he wanted. When his mother died, Frank went from a sweet mummy's boy and teacher's pet to a hardened rugby player and overall jerk. The personality change was literally overnight, as if something had possessed him.

"Julian is coming over on Friday," she added as she left for the kitchen.

Oh shoot. The one person I did not want to see. You may think that I was a horrible person for not liking my brother considering that he paid for my education. The thing is that Julian was a prick. A rich prick. Kind of like Frank, but not as bad.

I trudged off to my bedroom and psyched myself up to do some homework. Like a wounded animal, I crept up the stairs into my little igloo where I would reside for the rest of the evening.

My bedroom was relatively small. Papers were scattered across the room. All sorts. Many scrap pieces of work, some spider diagrams, failed tests: 45%, 62% 51%, C,C,C,B et cetera. My room had an overall stench of stuffiness. A combination of cheesy feet, deodorant and even the whiff of an egg. Not sure where the egg smell came from. I traversed over a sea of used pants and worn papers until my bed was reached. I sat on the large rectangle where the majority of my time was spent while I took in my surroundings and contemplated life.

I had a singular poster on my wall; Spider-Man, my role model in life. Whenever I was in a difficult situation I would think, *What would Peter Parker do?* Or WWPPD for short.

My arms were stretched out while I felt my tiredness and fatigue catch up to me. My pillow was calling for me, begging me to sleep but I knew I had homework to do. So much work, so much catch-up, such poor grades. *Very poor grades.* There was nothing that I could do. *Hard work does not result in success*, only luck. Julian had luck, why couldn't I. My surroundings blurred away whilst my eyes lowered. This was all too much to take in. *Just a quick nap and then Griffin's homework.* That was a promise.

Chapter 2: Fight for Survival

It was chucking down rain, with puddles strewn all across the pavement. The ground had a certain level of shine to it, revealing a skewed reflection of myself. My hair was currently dishevelled and mop like. My tie was lop-sided, and my shirt and blazer was littered with creases. The putrid, polluted smell of London rain smothered my nostrils. After leaping over a puddle, I was quickly able to get onto a bus. There was little to no wait, however I was dripping intensely, leaving a trail of water wherever I went. Slowly, I made my way over to a seat, and sat down, shivering. The cold touch of the rain breathed down my neck and slobbered over my matted hair. Fortunately for me, my bag was almost completely dry, protecting all of my notes. Getting those wet would be disastrous. It happened to me once last year, when all my GCSE notes were turned into papier-mâché.

The bus journey was a bit too long, with stops every couple of seconds. The darkness of the morning clouded everything through the windows which were speckled with dots of rain. The lights of the street would then reflect through the droplets creating a sense of a dark disco.

Eventually the bus pulled up at my stop. I took that moment to leave, careful not to slip down the stairs, covered in water. I held the bars as tightly as possible and waddled down. When I got off the bus, I was smothered by the smell of London streets. Intense car exhausts, rain, cigarettes were all combined together in a horrible blend of horror. I walked along the street, in a hurried fashion as school officially started in 2 minutes. With great strength, I hurried to my destination.

My journey was abruptly interrupted by a tidal wave in my direction. A colossal lorry smashed through a puddle, blowing a gust of freezing cold water in my direction. Similar to the ice bucket challenge, a huge splash of water smacked onto my head and gushed down my body in all directions. It was a ghastly experience as water spiralled around me, stabbing me with daggers of ice. As droplet of water trickled down my spine, they pierced me and froze my blood.

My hair had gone completely flat as if exiting a swimming pool. My shirt had gone transparent revealing my pale skin beneath. And the worst of it was that my bag was now sopping wet. Within a few minutes, the water would seep through. *Not again.* The results would be disastrous. Instantly, I rubbed the layer of water off my watch to see the time. Only one minute until school would commence. Above me was a huge hill, the final variable between me and the institution. Before I could think, adrenaline filled my body and my legs pumped, thrusting me up. Like a mountain climber, I clambered up the hill, racing against the elements trying to overthrow me.

After a couple of minutes, I was able to see the school gates. Rain trickled down my cheek, stinging me at the same time. The wind pushed against me as I trudged through a patch of muddied grass, watching as my already battered shoes became encased by a layer of mud. Instantly, I brushed the water off my face and powered on. The school gates loomed over me, looking like prison bars. If Mr Grove caught me being late, then it would be a detention. I did not have time for that.

The gates ahead were sealed shut, confusing me. I was in fact half an hour late as I checked my phone. My watch had deceived me with an incorrect time. I clasped the cold bars and yelled for somebody to let me in, however the entire school appeared to be deserted.

After a short while, Johnny the Groundskeeper locked eyes with me and headed towards me. Without a word, he buzzed the doors open. Like the doors of a castle, the gates, slowly creaked open, revealing the vast school site. It had always looked so much bigger when the grounds were abandoned. Immediately, I headed over to my classroom, traversing over puddles and lagoons. The rain still tortured me as I was pelted by drops from all directions and kicked by gusts of wind. In the end, I found myself outside Mr Grove's room. The room was entirely devoid of pupils, leaving the man alone, drinking coffee.

"You took your time," the man said, looking at me through the corner of his eyes. "Lessons have already started". My first lesson was physics and so I needed to bolt. My body was still drenched and it still felt disgusting, but it was best to get on with the day. Fortunately I got away scot-free.

Lesson 1: Physics. Today we were learning about Electricity and the class were just doing a worksheet in silence. Upon entering, I waved to the teacher, Mr Weaving, but he barely noticed me. Too engrossed in reading the book in his hands. I sat down at my desk, leaking water everywhere and quickly opened my bag. For the most part, my papers were dry however there were a few that had been obliterated. I ripped out my poor excuse of a folder and examined it carefully. The file was warped with non-hole punched papers hanging out. I began to contemplate the idea of working, when Raj leaned over towards me.

"Jason?" He murmured.

"What is it?" I said, unwilling to live any longer. This day had already hit rock bottom.

"I heard a rumour that Frank is back today."

"What?"

"Apparently Ted Clifford spoke to the school and persuaded them to shorten his suspension".

This was bad news, no, dreadful news. Frank had it in for me. I would have Economics and Maths later that day and we shared those classes. Amongst the freezing water, I could still feel the pain from the jab to the stomach and the cross to the face. Frank's immunity to punishment made him a formidable foe. But then again, I am Jason. *I fight bad guys on a daily basis.* Frank would be lightwork in comparison. Now I had 2 hours until Maths, where our paths would cross once again. It was time to prepare for war.

My phone started vibrating in my pocket and so it was fished out only to see a message from Julian:

'Hey Bro, make sure you finish all your homework before you come home, I've got an outing planned for the two of us.' I had almost forgotten that it was Friday and now Julian was coming home.

EURGH. There was no way that I was going to spend my free time with Julian. I would rather stay at school and do extra work. Honestly this day could not get any worse. But fate had other plans.

Mr Weaving, about 40 years old, had hair beginning to grey at the sides. He wore huge glasses alongside a thick woollen jumper. The man used to be a famous Aerospace Engineer for a decade until he suddenly had a change of heart and became a teacher. The guy was a great teacher, gave thorough explanations and was continuously hilarious.

"I will now be returning your recent topic tests," Weaving said. He grabbed a fat stack of papers from his desk. "And now, in no particular order". He looked around until he made eye contact with me. He slowly approached me and flattened my paper on to my desk. Instantly, I flipped it in order to see my mark.

48%.

You know, Mr Weaving was actually a terrible teacher. He spent all his time joking around rather than teaching. He should have stuck to being an engineer. My bad mark was a total reflection of his bad teaching. If everyone else had done badly then that would have made me feel better.

"Raj, what did you get?" I whispered.

"I messed up so bad and should have done much better," he whimpered. *There you go.* Someone else who had also done badly. If Raj had failed, then everyone would have failed.

"I got 88%", he cried. It was at times like these when I felt like punching someone in the face. If I had gotten 88%, I would have been dancing around in enjoyment, definitely not sulking. Now I needed to make sure that Mr Grove did not find out about this. The last thing I needed was a letter sent home.

At the end of the lesson, I raced out, unable to bare thinking about my failure any longer. My next lesson was maths. Surely my day had already hit rock bottom? But then again I had said that twice already.

I decided to get to Maths early, keeping my head down for the entire lesson and then I would leave as quickly as possible. That way Frank would not notice me since I sat diagonally behind him. I burst into the classroom and sat down on my seat, before chucking my textbook onto my desk with a heavy thud and then started doing questions. The aim of the lesson was not to look up. Slowly, members of the class started pouring in and I just kept focusing on my work, daring not to look up. That would be suicide.

My silence was disrupted when the sound of a chair being untucked came from behind me, as a boy sat down noisily, before drumming on the table. *Probably just Jermaine.* I ignored him and continued to study.

Once again, my silence was interrupted as the someone strolled into the classroom, singing in a muttered tone.

I did not recognise the lyrics, yet I knew that it had to be Manny with his trash singing voice.

"Ooh yeah!" Jermaine came in, finishing off the lyrics. Moments later an audible fist bump and a hug could be heard. "Bant and Dec, back together again". Jermaine and Manny were the two most lively people in the world. They would never stop talking and for the most part they were actually quite funny.

"So bro," Manny said to Jermaine, "do I have the tea for you?"

"What is it bro?"

"Remember I put the tea in banter, badda bim badda boom," he said, chuckling to himself. "Anyways, I have heard that Clifford 'The Big Red Dog' is back today. What do you think?"

"Shut the funk door," Manny replied. "Already?"

"Yeseroonie?" Jermaine replied.

It was at that moment that the pile of muscles stormed in, silencing the atmosphere. Even Jermaine and Manny stopped talking for a moment. The boy's steps were slow, heavy with each foot as his diamond shoes connected with the floor. On his way to his desk, he froze for a brief second, allowing not a single muscle in his body to twitch. Like something out of a horror movie, he cranked his head to the left, and made eye contact with me. For a brief second he stared into my soul whilst I may or may not have wet myself. Frank then strolled to his desk, sliding out his chair, allowing it to screech against the floor. The bully then took out his textbook and started to work as the class remained in silence. Even Jermaine and Manny stopped talking.

When there were only 5 minutes left of the lesson, Frank solemnly put his hand up.

"Excuse me miss; may I go to the toilet?" he said with a large smile. Fake kindness.

"Of course, Frank," the teacher replied. Within a second, Frank had stuffed all his belongings into his rucksack and bolted out of the classroom. Since the boy had taken his bag with him, he had no intention of coming back. Clearly Clifford was skiving. The thing is, when you have that much power you can do practically whatever you want and get away with it. The good news for me was that I no longer needed to worry about his presence.

At the end of the lesson, I leisurely walked out, smelling in all that fresh air, all that freedom. However, my temporary joy was crumpled by a strong force. A mighty hand clasped itself around my wrist, squeezing hard, crippling my it. Frank loomed over me like a colossus, fuming. He then started tugging me, away from the safety of the classroom. My bag fell to the floor as I aggressively fought back but he just kept on driving forward, dragging me across the floor. My wrist screamed out to me in pain while skin scraped off my back. Frank kicked open a door and tossed me into a classroom with ease. I looked up to see that the room was empty, with no teacher. Before I could get up, Frank latched onto my hair, grabbing a fistful of it and then raised me to the point where my eyes were level with his.

"You are dead Clyde!" he growled.

At that moment, four other boys appeared from the back of the room, having been concealed by the darkness. One of them locked the door, ensuring that there was no escape. I was petrified as these boys could do anything to me. Frank had gotten out of hand. This was too far. My head felt like needles were being stuck into it and still the bully showed no signs of letting go. I struggled and squirmed, only for Frank to punch me in the face with his other hand. Like a cobra, he extended his arm and retracted it within moments of the strike. I collapsed to the floor, with blood beginning to seep out of my nose. Frank was not holding back, enveloped by true rage. I clenched my fists to prepare for a counterattack, but instead was met with a large smack to the back. One of the bullies kicked me forward, causing me to land face first on the floor.

I mustered all my strength to try and get up again only for someone to grab my arm. My other arm was seized as well. Two more people then grabbed my legs, rendering me powerless. The group pulled me up with ease as they were all huge, muscular, rugby players. They carried me over with precision and slammed me onto a desk. My back was against the desk and they all stood over me as if I were on an operating table. The four of them were still holding my limbs and Frank was standing there.

Before I could think, Frank lunged his hand into my blazer pocket and ripped my phone out. He lightly held it in his hand as if it were a toy. Clumsily, he flipped it in his hands, appalled by age of my device. He tossed it into the air and caught it. He then hurled it into the air once again but this time did not catch it. The phone fell to the ground and clattered to the ground. Frank then looked at me dead in the eyes before saying:

"Next time you mess with me, this will be you." Suddenly he stomped on the phone and then again, and again. I watched in misery as my property was smashed to smithereens. The bullies then released my arms in unison, leaving me broken and battered. Frank then unlocked the door and stormed out, his goons not far behind.

I collapsed off the desk and crawled over to my phone, before cradling its corpse in my hands. The screen had a spiderweb of cracks. I switched it on and luckily it just about worked yet it flickered in places while chunks of glass fell off. That was the last straw, I was going to go to Mr Gideon and tell him what happened. That was when I remembered what Frank said, next time he would not let me survive. My arms ached and my nose was still leaking blood. He had to pay.

After leaving the classroom, I desperately tried to get to the school nurse as a trail of blood was left wherever I went. I was hobbling across the school site in agony, thinking that one day I would get my revenge on Frank. I could lock him in a cupboard overnight, or even stuff ice down his back. But then I could be tried for treason. While I was rushing through the site, almost sprinting, I almost crashed, headfirst, into Mr Grove. The man looked at me, slightly alarmed.

"Ahh Jason, there you are. I was looking for you and- Oh my God are you okay?" This was my chance to tell on Frank. Get him finally expelled from the school.

"Erm yes. I ran into a wall and am now on my way to the nurse". I spoke faintly. The words were heavy and stiff to release. Lies always were. My whole body ached even my lungs.

"Okay, well I was about to say that Mr Weaving told me about your recent Physics test. Jason you really need to pull up your socks. I have also rung your parents and told them about this". That bombshell was a punch to the gut, harder than any of Frank's attacks.

The man took a second look at me, "You sure you're okay?"

"Yes," I mumbled, fighting back tears. As soon as the man finished, I hurtled on to the medical room.

I burst into the School Nurse's office. Twice in the same week. A personal record for me.

"My goodness!" cried the school nurse. "Did you get into another fight?" The truth was there on the tip of my tongue, aching for it to be released into the world. However, Frank's threat echoed in my mind. I was not ready to be murdered in my sleep so should just play it safe.

"I was not looking where I was going and ran into a wall triggering the injuries from Monday." Cleary I was never the best at lying. The nurse just shook her head in disarray.

"I should patch you up" she exclaimed. My fake diagnosis had fooled her. She then took out some swabs and bandages and got to work. The nurse securely fastened a bandage over my nose.

Today had been a horrible day. My phone had gotten smashed. I never really liked my iPhone 5, but it did the trick. Well at least when you reach rock bottom, things can only get better.

"Jason, I think it is best you go home now and get some rest". Music to my ears. I could do with some free time. Maybe play some PS4 or watch some TV. This was perfect. My day had honestly gotten a lot better.

"Oh yeah that is an awesome idea. I should probably get going". I said excitedly, acting as if my body was damage free.

"No no, please stay. I have spoken to your dad and he said he will pick you up shortly", Ugh. I was hoping on going out before returning home. I could have easily fitted in a cinema trip. There was the new Terminator movie that I could have watched. Now I would be a prisoner at home. *Wait a moment, why would Dad pick up the phone?* His phone was always off during the working day. Surely the nurse spoke to Mum? Why would Dad leave work early when Mum was much closer geographically, working at the primary school across the road.

After about ten minutes, the telephone in the room sounded, and the nurse briskly answered it before talking. She chuckled before blushing and then put the phone down. Dad had never been one to joke? What was this.

"Your Father is waiting for you outside. Do you want me to come outside with you?"

"No," I said, playing down my injuries. The pain had died down a bit but I could still feel the impact of the punches. I trotted out of the back door and my jaw dropped. Right in front of me was a shining red Ferrari. It was such a rich red and it gleamed in the light. I could see a perfect reflection of myself through it. There was no way that Dad secretly owned a sportscar. He drove a Volkswagen. Who was this man?

One of the doors swung open and out came a man. He stood at over 6 foot with the Sun behind him, creating a majestic silhouette. He wore thin rimmed aviator sunglasses along with a blue suit. He wore a white shirt underneath with no tie and his shoes were polished to the extent that they were as shiny as the Ferrari. They were most likely polished together at the same time. The man had a large square jaw with a jawline that could cut through metal. He stepped out of the light and greeted me with a large grin. It was Julian. *Uggh.*

"So, you got into another fight," Julian said, leaning on his car. His voice was clear, slightly elevated from his posh tone. I suppose that is what would happen when you go to Oxford. But then again, him and I were related yet we sounded so differently.

"No, I erm ran into a wall," I replied bluntly.

"Don't lie, you got into another fight with that Frank person". It was no use lying. Julian knew me too well even though he was out of the country, saving lives most of the time.

"I see he grabbed a hold of your hair and gave you a right cross to the nose".

"What? Um-how do you know?"

"Just get in the car," he said dismissively.

I stepped into the car, which was insane. The seats were laced with the finest of rose-coloured fabrics. Machinery was dotted all over. To my right was the steering wheel which was a blend of yellow and black like a bumblebee. Honestly the word that came to mind to describe everything was 'slick'. The car gave off a wealthy odour such that when I sat down, I was embraced by pure luxury. Julian hopped into the driver's seat and the car roared into motion. With a push of the accelerator, the car whizzed off, leaving Queen's School as a distant memory.

"You like my ride?" he asked. "I picked her up last month. Showing up home in a Ferrari would honestly give Mum and Dad a shock. How are the folks by the way?"

"Yeah, they are fine, but you would know if you actually rang them once in a while." Julian laughed before changing the subject completely.

"So how did you get into the fight then? And before you say something dumb, just remember that you are a terrible liar. Complete lack of eye contact and constant fidgeting. Furthermore, you have no conviction in your voice. Way too hesitant. So please let the cat out the bag, before I inform Mum".

"How did you know I"

"But how did I know that you were hit with a right cross. Easy. The blood on your bandage is more extreme where the left nostril is. That means that Frank must have hit you with his right hand. Moving on to your hair. Your hair is unkempt and messy most of the time. Recently you have been putting gel into it and making some effort in order to get others to like you. Believe me, if you had any sort of charm or whit, then people would like you more. Try cracking a joke once in a while. Considering the fact that your hair is now ruffled, Frank must have grabbed you by the hair. You really should learn how to fight back. Now before you marvel in astonishment, remember that I am a genius so this is nothing to be surprised by."

I told you Julian was a prick. However, a smart one at that. The fact that he knew exactly how the fight went down astonished me.

The rest of the journey was filled by an awkward silence. Julian was incredibly judgemental and so talking to him was not ideal. Instead I took the opportunity to embrace the speed of the car zooming through the London streets. The roads were mainly empty however the footpaths were heaving with shoppers. People were rushing up and down, holding huge bags of clothes, people indulging into burgers and so on. However, I quickly realised that this high street was not the way home.

"Where are we going?" I stated.

"That new Terminator movie looks good". Julian smiled. He knew exactly what I wanted and so was pleasantly surprised. It was as if the man was psychic.

Julian drove through the town centre and pulled up outside the cinema. Movies were my favourite thing, especially Star Wars. I was impressed that Julian was taking me to the cinema as he would always say that movies were too predictable and that they lacked any element of surprise.

After parking up, the car doors swung open majestically and I stepped out. Julian stepped out gingerly, reaching for his can in the back seat before walking to the cinema with a slight limp in his leg. Julian was involved in a car accident when he was 8 and that did permanent damage to his leg.

Upon entering the cinema, I noticed how empty it was, mainly because it was a weekday afternoon.

"What snacks do you want?" Julian whispered.

Moments later, I lugged my huge box of popcorn into the multiplex where the entire room was vacant.

"Where are we sitting?" I asked.

"E7 and E8" he replied.

I looked up and to my surprise, those 2 seats were premium. They were huge seats with a built-in recliner feature. They were so soft to sit in, as if they had been ripped out of Julian's Ferrari. I sunk into the bottomless pit of luxury with the miles of leg room. For once, I felt ecstatic. The movie was going to be great.

So, the movie was great, yet Julian fell asleep halfway through.

"I can't believe they killed John Connor in the first 5 minutes" I said.

"It was predictable. It made sense to take the story into a new direction, even though they completely rehashed the original."

"How was your nap?" I asked dismissively.

"How was the film? Let me guess, Arnold's terminator sacrificed himself to kill the evil Terminator thus letting the heroes survive. Before you tell me I was right just remember that movies are not interesting to me. It is just people pretending in order to make people with low self-esteem forget about their dumb lives". Julian was always so straight with facts. He never cared if the truth hurt anyone and was always like this. His 'Supreme intellect' is what got him through life. However, I must not complain. Premium seats for a film when I should have been at school felt pretty great. The time now was 3. School still had another hour leftover.

"Where to next?" I jumbly asked.

"I am starving. Let's get some food". Julian exclaimed. He led me into the heart of the town centre where he pointed out a fancy Japanese restaurant.

While I was sitting down at the table eating, my phone went off. It was just Raj, asking where I was. I ignored it. However, my phone was still completely obliterated with its rivers of cracks travelling in all directions.

"What happened to your phone? Let me guess, Frank stomped on it while you were fighting".

At this point I was not even going to ask how he knew. I just nodded solemnly.

"Why do you have such a bad phone?" he asked.

"It used to be Dad's. He gave it to me". I commented.

"Well now that it is broken it needs replacing. Come on, let's go". At that moment, Julian casually dropped a stack of cash on the table and walked out. The world's biggest tip. He scoffed down a piece of sushi before saying "Keep the change" to the waitress. I awkwardly followed behind.

Julian led me towards the Apple store. I had never actually been to one of those before. There was a huge white glowing Apple sign on the outside. When we entered, I was astonished by the number of gadgets. The place was crawling with machines. Tables were covered

42

in hi-tech machinery like some sort of open museum. I had never seen this many phones at once before.

"I would like to see your latest model", Julian said to one of the store assistants.

"Sure thing!" the assistant replied. She then went to grab a few boxes and brought them towards us. "Here is the iPhone 11. You can choose between normal or plus sized. We have it in black, lime green, yellow, lilac, red or white."

"What do you want bro?" Julian said turning to me. I had never been more overwhelmed in my life. These phones were £1000 each and so I had to make the correct choice else doom. I was not even expecting a new phone as for my entire life I had been using second-hand phones. I finally got an upgrade from my Nokia brick two years ago and now I was being offered an exponentially better offer. The choice was too great, so many funky colours. It was clear to me that the plus size would be too big so I decided to go with normal. The colours were tricky though. Yellow, lilac and green were not the best choice. It would either have to be white, black or red.

"I will have a black normal sized phone". It was best to get the classic phone colour since if I ever wanted a fancy colour, I could just buy a new case.

"Sure thing" the assistant said. She went to the counter and Julian paid with a swift, effortless tap of his credit card.

"Thank you very much, please come back soon!" I was so happy with my new phone. The 11 had only released a month ago so it was super exciting.

43

"Thank you, Julian, I really appreciate it!"

"No problem. Just try not to get this one broken," he laughed. It was nice to have a rich brother. "Let's head home now". And with that, we headed back to the Ferrari and drove home.

By the time we got home, it was 5 o'clock, my usual return time. Now it was time to face my problems. Mum had kept quiet about my grades all week, despite Grove ringing her on Monday. Today she would definitely mention them and my Physics test result. When I entered the house, Mum was just standing there.

"What happened to your face?" she asked, both concerned and impatiently.

"He ran into a wall" Julian quickly responded. I was amazed at what he just said since he knew the truth about me and Frank and instead decided to lie on my behalf. I was touched. But then I realised that Mum must have already been told by the school nurse. That was when it hit me; Julian was the one who answered the phone call from school. He snuck out to collect me, pretending to be my dad and then took me to the cinema. As far as Mum was aware, I never skipped school. Julian was actually a life safer.

"You need to be more careful", Mum said, sighing. It was true. I needed to get my life together and avoid Frank. Mum still had not mentioned my grades. I had decided to get on with my homework as I still had some of Mr Griffin's Economics homework leftover. Mr Weaving had also set some Physics.

At 7 o'clock, Mum called me down for dinner. This was our first family dinner in a very long time. Mainly because Julian was always in and out of the country with work. At the table sat the 4 of us: Mum, Dad, Julian and me. Dad was 5ft 9 wearing black glasses and had short dark brown hair. It was strange how Julian had ended up being so tall considering the height of our parents. Dad had a moustache grown on his lip that was perfectly horizontal yet yearned to be a handlebar at the edges. He still wore his suit from work, with his tie loosened.

"How was your day, Jason? I heard you ran into a wall." He asked, trying not to laugh at my stupidity.

"Yeah, it was fine. I was late to maths and ended up running into a wall. The impact caused the bleed from Monday to open up." At that point, I had become a professional liar and should have become a spy. That would have been cool.

"I hope that Frank boy is enjoying his punishment. Nobody hurts my precious boy and gets away with it," Mum added. "A weeks' worth of suspension is simply not enough. He should have been expelled. What was school like today, without Frank?"

I frowned, about to answer, before she spoke again.

"Jason. I forgot to say before, but Mr Grove phoned me earlier this week". *Here we go.* "He said that your recent report was poor, with a C in economics." I could see Dad shaking his head in disarray. "He then rang again today and said that your recent Physics test was appalling with a mark of something like 48%." For a moment I felt great shame. I went to such a good school, yet still underperformed.

"Jason, this is unacceptable," said Dad. "Remember your teachers will be giving you predicted grades at the end of the year. If you do not get good predictions, then no university will accept you. Look at Julian, that boy is the result of hard work. Do you want to be respected like him, or end up like your cousin, Frasier?" I just sat there silently. There was nothing I could say and so expected to be grilled for the rest of the day.

"Do not worry about it," Julian said, calmly, slicing through the silence with a sharp knife. I was confused for a second. "I will personally make sure that Jason's grades are up to scratch next month." I did not know if that was a threat or an insult.

"Moving on," Mum said, "How have things been with you Julian?"

Julian then went on for the next 15 minutes going on about all the exotic things he had done. He spoke about the vast number of countries he had visited, and some of the elite medical procedures he had undertaken. I just switched off for that portion.

After dinner, I decided to do some more work before going to bed. It had been a long day and was fed up of everything. I collapsed into my bed with a loud thud. I took off the bandage on my nose as it had stopped bleeding and placed a fresh one on my bedside table. It was left there in case my nose started bleeding during the night. I waited in bed, thinking about what I would dream about. My dreams were always the most interesting parts of the day. I gently closed my eyes and prepared to sleep.

You know, Julian had been very nice to me today. I was actually proud to have him as a brother. He constantly defended me against Mum and Dad and he even took me to watch Terminator. Maybe he had changed into a better person. My thoughts swiftly changed to the more pressing matter. Frank was still at large at school. What would I say to him on Monday next time we would encounter? That boy was a public menace. My injuries still felt prominent as my face ached and my ribs hurt with every breath.

Within a few minutes, or maybe an hour, who knew, I slowly drifted off to another world. I would soon find out that this would be the start of a whole new saga in my life. But seriously, I needed to get out of the habit of falling asleep too early.

Chapter 3: The Dream

"I will now be taking in your homework", Mr Griffin exclaimed. Panic rushed through me. It was Wednesday and was convinced that the homework was due in for Thursday. The class proceeded to hand in their work. I was puzzled.

"Erm Sir, I thought it was due in for tomorrow" I murmured.

"Boy! Have you not done your homework?"

"No, Sir, sorry." Raj turned towards me.

"Kill him! Cut off his head as an example". He roared with enthusiasm. His eyes locked with mine, and he clenched his fists. His look of intent was utterly terrifying. The entire class started chanting. Frank walked towards me and thrusted his fist into my face. I fell back in agony. My nose began erupting with blood. It was a fountain of blood. I put my hand to it, trying to stop the bleed.

Wilfred and Haresh got up instantly and leapt on top of their desks. In perfect sync, the two of them clapped their hands and began to dance. Haresh flipped one hand out before slapping his head. Wilfred started spinning where he stood, while chanting.

"Kill him! Time to die."

Boris began slapping his desk, creating a beat. With a constant beat, his beats matched the chants and the two boys continued to dance on the desks. They violently waved their arms around as if they lacked any sort of skeletal structure. By Haresh's foot lay a candle. The boy, without warning, kicked the flame, knocking it to the ground. Like an out-of-control animal, the fire lit up the room. The heat stung me, singeing my hair, whilst light filled the room. It hurt for a moment whilst horror filled around me.

"This is the end Jason! No-one can save you now!" Frank screamed. I lifted up my hands to protect me. But that was when a cold hand grabbed my leg. Its nails dug into my skin and knocked me off guard. It yanked me with immense force. I tried to shake it off, but three more hands grabbed onto me. The hands were dark and shadowy, emitting a silhouette. They pulled me into the ground and into darkness, leaving the classroom a distant memory.

My body slammed to a hard concrete ground, where I could feel the cool rock under my fingertips, as my body wailed out in agony. The rain struck the ground around me and sliced my bloodied face. Water trickled down my bruises and tangled with my blood. My hair was matted by the weather whilst a gentle breeze brushed over me, freezing me in all corners. Ahead of me, a small light appeared amongst the vast darkness. It started to enlarge whilst the car approached me. Its light lit up the entire street and was truly blinding to look at.

The vehicle was heading towards me, moving at full force and I tried to move out the way but there were huge shackles tied around my body. I mustered up all my strength trying to escape, trying to move but it was no use. My body was pinned into position, making survival an impossibility. My heart began to burn in my chest as fear engulfed me. It felt horrific as the car got closer and closer whilst I stood there helpless. The driver started frantically beeping. The beeps filled the empty streets, echoing off the buildings around me. The sound rung through the dark street, getting louder and louder as the car got closer and closer. It was at that moment when it abruptly swerved to the right. The car screamed as it collided into a wall, crumbling upon impact. Scraps of metal, nuts and bolts flew in all directions creating an array of destruction.

Instantaneously, the shackles dissolved, letting me free. I walked towards the wreckage and that was when I saw two dismembered bodies. A man and a woman. Lying next to them was a small boy screaming with his hands sodden in blood. His cry was like that of a banshee. The boy's leg was sodden in blood with shards of glass sticking out. The child then looked at me, dead in the eyes, glowing red with fury.

"You did this!" he growled. I was perplexed. He stepped towards me and pulsed his hand out. My body was whipped back and slammed into a concrete wall as my spine shattered upon impact, crippling my body entirely. Before the pain could sink in, a flash of lightning struck, lighting up the surroundings, revealing a vast field riddled with dying trees. Within the field, I saw small stones littered throughout. To my right was a stone with the following words carved onto it:

'*Jerry and Jemima, beloved parents, died from car crash*'. I rested my hand on the stone and felt its rough worn face. This stone had been here for years, apparent from the fading words. Within a few metres, I could see the boy from before. He was standing with a group of people which resembled Mum and Dad. Their silhouette alone was not enough to identify them. Mum was holding a baby in her hands. I reached out my shattered arm and shouted. However, there was no sound coming out. It felt as if a pillow was in front of my mouth, muffling my voice. I shouted again and again but nobody could hear me. Once again, the ground felt uneasy beneath my bare feet. The solid ground wobbled like jelly as the situation got even worse.

A rumble could be heard, constantly getting louder and louder until my eardrums were squealing in pain. The ground tore open underneath the gravestone, causing it to fall into an abyss. The crack in the ground raced across the yard, creating a sizeable gap. Out of the crevice, a creature burst out bearing demonic claws that could slice through steel like butter. Its arms were built to lift entire buildings and its eyes were a deep red. The same red as the boy with the dead parents. The demon glared into my soul and opened its mouth to reveal a huge darkness. There were hundreds upon thousands of teeth there, contained amongst several rows of torture. They were terrifying in shape. A single bite would have burst me like a balloon.

I tried to run away, but my legs had completely given up. I wriggled but it was no use. The demon started approaching me., walking with slow but large steps. Whilst it approached me like a giant, my legs continued to fumble around. I started to walk, but each step felt like I was lifting a truck. Before long, the monstrosity was right behind me, its endless tongue hanging out. It lunged forward and one of its hands wrapped itself around my waist. The appendage was both cold and slimy in touch, making me want to puke. It squeezed so hard that my stomach began to ooze out blood in immense pain. The demon grew in size until it towered over me. It held me up, miles off the ground. The graveyard below was now a distant sight, as if I were looking down from an aeroplane. I writhed but it was impossible to break free and the shear pain I felt was detrimental. The demon pulled me up and towards its mouth. At that point, it dropped me into its void. As I fell, I could see it close its mouth, sealing me off from the rest of the world.

For what felt like hours, I was tumbling and turning, falling in endless darkness. Slowly, the speed of the fall caused me to heat up. My hands begun to sting from the heat, as if I had just touched a freshly boiled kettle. A few sparks flew off my boy as I quickly caught alight. I was like a meteor crashing onto a planet. My hands continued to burn and I could see them melting away. At this point I felt no pain as my body withered away. The skin on my hands dissolved, leaving bones which then blew into dust. My legs were torn off from the force leaving just my body and head. My eyes eventually started to melt away along with the rest of my body. My entire life slipped away in that instant, leaving nothing. The last of my body burnt away. And that was the end.

I woke up immediately and instantly looked to my hands, checking they were still there. I felt dazed as that dream was full-on. Everything felt so real, especially the pain and emotions. My head was whizzing like crazy, and my body felt odd. It felt tired and energised at the same time, whilst my heart continued to beat beyond control.

Glancing to my left, I saw the time. 7 o'clock. Wow, I had actually managed to sleep solidly for the whole night but had forgone an evening of homework. It went so quickly with just one quick dream. But that dream felt so surreal. Instantly, I raised my hand to my nose. It was no longer bleeding and the bandage on my bedside table had vanished. Perhaps it had been knocked over during my flurry of a nightmare. In fact my ribs were hurting no longer.

I leapt out of bed and stretched. My muscles vibrated and revved into action, burning off any sense of fatigue. Today was Saturday, the start of the weekend. Upon exiting my bedroom, I went to the kitchen to have some breakfast. Mum was standing there, but she looked different. Her hair was much shorter than last night. It was now a shoulder length bob. She must have had it done last night. It was a drastic change and honestly looked quite poor. But my better side took the better of me.

"Nice hair Mum," I lied. She spun around but had a confused look on her face.

"Erm Thanks, but I had it done 2 weeks ago". *Err What?* Last night, her hair was much longer. But you know me, always distracted. I probably did not notice the change. Frank must have punched me extra hard.

"It was worth another compliment," the words leaked out my mouth. Mum smiled. I was almost convinced that she had long hair the night before. Something was definitely off. And my nose had miraculously healed over night. Last night, my nostrils were clogged with dried blood. That sort of stuff does not dissolve over night. At that moment, it was apparent to me that the house felt awfully quiet. Something was not right.

"Where's Dad and Julian?" I asked.

"Dad is at his new job and Julian left some time ago". Dad's new job? He never mentioned that to me. And why was he working on a Saturday? Also when did Julian leave. He was here yesterday.

"What time did Julian leave, I asked?"

"Your brother has not been here all month. What are you talking about?" Mum said, her facing tensing.

"I thought Julian was here yesterday. Remember he came home from dinner and we had a family dinner and you told me off for my grades". I was getting increasingly confused. My chest began to feel tight, knocking out any previous happiness.

"Jason, baby, are you okay? That was a month ago. You must have had too much to drink yesterday." *A month ago? What?* I could almost swear that Julian was here yesterday. We watched Terminator yesterday. How could that have been a month ago? And also I drank nothing yesterday? A drop of alcohol had never entered my body. Something was off. There was only one way to sort out this mess.

"Mum, what is the date today?" I was so scared. My heart had stopped beating.

"11th November," she exclaimed, looking pale. At that moment, the pin dropped. Yesterday was October. Friday the 11th October. Today was November. Something had gone horribly wrong. Within the blink of an eye, I had run off to the bathroom.

I looked into the mirror saw that all my cuts and bruises from the fight had healed. A significant period of time must have passed since the fight. That means that it must have really been a month. Impossible. My phone jumped out of my pocket, revealing the date. Monday 11th November. I really had just skipped a month of my life. Furthermore, my phone was brand new yesterday. Now it was littered with small scratches. I frantically tried to remember all the things that happened in October but I honestly could remember nothing. The last thing I could remember was the family dinner yesterday and then waking up today. This was seriously bad. And today was not Saturday, it was Monday, meaning that I had school. *Shoot.*

After returning to the kitchen, I asked Mum, "Where have I been the last month?"

"What do you mean? You have been going to school as normal every day for the last month". I was stunned. That would mean that someone else was living my life or I had a terrible memory. This was petrifying. The fear of the unknown was utterly overwhelming. Slowly, Mum approached me and put her hand on my head.

"Sweetie, are you okay? The stress of school must be finally getting to you. Your father and I should never have sent you to such an elite school. It is not good for your mental health." I had no idea what to do and was in a state of panic. I should just go with the flow, attend school and figure out everything there. Raj should have some answers.

"I am fine Mum, just had a rough night. I'm gonna head to school early. My pile of work is not going to get rid of itself." Mum gently smiled but in her eyes, she knew something was definitely not right.

"Your father and I are so proud of you" she said while I left the room. My point exactly.

Outside, the house opposite was completely covered in scaffolding. Yesterday there was not a single trace of building works. It would take time to adjust to the new timeline. Perhaps I had accidentally time travelled a month into the future. That would explain my memory loss. But if that was the case, then there would be no version of me to live out my life a month ago, so I would be erased from existence. Time travel was trippy, so I assumed that was not the case. And where would I have gotten a time machine from? They don't exactly grow on trees. They should make time travel a topic in the A-Level Physics course. That would be a start.

The journey to school was nothing unusual. There had been no major changes to the transport system during my hibernation. (That is what I was calling it). The bus system was still super slow and unreliable.

Soon, the school stood right in front of me with the gates towering over once again. I gently stepped in avoiding eye contact with everyone. I walked along with my head down. A minute later, tall boy appeared in my peripheral vision. He wore a half sleeve shirt which unearthed his unruly biceps and forearms. *Shoot, it's Clifford.* I thought to myself and increased the pace of my walk trying to avoid him at all costs. Who knew what could have happened between us during that one month?

"Jason!" he shouted. I was done for. There was no hope.

"Jason Clyde!" he shouted again. I had a good run.

"How are you doing, my friend?" he said with a wide grin on his face. *My friend.* This was some sick joke.

He opened up his arms ready to embrace me. They stood there while his giant muscles itched to be set free. This had to be some sort of joke. In fact, Frank looked different. His usual buzzcut hair was now slightly longer, with actual texture. The front of his hair was propped up, most likely with gel. His eyes appeared bigger, hinting at more restful nights. In fact, even his uniform was in good shape with his shirt tucked in and laces tied. The boy then proceeded to hug me. And whilst I was within his embrace, there was an apparent smell of cologne. I felt incredibly awkward as this was the same guy that tried to kill me yesterday and broke my phone. Now all of a sudden he was trying to hug me and be my friend. Eventually I squirmed free from his giant arms.

"We had so much fun yesterday. That party was quality," he said, slapping my back. I winced, expecting to be overwhelmed by a sharp pain. There was surprise when there was no pain and even Frank looked a bit confused.

"Wow, those gym sessions have been doing wonders for you. No wonder you were so hesitant about drinking booze yesternight."

I had never been to the gym or a house party before. How could this have happened during my hibernation. This had to have been a Jekyll and Hyde situation. Maybe I had a dormant second personality. In fact what if I was the second personality of the actual host of my body and my life had been a lie.

"You don't look okay Jason. You must have a pretty big hangover from last night."

"Yeah, yesterday was so much fun". I stuttered. Seeing some footage of me at the party yesterday would actually be beneficial. That would definitely help me see what I was like during the hibernation, and maybe bring back some memories finally giving me some answers.

Frank led me to the Sixth Form Centre while I awkwardly followed. Everyone was seated in their usual positions. Raj was sitting down with my other friends on their usual sofas. Tim, Lewis and Yaseen were all there. In fact Bruce was sitting next to Raj, with the cast on his leg completely gone with absolutely no signs of it ever existing. As usual, I went to go sit with them when Frank interrupted.

"Oi Clyde! Get away from those nerds, sit with your real friends." This was finally my time to sit with the cool people. I felt so nervous walking over as eagle eyes followed my every move. But nobody was frowning at me, they were all smiling, as if welcoming me into the pack of wolves. Frank waved again, signalling the empty seat next to him and Wilfred.

"Wassup Jason", Wilfred said, smiling. Since when did I become so cool? Before nobody wanted to talk to me and now all of a sudden everyone wanted to be my friend. Honestly, what did I do over the last month? At that moment, Wilfred said,

"Jason, you lookin' forward to the rugby game this Saturday against St Pete's. It's gonna be a big game. I am sure you will score a few tries". So I also play rugby now? That would explain the muscles. In fact my entire body felt like a freshly oiled car. Getting out of breath from walking was just a long-lost memory now.

"I hope you are looking forward to making some big tackles." I did not know what to say. "Well say something, mate. Oh my, the alcohol has really gotten to you. To be fair you did chug a whole bottle of vodka."

"Frank, am I any good at rugby?" I whispered in his ear.

"Is that a joke Jay? You are the best, which is why you are in the first team. I am still not sure why you never tried Rugby before as you clearly are a natural."

"Jason, my boy!" I recognised Haresh's familiar voice. "How are you still standing? After all that alcohol yesterday, I thought you would be in a coma. Those dance moves as well." He gave an okay symbol with his hand as he said it.

Since when could I dance? So now I was friends with all the cool kids. This was going to be a very interesting day. At that moment, my phone started buzzing. I pulled it out of my pocket, only to see Julian's name, which filled me with joy because he may have some sort of idea as to what was going on.

"Hi Julian. Listen bro I need your help-"

"Jason, I can't talk for long. I am about to board a flight to New York. You won't be seeing me for a few weeks. Enjoy school little brother and stay out of trouble." And with that said, he hung up. Had he even heard a word of what I had said?

My first lesson of the day was Economics. I had struggled enough with the subject. Now there was an entire month of content in which I had missed. This was going to be tough. Raj was sitting down to one side of the classroom as usual. I went over to go and sit with him yet he did not even notice me. Haresh and Frank were already seated across the room and they waved for me to sit next to them. But I needed to talk to Raj, he was my actual friend after all.

"The seat's reserved", Raj said bluntly. This was my best friend, why would he not want to sit next to me?

"Erm who's it reserved for?" I asked

"For my friend, Jason. He died unfortunately and has been replaced by some douche who hangs around the cool kids. Go away." he said dismissively.

I was honestly perplexed. What did I do to Raj to cause him to turn against me? It had to have been something serious and so I solemnly walked over to the other side of the classroom and reluctantly sat next to Haresh and Frank who then took it in turns to slap my back and make some slang jeering noise. Was this what my life would be like from now on?

At that moment, Mr Griffin hobbled into the room, bearing a huge stack of papers. If those were tests then I would have been screwed. Griffin slowly walked up to me and slapped my test paper onto the desk.

"Nicely done, Jason."

I flipped over the paper and was pleasantly surprised by a top score. Whoever or whatever had possessed me was a genius. I flicked through the paper and was shocked at the fact that the paper was done in my handwriting, to the exact letter. Either I had done the paper and had gotten full marks but then forgot about it or someone had possessed me and done it in my handwriting. What kind of person could mimic someone else's handwriting so perfectly? But then this was not a person. This was something beyond human comprehension.

I sat there for the entire lesson examining every letter written by me during 'The Gap', the new name for my hibernation. I frantically tried to find a fault in the handwriting, something that this previous version of me would not be able to write. Perhaps an overly curly 'f' or a crossed 7. But there were no faults whatsoever. This mystery was proving to be impossible. And just when I thought things could not get any worse, Griffin interrupted my trail of thought.

"Jason, considering you got the top mark, I want you to come up to the board." I reluctantly did so, fearing what he may ask.

"Now, I want you to draw the following diagram: an AD/AS diagram showing the effects of a rise in Interest rates. Show the class how good you are at Economics".

This was bad. It was as if he almost wanted to catch me out. The old man looked at me, eagerly waiting for me to fail. Jason doing well was an impossibility for him. I would be doing him a solid as this question baffled me on so many levels. What was interest? The only thing I knew was that this lesson was of no interest to me. I gingerly lifted up the board pen and prepared to blag my way through the situation. From a quick glance at the class, Griffin and Raj were both there waiting for me to fail. My once best friend needed me to relinquish my spot of top economist back to him. Just as I opened my mouth to say that this was too hard for me, the following happened.

"Sorry Sir, I forgot to mention something," Frank interjected. Griffin looked at him, eyebrows crossed. "Jason isn't feeling right today since he had a bit too much to drink last night." *What*? Why would Frank throw me under the bus like that? The last thing I needed was a suspension for coming to school with a hangover. That was the last thing I needed.

"Thank you for letting me know Frank. Jason, you sit down and rest. Raj, you answer it instead". I forgot that the 'cool kids' were immune to getting into trouble. So now I could do whatever and simply get away with it, no questions asked. Frank did not throw me under the bus rather he pulled me up from under it. Perhaps he was actually a good friend. Impossible. The guy smashed my phone and almost beat me to death before threatening me. There was no forgiveness in that.

Raj then went up to the board and did the task, giving me evil looks while doing so. I must have seriously done something bad to him during 'The Gap'. As I sat in my seat, pondering my existence, a cold, pale hand appeared on my shoulder. It had veins popping out, contrasting the light colour. The fingers were long and bony.

"Jay, take some coffee to help you wake up," Boris added. Everyone was actually being so nice to me. It was surprising to say the least. The main focus now was getting Raj to be my friend again considering that he would be the only one clever enough to get me out of this predicament.

After the lesson I went outside only to be approached by none other than Mr Grove. He looked a bit different than he did last month. His stubble had now grown out into a short beard, alternating between brown and silver hairs. When he saw me, rather than smile, he spoke instantly.

"Jason, my room, now!". Had I done something bad during 'The Gap'? Perhaps Mr Griffin snitched on the fact that I was drinking.

The layout of Mr Grove's room was practically the same as last month except his desk was now a complete mess. Papers were sprawled across the desk with no sort of order. His bin was overflowing with even more sheets, looking like a volcano erupting paper. I sat down in my usual seat, and waited for the man to come in.

"Jason, I have something important to discuss with you. It is about your behaviour over the last month". Finally, some answers about what happened during the Gap.

"Your behaviour over the last month has been," he paused for a moment, catching his breath. "I am not sure how to put this. Your behaviour over the past month has been well - exceptional. I have called you here to show you your report. Look!".

He handed it over and to my surprise I had gotten A*s in all three of my subjects. How had this happened? On a usual day, I would have been ecstatic.

"It is almost as if you are a new person". That was when it hit me. He was right to an extent and he may have some more answers on that matter.

"Sir, sorry if this sounds a bit weird but erm do you have any footage of me from the last month? Is there any footage of me studying or playing rugby or anything like that? I just wanted to create a montage of how much I have changed this academic year."

Before the words had finished coming out of my mouth, he smiled. My impeccable results looked good on his behalf.

"That is a great idea, Jason. You are honestly a model student. I will have to have a look around. There must be some footage out there somewhere". This was good news. If I could get some footage then perhaps my memories would start coming back.

"Make sure you keep up the good work," Grove exclaimed. And with that said, I headed back out again. It was time to figure out what happened with my old friends.

My next lesson was Maths. Ms Dawson was even more pregnant now, only weeks away from giving birth. I entered the classroom and saw Yaseen sitting down opposite and so decided to go and sit next to him. Frank and Wilfred were sitting together with an empty desk behind them. Frank signalled for me to sit with them but instead I chose Yaseen. As I approached him, I could see Manny whispering something to Jermaine, giggling. The second the two locked eyes on me, they stopped talking, as if out of respect.

"Hi Yaseen,"

"Hey" he said briefly, without making eye contact.

"I take it we have not kept in touch over the last month."

"No we have not," he said hesitantly. Something had happened between us over the last month.

"If it makes you feel any better, I am sorry for everything." The second the words exited my mouth, my friend smiled, his face lighting up.

"You are forgiven Jason."

"Just like that?" I asked, puzzled.

"Forgiveness is very important in Islam. I understand that you wanted a shot at being Frank's right hand man and it did not work out for you. What is most important is that you apologised. And for that, you are forgiven." If only all rivalries could be ended like that.

"Yaseen, out of interest, do you know what I did to Raj to make him hate me. I seem to have forgotten.

"You really want to know?" Jermaine interrupted eagerly. I just nodded. Something had gone horribly wrong during 'The Gap' and I needed answers. "Basically, you beat him up over some petty argument. Frank joined in as well and now he hates you for it. I'm surprised you forgot about that."

Why did I beat up Raj? I thought to myself. The boy had been my best friend for almost 4 years now, carried through my GCSEs and done so much more. This could not have been a case of amnesia. I would never, of sound mind, lay a hand on Raj. Something had definitely taken control of my body. *But why? Why me?* I had no memory from the past 30 days. Nothing. I felt utterly useless. All my life I had desired some sense of adventure and now that it was here, I just wanted to turn back and cry. I had just lost my best friend. Julian was the one person who could help me but he was out of the country. Even though my grades had finally improved, I felt no happier. I desperately needed to get through to Raj and acquire his help. Like Julian, he was a human computer, able to solve absolutely anything. Either one of them could help me out.

Immediately I went through my phone to look for any potential evidence yet there were no new photos or any new messages or even phone calls from the last month. It was as if I had deleted all evidence at the end of 'The Gap'. Whoever or whatever was behind this wanted to cover their tracks. But why?

After the lesson, I rushed to Grove's office. Perhaps he had found the footage I needed. Abruptly, I swung open the door of his classroom. The man was sitting there, back hunched, endlessly typing. As he met gaze with me, he smiled.

"Jason, how are you doing?"

"I am good thank you, sir. Did you find any footage from that rugby game?"

"I am so sorry, but there is nothing. I even asked the Head of Rugby, but he said that filming sports fixtures can endanger child protection." That was all I needed. There were no videos, photos or even texts from me. The closest thing I had to evidence was my Economics test. That was when it hit me. There was an entire bank of footage sitting right under my nose.

Chapter 4: The Heist

Back in the Sixth Form Centre, I saw Frank, Haresh, Wilfred and Boris all having a laugh, sitting in a circle. Boris was downing another cup of coffee, pouring every last drop down his throat.

"There he is!" Frank shouted. "Where have you been, brother?"

"Sorry I just needed to sort some stuff out". This was my chance to get answers. "I was just wondering if any of you knew anything about getting into the school CCTV system?"

"Ooh Jason, that is big coming from you. The amount of information you could get" said Frank.

"You could literally spy on anyone," Haresh added. "When someone is slacking from a gym session you could find out what they were actually doing."

"I could find out what the school do with the leftover coffee," Boris said, smiling.

"I know some stuff about it," Wilfred stated. Of course, Wilfred knew. He was the tech-master at the school. "What do you want to know Jason?" he said, his eyes widening.

"Everything."

"Okay, so here goes," he said, bending forward, and started talking in a hushed voice. Everyone else moved in. "The school is littered with cameras in each room. All the footage from the cameras is broadcasted into a room directly above the History corridor at the top of the school. The room has several computers. There, if you were to plug in a USB stick you could download all the files. They will be in MP3 format so you can go through the footage when you are home." It sounded relatively simple. An in and out procedure. "However, there are always two members of staff in there at one point. Mr Wilson is one of them. The two of them are eagle eyed, constantly looking through the footage for any evidence of drugs, or any other illegal activity. We call them 'The Watchers'. When one of them takes a break, the other will always be there. The room is never left unguarded." Mr Wilson was an ex-police officer. He was the judge, jury, and executioner of Queen's. If he caught you doing anything suspicious then he would personally chase after you and bait you out.

"So how do we get in?" Frank stated. *We?* All of a sudden this had become a group mission. But the more we had, the better.

"The school officially closes at six every day. That is when the gates shut and all the staff finally go home. 'The Watchers' continue watching for a short period of time. Mr Wilson locks up the room and goes home at that point, before doing one final sweep of the site on foot. He then takes the key with him so nobody can get in. However, the room is sealed like a vault. First, you open the initial door using a passcode. The second door must be opened using the key. In case any of you are wondering, I do not know the code to the door."

This was a lot to take in. The deed seemed almost impossible. Emphasis on almost.

"So, all we need to do is figure out the passcode, find the key and get in after six", I asked.

"Oh, I forgot to say, if any of us get caught, it would be an instant expulsion." My jaw dropped. "The school deem stealing security as major theft which is punishable by expulsion." Was this really worth it? My entire school career was on the line just for some potential evidence to help rejog my memory This mission would ruin not just my career but the careers of all these other people.

"Sounds fun!" Frank exclaimed with a grin on his face. "Think about all the untapped footage we could get a hold of. We could use it as bargaining power against anyone."

Even though what Frank was saying was true to an extent, it was a horrible excuse to steal footage. However, if this got me the relevant evidence that I needed to figure out what happened during 'The Gap', then it would be worth it.

"So, when should we do this?" I asked.

"Tonight!" Haresh said extatically, clapping his hands. "We can go to the school gym up until 6 and then we can steal it."

"Alright, so here is the plan" Wilfred said. He tore a chocolate milk carton from Boris who scowled immediately. He then pulled black pin out of his pocket. What was that doing there? Wilfred then used the thin end to pick at the casing of the carton. After a bit of time, the casing gave way and Will peeled off a thin see-through film.

"This is a wax coating that goes onto milk cartons. One of us must take this to the vault and stick this film onto the keypad. When Wilson types in the passcode after his lunchbreak, his fingerprints will be left on the film where the correct numbers are".

"But how will we know the correct order?" I interrupted.

"If it is a 4-digit code then the number of possible combinations will be 4 factorial which is 24". Haresh said. Everyone looked at him oddly. "What? I know my maths."

"Luckily the lock has an infinite number of tries. It will not disable if we keep getting it wrong. Now, who wants to apply this to the keypad?"

"I can do that," I said. Frank nodded.

"That's the first door sorted. For the second door, follow these instructions carefully. Mr Wilson drives a BMW which he parks in the teacher's carpark. Boris can get the key off him when he goes to his car. Then he will throw it to Frank who will give it to you, Jason. You then have to break in and download all the files. Haresh will create a distraction outside for you so you are safe. And then we bail out and give the key back to Mr Wilson before he realises."

"Wow, you really know your stuff, Will. How do you know so much about the CCTV?" I exclaimed.

"Promise you will keep this a secret. I have been planning to break into that room to delete some CCTV footage of something I did. I need to destroy the evidence before anybody finds out the truth". He sounded very ominous. "Now, back to business. I actually have a set of walkie talkies that we can use. They are in my locker." This guy was full of surprises.

The plan was solid. Fault-proof you may say. "So, when do we start?"

"In 10 minutes. When Wilson goes for his lunch break, Jason, you need to place the film on the key code."

9 minutes and 30 seconds later, 'the gang' and I were in an empty classroom. Wilfred had hooked up a system so that everyone could hear what I was doing. All I had to do was stick some plastic onto the keypad.

69

Outside, a giant figure could be seen marching across the pavement, towards the dining hall. Mr Wilson was bald with giant arms, equipped with mountains of biceps that poked through his T-shirt. Even in peak cold, the man was immune to the elements. As he moved, he kept his eyes locked forward, like a lion locked onto its prey.

"Ok GO!" Wilfred said, pushing me out the room.

I rushed up the stairs, to the top of the history block. The area above the school was dark and dingy with cobwebs sprawled across the ceiling. At the end of the room was a large steel door, looking as if it had been ripped straight out of a bank. To the side of the door was a tiny keypad, that looked pathetic when compared to the marvel of the door. I simply stuck the film onto it, looking completely seamless.

"It is done," I whispered into the microphone in my shirt pocket. However, as I was heading back, a tall silhouette blocked the end of the corridor, sealing me in.

"What are you doing here?" The voice boomed. Wilson was supposed to be on his lunch break.

"Erm sorry, I was looking for the toilets."

"No toilets down here," his voice boomed. "Don't let me catch you here again."

Mr Wilson simply groaned and stormed past me, leaving a nasty stench of sweat behind him.

"Phase One complete," I said, re-uniting with the others, trying to catch my breath.

At 17:45 we were all back in the same classroom. Wilfred held the wax film, cradling it in his hands like a child. The were 4 different fingerprints. One was on the top middle (2). Another was on the right end of the first row (3). The next one was on the left of the second row (4). The last fingerprint was on the left of the third row (7). That means that the 4 numbers were 2347. Haresh was sitting down writing out all the different number combinations. They were:

2347

2374

2473

2437

2734

2743

And those were only the numbers starting with 2. This was going to be tough.

The plan went as follows; In 15 minutes, Mr Wilson would head to his car. Haresh would distract him while Boris stole the key from him. Boris would then give Wilfred and I the key. We would unlock the 2 doors and then enter the vault. At that point Wilfred would copy the footage onto a USB stick and we would leave. Frank would be on guard for any teachers. Then we would sneak the key back into Mr Wilson's pocket before he would finally drive off.

Wilfred was looking at his watch tirelessly and his gaze would occasionally flicker outside the window. It was dot on 6 and just as planned, Mr Wilson was walking towards his car. He marched towards the vehicle with a completely blank expression, yet still looked as fearsome as ever. His eyes were wide open, devoid of any tiredness which was surprising for a man who would stare at screens all day.

"Haresh, you are up, over" Wilfred whispered into the walkie talkie. The boy acknowledged the request and did the unthinkable. All of a sudden, Haresh started breathing heavily and then erupted into endless coughing. At first Mr Wilson made no remark. Suddenly there was a loud thump from the walkie-talkie, followed by static.

Swift and heavy footsteps followed.

Haresh moaned and grumbled before suddenly going silent.

"Wilson is going in for the CPR. His back pocket is exposed, over," said Boris through the microphone. "What happened!" he shouted to the teacher.

Mr Wilson was getting nervous. "He is going into Cardiac arrest. I-er have to do CPR and bring him back to life". Wilson then pushed Boris out the way and started compressing Haresh's chest. Sounds of banging could be heard.

"I will go and call the school nurse," Boris exclaimed before running off with the key." The excitement in his breath could be heard.

"Don't die on me kid!" Wilson cried, thumping at Haresh's chest with full force. The boy was doing an amazing job at keeping still. This was Oscar level acting.

Back in the classroom, the rest of us were joyful as the plan had gone exactly to plan so far. In my hand was the sheet with all the possible codes. Boris soon approached the classroom before chucking the keys through the open window. Frank caught them clean and handed them over to me.

Wilfred and I paced towards the vault, skipping up the stairs. The huge steel door stood still with all its might, towering over the two of us. To the side, the keypad caught my eye. 2, 3, 4 and 7 were the possible digits. Will began plugging in every possible combination, first trying all the numbers staring with 2. There were six different numbers beginning with 2. None of them worked. Then he began with all the numbers for 3.

Haresh had left his device on, so we could hear everything that was going on. From the banging to the nervous remarks of Wilson.

"I am sorry kid, but you have left me no choice," he said taking in a deep breath. I cringed in disgust.

The second their lips connected, Haresh got up and started spluttering. Mr Wilson sounded relieved however it was at that moment that Haresh knew that his distraction was over. We now only had a matter of seconds to finish the job and give him back the keys.

"What was that all about?" Mr Wilson said.

"Erm, well I choked on some food. Sorry about that sir." Haresh said, his acting cracking under pressure.

By this time, Will had finished trying all of the numbers starting with 3. He then started with the 4s. We were desperately running out of time.

"I should be on my way" Mr Wilson said.

Haresh knew that now was the time to act, so he shoved his hand down his throat and projectile vomited all over the floor.

"Jesus!" Wilson cried. "Are you feeling okay".

"No, I am not, I have been food poisoned. I knew that fish at lunch smelt off," he said before tumbling back to the ground buying us some more time. I peered over to Wilfred to see his progress. 4273 wrong. 4327 wrong. 4372, the keypad glowed green and buzzed. Bingo. With a mighty shove, the door swung open revealing the second door. I took the key and slotted it in and unlocked the door. The vault opened to reveal our treasure.

The room was filled with all sorts of computers and an array of different coloured lights. There were buttons and switches all over on the wall, as if we were in the cockpit of the Millennium Falcon. I could see Wilfred gloating at the place, fiddling around with some screens. This was heaven for him.

On the main computer, there was a grid full of different places at school. The main areas were the Sixth Form Centre, the Dining Hall and the Library. Other classrooms could also be seen on separate tabs. I went over to the biggest computer and opened up the footage for the sixth form centre. Wilfred gently pushed me to the side.

"Give me a second to sort out some personal business," he said before putting his hand onto the mouse and then he started flicking through footage. He fast forwarded through many days, a blur of images on the screen. His eyes flickered from left to right. Somehow, he was able to navigate this huge web of footage. Eventually he pulled up the footage for Tuesday 5th November and then skipped to 10:05. What happened next shocked me.

It was 10:05 on a Tuesday. The Sixth Form Centre was relatively full. Wilfred was sitting on a sofa just relaxing. However, a moment later he began to rummage through his pocket with a confused look on his face. As he pulled his hand out, a small container rolled onto the floor containing an array of pills. Realising what he had done, the boy dashed to the container and put the drugs back in his pocket before looking up at the security camera. How had this flown over Mr Wilson's head? Will then clicked a few buttons and deleted that short clip.

"Your secret is safe with me." I said, smiling. So Wilfred had cannabis in school? He then proceeded to plug in the USB stick into the computer. He then selected the entire footage from the last month and copied it onto the stick. Proceeding that, he removed the stick and placed it in my hands.

"This is what we came for. Now, let's scram." Within the blink of an eye, the two of us had left and then locked each door individually. I looked out the window, to see Haresh who had now stopped vomiting and was sitting down. Mr Wilson suddenly checked his pockets before looking totally alarmed.

"I have to go. This is an emergency!" he shouted. He left Haresh on the floor and paced back towards the school site.

"Code Red!" Haresh whispered into the microphone. Wilson was storming in our direction, unaware that we were outside his dwelling. I grabbed the key off Wilfred before making the perfect throw to Boris, outside the window. He grabbed it and sprinted towards Mr Wilson.

There was a corner in between the two of them. Boris chucked the keys to the ground, making it look like they had been dropped.

However, Mr Wilson was just about to turn the corner. If he saw the boy standing next to the keys then he would be a goner. At that moment, Boris did the unimaginable. He lifted the lid of the huge bin next to him, and leapt in, closing the lid nanoseconds before Wilson had turned the corner.

The member of staff caught sight of his prize and then gingerly raised them before looking left and right. There was nobody there. He just assumed that his keys had fallen out of his pocket. Upon returning to his car, he noticed that Haresh had fled the site, leaving the carpark deserted. Wilson just shook his heads. "Millennials," he murmured. With a revving of the engine, he drove off into the night. The heist was successful and now both Boris and Haresh stunk.

Chapter 5: The Footage

Later, that evening, I sat at home flicking through the footage on my small laptop in my bedroom in which the USB was plugged into. I was watching all the footage at the Sixth Form Centre diligently, starting off from the very beginning. The first Tuesday was when I was in full control of my body, when Frank beat me up and smashed my phone, allowing me to go home early and watch Terminator with Julian.

The first two days of 'The Gap' were the weekend followed by Monday 14th October. I would usually get into school for 8 o'clock, however at 8:10 there was still no sign of me. These security cameras recorded in such good quality and even recorded sound. This allowed teachers to monitor any sort of potential drug trafficking. The sound of the centre is usually that of a hubbub of teenagers, sounding like a carnival at times.

The ruckus was silenced when I leisurely strolled in at 8:15, without a care in the world. This occasion was completely blank in my mind. Everybody looked towards me as I still had bandages on my face from the fight on Friday. The person that was supposed to be me walked up to the middle area of the Centre and roared "FRANK!" sounding enraged. From amidst the crowd emerged Frank with a bloodthirsty look on his face. "This ends now!" I shouted again. Frank just smiled and licked his lips, looking like a serial killer.

This entire spectacle was truly a sight to behold. Whoever had taken control of me was a force to be reckoned with. Out of nowhere, he hurled a punch that plummeted into Frank's cheek who then squealed in pain. He did not expect anyone to hurt him, especially not Jason, that little squirt. All of a sudden, I was in a boxer's pose with my arms bent at 90 degrees blocking my face. Frank returned with a right cross but it was blocked precisely before parrying back with a jab to the stomach. The enemy was knocked back by the force but looked oddly happy. Finally, the bully had a worthy opponent and the perfect video for his social media.

Frank tried to clamber back onto his feet yet was met with a swing from my right leg, cleanly sweeping him to the ground. On the ground, he whimpered, and his grin slowly faded and moulded into a look of fear before he raised his arms to protect himself. Instead of striking down the wounded animal, I put out my hand, a gesture of a truce. I was astonished at my behaviour. The son of the Prime Minister grabbed my hand and pulled himself back onto his feet.

"No hard feelings, mate," I said before disappearing off into the crowd. The entire year looked around in confusion. What had they just witnessed? Some nerdy kid just walked in and whooped the school bully's arse before casually walking away. Rather than run away from embarrassment, Frank just smiled

So that was how Frank and I became friends? After beating him in a fight, he admired me enough to make me a friend. *How unusual?* And yet there was absolutely no memory of this in my head. The hope that watching footage would bring back memory had gone. However, this 'thing' that had possessed me had some sort of plan. An agenda. He wanted to befriend Frank. That had to be his priority. But why?

I finished cycling through the Sixth Form Centre footage for that day before going on to look at what happened in my Economics lesson, that same day. At 09:05, I skipped in, late, and headed across the room, without a care in the world. Raj gestured for his best friend to sit next to him, yet he was ignored. I then walked up to Frank, before signalling for Haresh to move aside. The boy moved, out of fear, leaving the seat next to Frank empty. This new version of me then sat next to the school bully and prepared to begin some work.

Griffin looked at me, confused, before saying, "Okay everyone, it is time to hand in your homework." Frank frantically rummaged through his bag but brought out nothing. First Raj handed in his papers, followed by Yaseen, Boris and then me. "Frank where is your work?" the teacher asked.

"Erm well you see. You see"

"You see, Frank lent me his work but I forgot to return it to him," I interrupted. "His lack of homework is entirely my responsibility and any sort of punishment in my direction will be accepted with due diligence". *The heck did I just say?* Rather than question my excuse, Griffin just grumbled a bit and then walked off. Frank was puzzled as to why some guy who beat him up was now covering for his work. He just shook off the thought and got back to work.

That same day, Frank put out his hand to me. "Nice to meet you, partner. The name's Frank." This just kept getting stranger and not to mention a tad cheesy. The bully then shoved Boris to the side, spilling his coffee, making space for me next to him on the sofa. I had officially become friends with Frank in just one day. And yet there were still twenty-nine more days of activity to go through. This was going to be a chore.

During the next day of footage, in Physics, I had sat next to Wilfred. Mr Weaving proceeded to give us a test to do and the person using my body worked through it diligently. It was hard to zoom in enough to see him write, but I was able to pick out something peculiar. When he wrote my name at the top of the paper, he wrote J, paused for a split-second before writing 'ason'. The being was still adjusting to using my name. At the end of the lesson, Weaving gave us back the papers, marked, and unsurprisingly I had achieved full marks.

In Maths, rather than sit with Yaseen as usual, I had sat behind Wilfred and Frank. They were constantly chatting with me all lesson and Ms Dawson was just oblivious to our distractions. Rather than focus on me all day long, I decided to look at some other people, mainly my old friends.

In the Sixth Form Centre, at lunch, Yaseen was talking to Raj and a few of my other friends.

"Is it just me or is Jason acting very strangely?" Raj asked.

"You are right, Raj. It may just be a phase." Yaseen responded.

"I just cannot believe he is hanging around the 'cool' kids. Frank publicly humiliated him last Monday and now they are acting like BFFS."

"Very strange," Yaseen muttered. I felt sorry for the two of them. They were trying to look out for me and had no idea about my possession.

This was enough detective work for one day. It was time for some well deserved shut-eye.

The next thing I knew, I was back at school, sitting next to Frank in Economics.

"Hey Jason, how are you doing?"

"Erm I am fine, just a bit concerned."

"What is there to be concerned about? You are my friend. Anything you want, it's yours. Not only that, but my father can get you anything. A chauffeur to school every day, a small island in the Caribbean. Anything."

"You see well there is this thing that I want." My speech was cut off by some noise. I looked up to see everyone holding weapons. Frank's face was smudged with dirt, while he clasped a weapon.

"Save it for later Jay," Frank whispered, chucking over a pistol. Without a second thought, I reloaded it and held it pointed to the door. There were thumps at the door and groans. Haresh was standing there with his tie around his head, holding a sledgehammer in his hand which was wielded with a firm grip, ready to obliterate any incoming threats.

"Why are you so scared?" Boris said to me, aware of my pale expression. "Have some coffee, that will help". He handed over a huge cup of coffee and it burnt in my hands. It slipped out of my hands and smashed on the ground. Rather than coffee spilling out, thick red blood oozed. The sludge spread across the ground before it started wriggling like a slug across the room.

"Everyone ready!" Haresh shouted and everyone nodded in agreement. He swung his hammer preparing to smash the door open when a bright light burst through the door and tore through the boy. Haresh looked at me, his life slipping away as his skin melted. At that moment, his body fell into ash and his skull thumped onto the ground. From within the hole in the door, a figure emerged. He had a mechanical head full of cogs and wires. Its head had a huge dent in it as if it had been hit hard. It spun and looked towards me with its devilish eyes.

"You killed me!" it roared before reigniting its hilt causing fire to erupt out. The flame swiped through Boris killing him in one quick blow.

The moans of zombies got louder as hoards of undead monstrosities flocked into the room. One gazed at me, its face grey and hair like string. Any remnants of teeth had been yellowed and there were remnants of bloodied flesh stuck between the teeth. Their fingers were long and strewn, with the occasional one missing.

Now I had zombies and a killer robot to worry about. Frank was shooting zombies, one after the other, blood bursting in all directions. With his other hand, he had a knife and was gutting them.

The Android stormed towards me, melting everything between us. Its eyes were set on complete destruction. Without warning, it picked up Wilfred and hurled him across the room like a doll. The boy landed, incredibly mangled and before he could get up, he was dissected by a swarm of creatures. He let out a shrill cry as his spine was yanked out leaving his flesh a jelly that wobbled to the ground, blood spurting out in all directions.

There were only a small handful of us left as the undead creatures tore into the classroom and savaged their way through the dead pupils. From within his rucksack, Frank fished out a can of deodorant. From his pocket he got out his lighter and he sprayed the can into the lighter creating a Hellish flame that melted a large portion of the zombies. The Android approached me and was about to burn me when the indescribable happened.

Each one of the machine's limbs began to fade. It began to lose colour before it was entirely gone. The Droid just bubbled into darkness. One second it was there and then it was gone the next. It just dissolved into nothingness, leaving me deeply puzzled. But before we were safe, a hand reached out of the ground, demonic in its nature with huge claws. The arm reached out of the ground and decapitated Haresh with one quick blow. His head dissolved into nothingness as he fell.

"NOO!" Frank screamed, echoing like a banshee. He pulled up his gun and shot the creature's hand multiple times, yet it did not flinch. A small blue flame emerged from its palm. The flame danced within its demonic fingertips before it sped forward and collided into Frank, whose body was engulfed, melting his skin as he collapsed.

As my new friend lay on the floor, dying, he reached out to me. "I see through your lies! I hope you die a long and painful death," he said as he disintegrated. Everyone was now dead except me. The demonic hand that came out of the ground stretched out even further and its body crawled out of the ground. From its red eyes to its fangs, I recognised it immediately. This was the monstrosity that attacked me during my dream yesterday. This was the thing responsible for all of my problems.

"You!" I cried. "You did this to me!" The monster just looked at me blankly. "Why did you take my body! Who are you!" The monster just put a finger over its lip. "Why should I shush!" I screamed. That thing had no authority to tell me what to do. With a flash of movements, I reloaded my gun and shot the creature between its two excuses for eyes. The bullet just bounced off like a pea.

"Answer me!" I cried. "What are you? Why have you done this to me?" The silhouette just shook its head.

"I am not the one you should be looking for," it said with a sombre tone. Its voice was thick and gruff, yet it had a creamy sound to it, like dark chocolate.

"What do you mean? Who should I be looking for?" I cried out.

"I am just the messenger. Find the source of the message and you will have your answers," it said in its powerful voice. Having said that, the being just blew away into dark, dust particles and then ground into nothing, leaving me in a room full of dead creatures and deceased friends.

And so I sat on the floor and began sobbing. I had had enough of all these games with no answers and so sobbed so hard, to the point where my eyes ached. Nobody could help me in this field of tall grass. There was no hope, nothing.

Moments later I woke up, back in my physical body which was burning hot, throbbing, and doused in sweat. My cheeks were stinging from the tears and my muscles ached. *What the hell was that?*

The next day at school was pretty standard. As in the new standard where I was cool and hung around Frank and his crowd. Now I was a genius and was treated like one. Jason was truly embraced by the pupils of Queen's. Had I done anything to deserve this? No.

While walking to the Sixth Form Centre, I was stopped by a teacher. It was Miss Young, my old GCSE French teacher.

"Bonjour Jason," she said. I had not practiced any French for the last two years. I barely remembered any of the vocabulary and so simply waved back.

"*ça* va?" She said. I could just about remember that phrase.

"Bien," I stated bluntly. Today was more of a 'mal' day but it was always better to give a good answer in order to avoid further conversation.

"So, I was hoping to write a piece on you for the school magazine." Queen's does have a monthly magazine that commemorates the best pupils and ignores everyone else. It is honestly an elitist system where only the good people are celebrated and everyone else is treated like dirt. "So, would you be interested?" Before you ask, no, I have never featured in the school magazine. I am just too good for them.

"Erm why me?"

"Follow me. Monsieur Grove and I have something to show you." Mr Grove also had a part to play about this interview? Perhaps I should just tell them the truth, about everything. In Miss Young's classroom, Mr Grove was sitting in the corner reading a French magazine. When he heard me come in, his face lit up.

"Jason! So good to see you." I just waved back with minimal effort. "I was looking at your recent performance and thought that it would be best to celebrate your achievements. In response to that, I invited Mademoiselle Young over here to document it in the school magazine. What do you think?"

"I think that's a great idea," I said with fake enthusiasm. It was clear that I had cheated my way to success, but it was fun to see me finally be remembered around the school site.

"Jason," said Grove, "I found some of that footage you wanted." He reached to a remote control and turned on the smart board. "This is from your concert last Friday." *I performed a concert?* I did not even know the first thing about music. On the screen, there was a boy reminiscent of myself who walked onto the school's concert hall stage. Thunderous applause loomed around him. The boy had slicked-back hair and wore a fancy black tuxedo. I was supposed to be this person? The boy (me) bowed before the audience and seated himself behind the Grand Piano. All of a sudden, there was dead silence which then broke into dramatic music. My Gap-self swept from side to side on the keys, making beautiful music. I recognised the piece as 'Moonlight Sonata 3rd Movement' which is easily one of the hardest piano pieces and yet my Gap-self played it with such majesty and pride. He made the impossible look seamless as he blasted out Beethoven. I could see my scrawny fingers bouncing up and down the piano. I did not even know if I had the finger strength to play such a piece. I took a quick glance at my hands and realised that I had not used them to their true potential.

After about a minute, Mr Grove paused the video. "I can send you the footage if you would like?" I nodded vigorously. My jaw had dropped in astonishment to my Piano skills. If my Gap-self could do it then so could I because technically we were the same person.

Miss Young went on to say, "I want you to tell us about your recent claim to fame. This 'Jason-fever' should we call it, where you have gone from a nobody to an absolute hero." That is what I was saying about elitism. Nobody cared about my existence a month ago. I literally stood up to the school bully but everyone forgot that. And now all of a sudden, I did well in a few tests and everyone wanted to be my friend and have me be a representative for the school. Mr Grove stood next to her, recording me with his phone, eagerly waiting for me to talk with his ear-to-ear grin.

"Last month I was not exactly a nobody," the words fumbling out of my mouth. "I still tried my hardest to be likeable, going out of my way to make friends and I even stood up to the school bully, Frank Clifford, if any of you remember that." Grove's grin gently transitioned into a modest scowl. Insulting Frank would be a poor move on my behalf, ruining our 'friendship'. I needed to tell some more lies.

"But the thing about Frank is that we never saw eye to eye in the beginning and I have warmed up to him within the last month. About a month ago I had the realisation that trying my hardest in school was not good enough. I needed to extent my boundaries and so came to the conclusion that I was capable of so much more. I got into Rugby and thus discovered a natural talent. Spending more time with Frank resulted with his good being rubbed off onto me." *More Lies.* "Piano has also been a hobby of mine. I secretly have been attending classes and slowly learning and I thought now would be the best time to show off. My message to everyone would be to know your limits and extend them because we can never reach our human limits. It is all psychological. I hope that answers your question."

"Thank you for that Jason." Grove stopped recording and put his phone away. Miss Young had made a few notes during my talk. She was jotting so much down, more than had even come out of my mouth. *What is she writing down?*

"The new magazine comes out next Wednesday. Come to this room for your free copy," she said. *Do they seriously charge people for this junk?*

I waved goodbye and strolled out of the classroom. I was now some sort of celebrity within the school. And could play piano? The situation was getting crazier by the hour.

There were still another 30 minutes before my Maths lesson and so it was time to take a trip to the Music School.

The New Music School was opened in 2018. I had only ever been in there once to tour some prospective parents. Now you are probably wondering, *Jason why were you helping around the school, you are too cool for that?* The short answer is that I was 'volunteered'. Shame. There were so many better uses of my time that Saturday morning.

Upon entering the Music School, I was overwhelmed by the positive ambience. Some smooth Jazz could be heard through the halls. Across the wall, there were dozens of photos of pupils playing instruments. From saxophones to violins, all sorts of music. One photo showcased a huge choir of students. At the front, there was a boy who was absolutely belting out with his mouth was wide open. I did not know a child could have so many teeth. At the main desk, there was a receptionist. The whole room gave off the odour of fresh paint and the ground was polished to such extent that I was almost struggling to walk without my shoes squeaking.

At the main desk there was a receptionist. When she saw me, she smiled.

"Jason, so good of you to come here again. Your performance last week was breath-taking to say the least." I just smiled in response. *Who is this person?*

"I was wondering if you have any Grand Pianos that are not in use." My plan was to play on the piano the same piece from the concert. Perhaps I could play it. Depending on muscle memory.

"Yes, of course. You can use the one in room M5. Use it for as long as you like". I then proceeded to head over to that room. Room M5 was a generic classroom with a grand piano at the front. The room had a timeline that covered the entire back wall, showing off all the eras of music. On the whiteboard there were some musical notes written down. All beyond my understanding.

The Grand Piano was so shiny that it could have been a mirror. The elegant keys stood there, ready for me to play. I stroked my fingers across the ivory and prepared to sound the machine. In my mind I pictured the video of the concert. I needed to trust my muscle memory and so relaxed my fingers before beginning to play. I pushed the first key and a smooth sound was made What was the next note? I hit the keys at random hoping to recreate Beethoven but instead ended up playing 'Mary had a Little Lamb' before walking away in shame.

"That was quick," the receptionist said on my way out.

"I did not feel like playing today" I mumbled.

"Oh well. I was going to ask. how would you like to play in next week's concert? Everybody loved your performance and we would like to see you play again. Your performance was the best selling concert since your brother Julian's concert all those years ago. Those were the days," she said, rambling on. "Your brother's concert was the first concert I saw at this school. Anyway, how would you like to play next week?" That was the last thing I needed; to show myself up in front of hundreds of audience members. The truth about my lack of memory needed to be concealed for now. If someone found out, they could diagnose me with schizophrenia and send me to a psychiatric hospital or something like that.

"My apologies, but my work-load is quite high and I need to do some more revision." That statement was true, from a certain point of view.

In Maths, I was given my latest test back and scored 100%, unsurprisingly. I expected nothing less from my Gap-self. The problem was now that I needed to catch up on thirty days of missing work in order to maintain this streak. Ms Dawson would be onto me if my perfect test scores suddenly dipped down to the 60s.

In that lesson, we were looking at Binomial Expansion. The problem was that I did not know any previous month's content, so this lesson proved to be extra difficult.

That Break Time, I had a lot to think about. There was this event in the Marvel Comics called 'Secret Invasion', where a bunch of shapeshifting aliens, Skrulls, pretended to be the superheroes. They hid themselves in plain sight and start taking over Earth from the inside. I could have been the centre of a potential alien invasion. But why would anybody want to be me? Apart from my dashing good looks and muscular physique, what else could I possibly offer? My thoughts were then interrupted by the loud voice of Frank.

"Jay, get over here!" he shouted, sitting amongst the usual gang. I had not spoken to them since the heist last night. I waddled over to where they sat.

"How are you feeling, Haresh? You really went all in last night." He just scoffed in response. I could tell he was still emotionally scarred from having to do mouth to mouth with Mr Wilson.

"So," Frank said, "Did you find anything interesting amongst the security footage?"

"Nothing interesting yet. Just a bunch of boring conversations."

Frank just gave out a laugh. "Moving along, are you ready for the Rugby match later?" Haresh, Boris and Will just nodded in agreement. "What about you Jason?" That was a no-no. When was the last time I played rugby? At least 6 years ago. After my lack of muscle memory on the piano I highly doubt that my skills lay in rugby.

"Well, I am going to take a rain check today. My work is piling up, but you can bet I'll be in the match next week." Frank gave a look of disarray before saying,

"Jason, I know you are new to rugby, but you have to understand that you simply cannot skip a match. Especially since you are our star player. We need you today against St Peter's." St Peter's and Queen's were long time Rugby rivals. The members of the opposite team were all built differently. The school was famous for being the breeding ground for Harlequin players.

"Good point but I forgot my kit. Real shame," *think of something to change the subject.*

"Oh well, luckily I have some spare kit" Boris interjected. "It should probably fit you."

"Well, how about a mouthguard? I don't want my teeth to be knocked out." Haresh reached over and passed me one.

"It's brand new and has not yet been moulded. It should do the trick." Even though the mouthguard was new, I did not want that thing in my mouth. However, everyone was staring at me.

"Fine, I'll play." They all cheered. Peer pressure at its finest.

The kit hung over me like a bed sheet. While running, it acted like a parachute. It sucked.

The world needed to know the truth, that I was still Jason, not some school celebrity. Honestly, I should have never agreed to wear Boris' kit and should have just gone home early. Luckily this was a Home match, so I did not have to worry about travelling. Time to get this over and done with quickly. How bad could this be?

Amongst our team was me, Frank, Wilfred, Boris, Haresh, Bruce and a few others. Within our team I was by far the skinniest. Haresh pumped his biceps in preparation, tensing all his muscles whilst his overly tight T-shirt struggled to fit around him.

From across the field, the opposition walked over. The boys from St Peter's ran over in a slow manner as if they were in 'Baywatch'. Ever member of their team was at least 6 foot 5 and they towered over us. In fact, they did not even look like teenagers, looking like they were the official England team. From within their ranks, a giant stepped out and stared at Frank. I had to crank my neck just to see his face.

"You're dead Clifford!" He growled, cracking his knuckles followed by his neck in a clichéd manner. I assume Frank had made some enemies on the rugby pitch. It also didn't help that his Dad was the Prime Minister, bringing home an army of haters. Frank just ignored the giant. He was in his own element now. Me on the other hand, not so much. I looked like a deflated balloon with such large clothes and the mouthguard did not settle in my mouth. I could not talk without either spluttering or choking.

The referee held the ball in his hands. I could just about remember the rules, no forward passing. That was when it hit me.

"Psst Frank, what position am I?"

"Prop" he simply put. *Prop?* That's the position that goes in the scrum. That was impossible. However, the idea of possibility was challenged yesterday. Here goes.

Several minutes later I found myself huddled against others in a gridlock position. The opposition pushed against us, creating an arch. The ball was rolled into the scrum and a war began. The St Peter's boys pushed with all their might. Frank was able to swing his leg onto the ball and roll it back. Boris picked it up and sprinted forward.

I awkwardly ran after him, pretending to know what to do. The entire opposition was at least double my height. One push from them could cripple me. My shoulders were still aching from that scrum.

In a quick transition of events, Boris passed the ball to Frank who then chucked it to me. The ball slammed against my chest and into my arms. For a brief moment I stood still, not knowing what to do. The try line was all the way at the end and there were about five Pete's boys standing in my way. Instead, I decided to go for a heroic stand, clutching the ball tightly and charging towards the goal. I sprinted past many boys until something smashed into my legs. One of the opposition had hugged my legs before lifting me up and hurling me backwards. I fell to the ground, before rolling like a coin slipping out of a wallet. On the floor I lay dazed for a second before getting up. They had gotten a hold of the ball. Frank put out his hand and said,

"You alright mate?" I took a hold of his hand and jumped back onto my feet, hoping to look like an action hero. It was time to win this game. A Pete boy was running towards our try line and so I jogged towards him and prepared for a tackle, only for him to shrug me off with ease. He then ran to the end and scored a try. The boy went on to do a victory dance around the pitch. At the end of it he tore off his shirt and chucked it to the ground revealing a shredded pack of abdominal muscles. His body was oddly shiny, as if he had greased it in preparation for this moment. From within the crowd, there were screams of joy.

This match was tough. The opposition was too hard for us to handle. It must have been nearly time to stop now as this match felt like it had gone on forever. However, when I looked at the clock, only two minutes had passed.

About a minute later, Frank had the ball and passed it to me. The ball collided with my ribcage once again. I held it with dear life, like a dinosaur holding its egg. *Wait, can dinosaurs hold their eggs?*

This time, instead of trying to score, I would actually pass the ball to someone who knew what they were doing. Looking around for someone to pass to, I noticed Haresh a couple of metres away, standing in the open, with his arms ready to catch. I motioned the throw in my mind, visualising the parabola. Yet as the ball left my grasp, an impact knocked me clean off my feet and the ball tumbled away towards the opposition. *No!* My one chance at being good was ruined.

However, before my head hit the ground, the ball rolled back towards me and into my hands, while my body was propelled back onto its feet by a guiding hand. I looked around to see that nobody had pulled me up. Instead, the same St Pete's boy collided with my legs, and the ball rolled away just like before.

My head smacked against the ground. What the hell had just happened? My vision went fuzzy for a moment whilst my head tried to make sense of the last couple of seconds.

"You alright Jay?" Wilfred asked. My head screamed in pain yet my brain still whizzed.

"Will, what just happened?"

"You got tackled bro. Now get up, we have to win this match."

I tried to get up but instead was met with a splitting headache. This was not good. Was I concussed? My brain must have slammed against my skull causing some damage. Twice in fact. Oh well there goes my chance at being good at rugby.

Within a short amount of time, I had been transferred to the School Nurse. For me, this was my third trip in two weeks. For everyone else, this was my first trip in just over a month.

"Here you go Jason," the nurse said, placing a packet of ice on my head. I still failed to see how cold ice would help my damaged head. It was not some sort of magical elixir that would diffuse immortality into me. My head still felt dazed from the fall and upon glancing at my hand, I could see it split into two. At this moment I desperately needed a nap to recharge. My batteries had been completely drained, leaving me on reserve fuel.

I lingered around till the end of the game where St Peter's School won unsurprisingly. Our team was greatly disheartened by it. Me on the other hand, could hardly care. I needed to get home as soon as possible to look through the rest of the footage. Hopefully this migraine would go away.

Upon being released from prison, I raced home to churn through some more security footage. That was my only hope of salvation within this whole mess. *How hard can it-*

My thoughts were instantly silenced by the blaring of a car horn. I spun to see that a car had almost hit me. I had crossed the road without thinking and had almost lost my life. The driver braked his Range Rover before poking his bald head out the window to start cussing. Listening to him would be a waste of my precious time.

Yet his words were loud. Too loud. Like a buzzing in my ear waiting to burst at any moment. He was holding up the traffic. Horns blared whilst I slowly dawdled across the road. Each horn felt like my eardrum had just burst. Something was not right. In fact, many things were not right. But home was my destination.

My surroundings appeared to fade as I approached my house moving in a drunken ramble. It stood there right in front of me yet my ears rang like crazy, as if a gun had just been shot right next to me. The sound of a dog barking sounded like a wolf howling at the moon. The beep of a car appeared as the blaring of a ferry horn. My feet could no longer feel the earth beneath me as it sunk through fluffy clouds. Immediately I jammed my keys into the door and unlocked it, before collapsing into the entrance.

Like a fish being pulled out of the sea by a fisherman, I was pulled out of my sleep by the sound of my Mum.

"Jason, sweetie, wake up." I looked around, confused. "The Nurse told me about your accident. Let me know if things get worse, and we will get you to A&E. I was in the comfort of my bed, in my bedroom, away from all the pain outside. However, something felt like it was missing. *The mystery, that's it.* There was no time to sleep. This nightmare needed to end first.

To my left, on my desk, was my laptop where Wilfred's USB stick was still plugged in. Once Mum had left my room, I clambered out of my bed, kicked my door closed and threw myself onto my chair before whipping the laptop open. My brain felt like sludge. But there was nothing that could distract me from getting to the bottom of this whole matter.

Back to the footage.

There was a day in which my Gap-self walked into school with a black briefcase. *Did I even own one?*

On that day, I carried it with extreme caution as if there was a baby animal inside. I would not get close to anyone else, and just acted oddly suspicious.

Later, that day, I sat with Frank and Wilfred in the Sixth Form Centre, but the briefcase had now mysteriously disappeared. I had no idea what was being said mainly because the ruckus of the year group drowned out the conversation. I focused hard to notice anything out of the ordinary and even sped up the footage to five times.

After a few minutes someone walked along the centre, looking ticked off. It was Raj.

Raj walked up to the group of us yet my Gap-self completely ignored his presence. I still could not make out what was being said. Raj put his hand on my shoulder and spoke to me. And then in a flash of actions, my Gap-self seized his arm and threw him over my shoulder. His body slammed against the wooden floor and the hubbub of noise was instantly silenced.

"Say that again to my face!" I roared.

Raj lay on the floor with his glasses wonkily resting on his face. He looked incredibly apologetic but that was not enough for my past anger. I connected my foot with the boy's jaw as he flew backwards. His glasses slipped to the ground where the beast obliterated them with a single stomp. A few drops of blood trickled from Raj's face and down his neck. His eyes were squinted and I could see the pain on his face. What had he said to cause me to go berserk? I honestly did not know that I had that much anger and strength within me. I turned my back on Raj, leaving him injured on the ground. He tried to scramble to his feet, only for Frank to approach him.

"You mess with Jay, you mess with me," he exclaimed as he marched towards the wounded boy. The crowd was so quiet that the footsteps of Frank could be heard. Wilfred, Boris and Haresh followed behind him, forming an arrowhead formation. When they got to Raj, they circled around him like hyenas about to feast on an injured animal. He reached out his arm, begging for them to stop but it was no use. Frank led in with the first attack, a swing of his leg. His foot slammed into the boy's stomach, knocking the wind out of him. Then in synchronised fashion, the thugs kept on kicking him. Each kick resulted in a sharp squeal and a gasp for help. For a solid minute, there was no sound except the noise of shoe against flesh, bones shattering and moaning. The year just looked in sheer terror as they dared not intervene. Eventually Mr Gideon stormed into the Centre screaming,

"Everybody stop now!" the veins on his neck were bursting and his face was beetroot red. "The five of you, go to Mr Ford's office. You will be extremely lucky if you are not expelled" he spat. The bullies and I dispersed from Raj and walked off together. We looked barely phased by the threat. The boy on the floor was a sorry sight. His face was caked in blood and his body was incredibly mangled. Mr Gideon just looked to the floor, in shame, knowing that this was his fault.

"Alright, one of you lot call the nurse. This is *equally* your fault for not stepping in." I could not believe that this had actually happened. I had not only turned on my best friend, but was responsible for almost killing him. The Nurse shortly rushed in afterwards and cared for the near lifeless body. Everyone was chatting to one another in a fearful manner. Hushed whispers swept through the Sixth Form Centre which were then silenced by the wailing of an ambulance. Three paramedics burst into the school and carried him away on a stretcher. A bloody sight to behold.

I turned off the screen as I could not possibly bare to watch anymore. My heart had gone mental with its beating and my body was drenched with sweat. This was a horrid situation. It was even worse that both the bullies and I actually got away with our crimes. In the end we were not expelled and continued to attend school. There was nothing that Raj could have said to cause me to go berserk. What about the briefcase? Did that have something to do with Raj. It was clearly something of immense importance. These questions riddled my mind to the fact that I had almost forgotten about my concussion. My migraine eventually returned signalling for me to take a break.

Chapter 6: The Briefcase

I started the next day by switching on the TV. The first thing that came on was BBC News, live at Downing Street. Ted Clifford stood there in an oddly dapper looking blue suit, with an odd checked pattern. The design did not entirely match his personality. Speaking of the Prime Minister, I was now best friends with his son so maybe we had had a run in. Perhaps I had even shaken his hand. Come to think of it, Frank said that I was at his house for a party not too long ago. Not 10 Downing Street, his second house nearer the school.

Today I was on the hunt. The plot of this mystery had only thickened and so the desire for resolution had only risen. What was in that briefcase making it so important? I also needed to fix my friendship with Raj.

I leisurely strolled into school and kicked open the doors of the Sixth Form Centre. Now, there is an art to kicking open a door. There is the 'break-in' method which is what the FBI do. There is also the grand entrance method. This one involves kicking open the door and expecting thunderous applause on the other side as the whole world revels in your celebrity status. The latter is what I did when entering.

"Welcome back Jay!" Frank yelled. I waved back to him. This popularity suited me. It felt good, like a wave of fresh air. *Focus on the mission Jason.* At that moment I went up to my new 'friends' and enquired the following,

"Hey guys. Do any of you remember when I came into school with that big briefcase?"

"Oh yeah", Haresh said. "You held that thing with your life, like there was the cure for cancer in there."

"Well, what did I say was inside of it?"

"You said that you had the answers to the upcoming Maths exam," Wilfred added. This was getting stranger. Why would I steal answers to papers? Considering that my Gap-self was a genius, test answers would be the least of his worries. I then thought back to the footage. The briefcase was in my possession all morning that day but then in the afternoon, it was gone. Maybe these guys saw me place it somewhere.

"Do any of you know where I put it. I can't seem to remember."

"Oh yes, I remember," Frank interjected. "You left it at the back of Griffin's room." I had economics yesterday but the briefcase was not there and so it was worth another look though his classroom.

Economics was the first lesson of the day. I endeavoured to get there early, in order to look for the briefcase and so after registration, I paced to the top floor where my lesson would be and kicked down the door before entering. This was an FBI kicking rather than a social one. I leapt into the empty room and did a full sweep, examining every nook and cranny of the room with eagle eyes. Griffin had still not turned up yet, so I had some time to investigate.

Upon inspection, the room appeared perfectly fine. All the seats had been tucked in and the desks were cleared of stuff. The whiteboard had notes on it from yesterday's lesson, sprawled in all corners. The floor was completely empty, sparkling clean in fact. There was no evidence of the briefcase whatsoever. A sense of dread filled me. It could be in lost property else it would be gone forever along with the answer to this mystery. I peered underneath all the desks but there was nothing. Even the space under the teacher's desk was empty, apart from a lone pair of shoes. I glanced at my watch, only 6 minutes until the lesson. Griffin would certainly not like me snooping around his property.

The last place to look was the cabinet at the back of the classroom. Usually, it was filled with large textbooks, exercise books and the occasional test paper. I lifted open the door as it let out a shrill creak. To my joy, the briefcase was right there. I quickly reached out to grab its handle but was shocked as to how heavy it was. I hauled it upwards with all my strength and slammed it onto a desk, making a huge metallic clang as it collided with the table. Now I looked over it, studying its intricate design. The shell itself was made with carbon fibre. It had a handle secured to the top and next to the handle was a four-digit padlock. In order to unzip the bag, I needed to crack the code. The contents of this bag must have been extremely important to license such security.

My birthday was the 8th of May. That seemed like a good place to start. I spun the first digit to 0, The second to 8 and so on. 0805. I gently pulled at the padlock but nothing happened. I then tried the American version of the date. 0508. That did not work either. I then tried 8503 with 03 being my year of birth. Once again there were no results.

There were only four minutes left until the lesson started and I needed to get rid of this bag before Griffin bombarded me with questions. The case had two golden locks on it, one on each end. If I could smash them, then the case would open, revealing the treasure. I performed an about turn and frantically looked for something heavy, like a hammer. It then caught my eye.

With some oomph I yanked the fire extinguisher off the wall and brought it towards the table where the case lay. I would just have to smash my way in. The red canister was heavy above my head, causing my arms to ache as it was begging to be lowered. And so I thrashed it downwards demolishing one of the golden locks. It popped off the case like the cork of a bottle of whisky. A small gap opened, and I pushed my fingers into the case before prying it open. The case eventually opened, and I stood there, gobsmacked.

There was only one minute left until the lesson and that was bad. Dreadful in fact. The case was filled with wires stringed around alongside small parcels of what I imagined were explosives. I had just discovered a bomb on the school site! Even worse, it was planted by my Gap-self. The school would easily trace it back to me using CCTV footage. What was my Gap-self thinking? Why would he want to frame me for murder? The school would not believe my story and so if I survived this, my next home would be a prison cell.

Within the bomb I could see that there was a timer displayed using large red digital numbers. 02: 32. I had 2 minutes to dispose of the bomb. It was set to go off during our lesson and wipe us all out. But why would someone do this? Did my Gap-self want the entire set killed or just one specific person? Who from our set was worth killing? Haresh was the son of a wealthy CEO. Erm Wilfred's mum was some high up at Apple. Frank was the son of...

Oh no!

Now the lesson had officially started and the bomb would go off in just under two minutes. I needed to stop anyone from entering and so sprinted to the door and tried locking it but that was impossible without a key. Instead, I grabbed a chair and wedged the seat rest under the handle. Within an instant of placing it down, banging had ensued.

"Hey, let me in!" Boris yelled. I just ignored him since the aim was to diffuse this bomb and keep the entire set out of danger. The kicking at the door got louder and more evident as more members of the class showed up, baffled as to what was going on.

Upon inspection, the bomb perplexed me. Usually in movies, the main character would cut the red wire 1 second before detonation. I had just over a minute and there was no red wire. The bomb contained an entangled web of 5 different black wires. Each led to a different thing. I watched the numbers slip away while questions riddled my brain. Who did this? Was I framed? How powerful will the blast be? Would I live another day? I needed to say goodbye, to Mum, Dad, Julian.

"What is going on here?" Mr Griffin asked, knocking on the door impatiently.

"Jason has locked himself inside the classroom" Haresh said bluntly.

"Jason, this is not funny!" Griffin shouted. "Open this door now or there will be consequences". I quickly grabbed a pair of scissors from his desk and prepared to cut a wire, taking a gamble. It was either my life or theirs. There were only 20 seconds left now and the banging at the door got louder.

"Come on Jay, open up" shouted Frank. A tear rolled down my face which then mixed with a bead of sweat. My face steamed as hot blood pumped through my vessels. This would be the end. I opened the scissors and put them next to a wire, ready to cut. My hand was shaking vigorously as my heart skipped beats. I just wanted to run away from this and go home. Why did this have to happen to me? Why?

10

I held the wire, ready to cut. It was now or never.

9

My hands dripped hot sweat

8

"JASON! Open up!"

7

So, I guess this was the end

6

I prepared to cut. The scissors began to cut the wire when-

5

The door smashed open.

4

Frank erupted in, the class not far behind.

3

He glanced at what I was doing, "What the F-"

2

Before he could finish, I hurled the briefcase out of the window

1

"Everyone duck!" I yelled

I watched as the case smashed through the window, causing a ripple of glass to fly outwards, as the briefcase spun in the air, high above the school. My biceps ached from the throw and my breaths were short and fast.

0

The case was quickly enveloped in flames as it breathed out destruction. A ring of hell was conjured up and blasted in all directions. The sound of the boom deafened me as I witnessed the destruction approach me. A wall of heat pulsed into the classroom and chucked me backwards. My skin screamed in pain as it was singed, and shards of glass punctured me. I tumbled back and smacked my skull onto a hard table.

Darkness

"You did good, kid," he said. "You saved the day. Nicely done. Now enjoy Hell". *Wait what?* I was not ready to die yet. I tried to muster up the strength to talk, but my body started slipping away.

"Wha-" I mumbled as my tongue fumbled to convert my thoughts into words. Blinded, I felt around. There was nothing except a large void and a sharp cold. My blood froze as it pumped around my body causing a thin layer of ice to be laced around my skin. My muscles had stiffened to the point of no return and my lungs had shrivelled into autumn leaves. I gasped as no more breath was coming out. A final breath escaped my mouth, a visible cloud in the air before it dissipated.

And that was the end of my life. I died a hero, saving the Prime Minister's son. Now I wait in anticipation for the afterlife.

"Let's try 200. Okay that should do it. Ready…"

Boom

"Okay, still nothing. 220. Ready ..."

BEEP

The ice around me shattered and my heart manically pumped hot blood back into me. A huge gust of air was sucked into my chest, revitalising my lungs as my fingers regained their touch. The weight on my eyelids was removed revealing the world again.

"We have a heartbeat!" Several sighs of relief followed. The beeping on the machine continued as I took in my surroundings where there were paramedics wearing bright green alongside Frank? *What's he doing here?* The sounds of the chatter was drained out by the sound of the sirens.

"Mate, you made it," he said getting excited. "You saved my life! My father will be thrilled to hear about that. Jason, great things are coming your way."

My neck was stiff, making it impossible to look down. *Is my body still in one piece? How did I survive such a blast?* My entire body felt oddly numb and painless. All my injuries appeared to blend together.

"Get some rest now," one of the paramedics said calmingly. And with that said, I drifted off again.

"We are trying the best we can, but there is little hope."

"Please, you have to save him."

"I came as soon as possible. How is our son doing?"

"He's in critical condition, he is constantly in and out. But he is a fighter and a hero and I know he will pull through".

"I can't believe this has happened, Graham. One day he was fine, next day he tries to diffuse a bomb. What was our son doing?"

"More importantly, who tried to blow up the school".

"Well considering that the Clifford boy is in his class, who knows what grudges someone might have against the Prime Minister."

"We should pull him out of that school before anything like this happens again."

"But this school has the best education in the country."

"Sarah, remember. We promised Jemima and Jerry that we would take the best care of him. We simply cannot keep him at a school where his life is at risk. Look at him. Look at our son!"

"Oh no! How did this happen?"

"Don't cry, darling. He is a strong one, like his brother. Speaking of Julian, I tried ringing him, but there was no response."

They kept on talking but their voices got fainter and fainter. I tried to hone in on their words but my ears were failing me. I just needed to hear more. *Who are Jemima and Jerry?* I had never heard of them before. I tried to raise my arm, trying to give a signal to Mum and Dad, but it was no use. It felt like my limbs were strapped down to the bed with chains. Such tight chains around my wrists and they stung. I tried to move any part of my body, anything. Even my tongue was completely limp. I could not bare to hear the sound of my parents crying. *Focus Jason.* But before I could try to move, drowsiness once again overwhelmed me.

"His eyes are opening".

"Give him some space, his body is still in shock. It will take weeks for him to recover from the surgery."

"Welcome back to the land of the living," Dad said. My vision slowly unblurred itself. My right hand was covered in bandages. With some effort, I was able to raise it to my face, where I felt a thick bandage over my right eye. Was I blinded? Did a shard of glass penetrate my eye?

"Nice to meet you Jason, I am Dr Wu, the one who fixed you up. What you did back at school was truly breath-taking. Both your parents have been here the whole time. Also, some guy has been hovering around."

The door opened and Frank strolled in.

"I specifically stated that only family was allowed in, but he was relentless."

"Jason, my boy! Could I have a minute with the hero?" Mum and Dad simply shrugged before leaving alongside Dr Wu.

Frank proceeded to embrace me with a hug. "I can't believe you saved my life. In fact, you saved the whole set. School ended early that day and I got away without doing my homework" He said grinning ear to ear. "You are a legend Jay."

"Thanks" I croaked. My throat felt dry and my voice was hoarse.

"Did the Doc give you the news?" He asked

"What news?" Was this about my eye?

"Basically," he said. "Some shrapnel flew in between your legs. The doctors tried to help you, but your testicles were removed. I'm sorry Jason but you are never having children."

No, this was too much. I had not even thought about having children, but the fact that I had lost my balls was detrimental. Any chance of a future lineage thrown out the window. Nobody would marry me. Life was now meaningless. How could this have happened to me? What had I done to deserve this?

All of a sudden, Frank cracked up. He started to hiss and then blew up into roaring laughter.

"I'm joking mate! You should have seen the look on your face." I was overwhelmed by a sense of relief. Frank really was a horrible person with a disturbed sense of humour.

"Buddy", he said, "you will be perfectly fine. Don't worry about it". I quickly lifted my hand and placed it between my legs. *Just to check, you know*. Fortunately, it felt normal. This interaction was getting very strange now.

"Anyway", he said, "my Dad says that he will be coming to visit us very soon." The Prime Minister wanted to see me? For saving his son? I was not ready for this. Was I about to be knighted? Sir Jason Clyde. *Has a nice ring to it*.

My parents then came over and hugged me a lot before saying some stuff about being proud of me. It went on for longer than I would like to admit. The moment got interrupted by the cries from my new friend.

"Quick, he's here," Frank said. I looked out the window as a black jeep pulled up outside the hospital doors. Out of the driver's door came a man dressed in black, wearing sunglasses. Obviously, a security guard. The passenger door opened and another guard came out, dressed exactly the same as the first. The guard then walked over to the back door and firmly pulled it open. A leg emerged from the car and at the base of it was a shoe that was so polished that it reflected the sun into my eye. The leg stood up and the rest of the body followed. A tall, plump man stepped out, wearing aviator sunglasses. His brown hair was neatly combed to the side and his navy blue suit was impeccably clean. The guards stood in front of him and led him inside.

Frank Clifford opened the door for his father and Ted walked in. When he saw me, he looked at me, blankly.

"Is that the kid?" he whispered audibly to one of the security guards. He just simply nodded. Ted then motioned to the other guard, who took off his sunglasses for him. As soon as his sunglasses were removed, he had a wide smile on his face surrounded by the odd wrinkle. The man in person was less impressive than on TV.

"Jason, it is so good to finally meet you!" he said sticking out his hand for a handshake. I feebly raised my bandaged arm and was greeted by a strong squeeze. A bit too strong in fact. He caused my hand to start hurting badly as it was still wounded from the blast.

"I just wanted to come and say thank you for saving my son. I never tell this enough to Frank, but I sincerely love him. Ever since his mother passed away, he is all I have left. You saved him and for that I am eternally in your debt. You are a good man Jason, and a positive influence on my boy."

"Thank you, sir," I said, trying to make my voice deeper and more manly.

Ted then turned around. "Alright then, all of you, please get out. Including you, M-Sarah and Graham."

"How do you know our names?" Mum asked.

"Darling, I know everything." She looked at him a bit weirdly before heading out.

After a few seconds, everyone had left. Everyone except Frank. He was sitting on a stool next to where I lay.

"Even you, *boy*," he said to Frank who let out a little moan before walking off. Once Frank had left and the door was closed behind him, the security guards closed the curtains leaving just me and Ted.

"Right Jake," he said.

"It's Jason," I replied. My response did not even phase him.

"The real reason I am here is to find out more information. What were you doing with a bomb in my son's school?" I gulped. This was about to get really bad.

"By the way, the two people out there are MI5. Try anything funny, and they will be on to you. And trust me, they are not as nice as me." *Should I tell him the truth? About 'The Gap' and the rest of that. No. He would just scoff.* This was not the kind of man to believe in fairy-tales.

"So here is the story," I said, my voice shaking. I was a terrible liar so the only way to get through this was by telling part of the truth. Concealing the full story is not technically lying.

"I was on my way to Economics, 5 minutes early, so that I could get some homework done. However, my lined paper had run out so I went over to the class cabinet to grab some more. A briefcase was inside said cabinet. Curiosity took the better of me and I tried to open it, realising that it was locked. There had to be some sort of important documents, maybe some exam papers. To my despair, I found a bomb within the case. With only minutes before the start of the lesson, I locked the door to prevent anyone getting in and possibly dying. It was impossible for me to diffuse it. At the last moment, Frank walked in and I realised that the only way to save him was to chuck the bomb out the window. And that is all I remember."

Ted Clifford just nodded intently. "I believe you kid, you don't seem like the kind of person that would try and assassinate my son, only to get yourself blown up." With that said, he clapped and the two agents waltzed back in. The one to his right handed Ted his sunglasses who then put them on.

"Thank you for saving my son. I will get to the bottom of this and can assure you that whoever is found guilty will wish that they were dead," he said with a smile before heading out, his goons behind him. But something interesting happened as he walked away. The man usually walked with precision and determination like that of a soldier. However, as he started walking, his march sagged into a limp for a single step. As his right leg led, his left leg just dragged itself across the floor. He quickly readjusted and kept on walking as normal. The Prime Minister's legs looked perfectly fine, a bit fat if anything. Why would he limp?

Everyone then came back into the room and pretended like nothing had happened.

"Where's Frank?" I asked.

"He went home with his Dad," Dr Wu said.

I needed to get a few things straight in my head, I lived my life as normal in October 2019. On Friday October 11th, I watched Terminator with Julian and that evening I went to bed as normal. That night, I was possessed. While possessed, I became close friends with Frank Clifford, son of the Prime Minister. I then went on to plant a bomb in my Economics classroom to kill him. The possessor then unpossessed me and I returned to my normal self. I woke up the morning of Monday 11th November having missed 30 days of my life. At school I found a bomb and whilst trying to diffuse it, I was severely injured, leaving me in my state now.

What confused me, is that I was supposed to die in that explosion. The Demon that possessed me, was planning on blowing me up alongside Frank, to destroy evidence. But where did Frank come into all of this? Why did the Demon make friends with him and then try to kill him? It tried to kill two birds with one stone, literally. Why did it want the son of the Prime Minister dead?

The next day, I switched on the TV to watch the news. My aches and pains were still there, but now they were less severe. The bandage around my eye was now gone, so I could see properly again.

"It has been a day since the explosion at 'The Queen's School'." The Reporter said. The camera panned over my school showing it. The Economics block was smoking and there were fire fighters surrounding it. A large chunk of the block was missing, having been burnt to ash.

"The school was saved by a brave, young pupil who put the lives of his classmates before his own. He is now in hospital and is fortunately on the road to a steady recovery. We now go live to Downing Street where Mr Theodore Clifford will speak about the matter. His son, Frank, attends the aforementioned school and was close to being killed."

On the TV was none other than Ted who stood in front of 10 Downing Street, surrounded by Press. This was his first time going live since the explosion. He cleared his throat, straightened his tie and began to talk.

"Hello everyone. Now I know you all will have many questions for me and I will try and answer them all."

"Is it safe for us to send our children to school?" Somebody shouted out.

"I will get onto that if you will excuse me," he replied. "So as you all know, my son's school was attacked yesterday. Upon further examination, we realised that the bomb was planted inside of his classroom intending for him to be killed." Ted wiped the sweat off his brow, unable to maintain eye contact with the crowd in front of him. "My son was almost killed yesterday and I see that it was an attack on me. Like all politicians, I have many friends and enemies. However, it is completely unacceptable to come after my family like that!"

"Did you find out who planted the bomb?" another person called out.

"Unfortunately, at this moment, we have no further evidence on the matter. All we can assume is that one of my enemies has tried to break me by killing my one and only family. The rest of you do not need to worry. My enemies came after me, not any of you. This is between me and them and so schools are still safe for all of you." Ted said before signalling for somebody.

"The Prime Minister is done for today," came an authoritative voice. It was the same MI5 agent that I met yesterday. The crowd still shouted questions but they were all ignored. Ted left the stage and retreated to his house.

I thought about Frank for a moment. He was in severe danger and I paid the price because of it. I needed to do something but I felt utterly useless against the world. Somehow my life was intertwined amongst all this political madness. Who were the 'enemy' that Ted kept on talking about? Maybe Frank had some more information on the matter.

A little later, Dr Wu popped in.

"How are you doing Jason?" he asked solemnly.

"I am feeling much better. Do you think I will be able to go home soon?" I was dying of boredom in this hospital bed although my body still writhed in agony.

"Don't get ahead of yourself. You need to rest so you can get back onto your feet. Some of those wounds may take weeks to recover. On a separate note, you will be happy to know that your school is closed for this week, so you don't have to worry about catching up." Honestly I had not even thought about catching up on work. I still had a month of work during 'The Gap' to do.

My phone somehow survived the explosion. It was cracked on the outside but still fully functional. Julian would probably need to buy me another. I flicked through my phone for anything interesting. Little did I realise, that I had been bombarded with messages. First up was Haresh.

Bro, I hope ur good. Because of you I now get to bunk a whole week of school. Thanks :)

That was nice of him. Next was Wilfred.

Jason, my guy. Get well soon. Looking forward to seeing you back in action. There were some automated balloons that flew across the screen. The latest IOS update?

Bruce sent a nice message

You saved the whole school from blowing up. I am pretty sure you are now a superhero. And you became one without the tragic backstory. Nicely done.

Boris was next,

I still have not done Mr Griffin's homework. Now I have an extra week to do it. Thank you :)

My old friends also all sent messages, Lewis, Tim and Yaseen all sent words of support. In fact, even Raj sent a message.

I knew there was still some good left in you ;)

That was the nicest thing he could say despite what I did to him.

My popularity at school had gone through the roof.

That was the last of the messages. I sincerely hoped that Frank was okay. His father acted harsh towards him yesterday. Hopefully he did not blame his son for almost dying.

Chapter 7: Back to School

I had always dreaded going back to school. The thought made me feel sick. Whenever I would go shopping and would see the 'Back to School' line of clothes, I would almost cry. The closest analogy to school I could think of was prison. A prisoner wrongfully arrested for murder who wanted to get away from captivity however they could not escape their fate.

Today was 'Back to School Day'. It was a Monday 18th November and Queen's had reopened again. They had removed all the rubble from last week, making school safe again. The pupils probably now feared for their lives at Queen's. I would not be surprised if several parents had pulled their children out of the academy. If I asked my parents to transfer schools, I would be shut down immediately. I would then be told something about being 'privileged' and thus should be more grateful for my situation.

I stepped onto the school site and felt chills down my spine. Last time I stepped foot here was during my close encounter with death. My hand rested over my bandaged stomach. I was only 16 and had a lot more to live for. Dying in my final years of school would be insulting. It would be like dying the day before the end of a prison sentence. Over the last few days, while recovering, I had been thinking a lot about this mystery.

The 'Mystery of the 30 Lost Days' was a good name for this conundrum. I had been searching for answers but had found none. My inability to solve this mystery before almost resulted in my death, alongside the rest of my Economics set.

Speaking of explosions, the school looked different. The entire Economics block was now caked in scaffolding from top to bottom. With the amount of wealth that the school had, it would have been a matter of days before the block would be rebuilt. The school playing fields had now been converted into an outdoor classroom. A whiteboard was set up with chairs and desks spread out in normal fashion. Outdoor lessons? Economics could not get any worse. Actually, I take that back. A lot of things could make it worse.

Upon entering the Sixth Form Centre, the hubbub of noise dispersed. It then converted into applause and cheering. I was a celebrity, a hero in fact. I was instantly surrounded by others as they jumped up and down in celebration and then was greeted by a large smack on the back.

"Good to have you back Jay," Haresh said.

"You saved my life," Boris cried. "If you ever want coffee, just let me know and I will buy some for you." Everybody was being so nice to me. Luckily, I was not grabbed by the crowd and thrown into the air like a rock-star. If Frank were here, then that would definitely have happened. Speaking of Frank, he was nowhere to be seen. He must have been under full security in some underground bunker somewhere. This whole situation was madness. Even though everyone seemed happy to see me, there was still a sense of dread in the atmosphere. Today school was back, but things felt worse than ever before.

Outdoor, Double Economics with Mr Griffin, first thing on a Monday morning. *EUGH.* I sat on a chair in the middle of a field, surrounded by everyone else. Did I mention it was mid-November? My hands had gone entirely numb and my nose was probably blue.

"I know this is not ideal" Griffin exclaimed, his breath turning to mist, "but it is the best we could do" He suddenly halted and looked down at his shoe. After a moment, a look of disgust formed on his face as he said. "I think I just stepped in poo!" His immaculately polished shoes were now smeared in faecal matter. A foul stench was emitted and polluted the air. Rather than clean his shoes, the man kept on talking. "As I was saying, I will now be taking in your homework due in last week. You had a one-week extension, so no excuses."

There was a brief rumble as everyone scrambled through their bags to find it. Everyone succeeded and pulled out a piece of paper. Mr Griffin went around collecting them all in. Boris handed in a piece of scrunched up paper that looked like it had been driven halfway across the world.

"Boris, you have only written half a paragraph?" the old man grumbled.

"Erm yes, well it is quality over quantity," he replied, fumbling for words. Griffin shrugged it off and moved on.

"Wilfred, where is your work?" he questioned.

"I am emailing it to you now, Sir."

"Wilfred, you know that I do not mark digitally. Print off your homework by lunch else you will be in detention!" Will smiled smugly. He had bought himself three hours to do the homework.

The teacher strolled on towards Raj and Yaseen. Yaseen swiftly handed in his work followed by Raj who handed in an entire stack of papers. The fat booklet was whole-punched and neatly stapled at the top.

"Thank you, Raj, I look forward to reading this." When Mr Griffin came over to me and Haresh, my friend handed him a single sheet of paper. The teacher nodded before gazing at me.

"Jason, where is your homework?" he said. The audacity of this man. I had only just left the hospital after saving his life and he wanted my homework. I wanted to spit on his face.

"I am sorry sir, but it got burnt. You know when there was a bomb in our classroom. Remember that?" I said starkly. Griffin just ignored me before heading to the front of the 'classroom'.

"Okay, class, get out a piece of paper and start taking notes."

I opened up my new rucksack and pulled out a pad of paper before taking out a pen. At that moment, a huge gust of wind came and blew my work away. The paper then rolled off into the distance. It was instantly replaced by another sheet which was also blown away within minutes. Eventually it was replaced by a third piece of paper, which had a pencil case weighing it down. Shortly afterwards, a ladybird placed itself on my sheet. Within moments, I had swatted it, leaving a splodge of insect blood on my notes. My nose dribbled from the intense cold. To take my mind off things, I puffed out a large breath and pretended to be a smoker, watching my puff of smoke fly away and dissipate into the atmosphere.

In the end, the entire lesson was a waste of time as my economical knowledge had barely changed. My blood was still frozen and my hands had gone red. Now it was Free Period time, the best part of the day. I should have been using this time to study but I could not have cared less about my grades at that moment. The school believed that I was some sort of prodigy and the thing about prodigies is that they never work. It had been a week since the explosion at school and I was in no way closer to finding out the truth behind everything.

"Jason, have you heard anything from Frank?" Haresh asked. Nobody had heard from him in a while. He was probably being kept inside some secure facility where he was safe. In fact, he had to have been missing his friends. He would not ghost everyone like that. Ted had probably confiscated his son's phone off of him. To be fair, I was missing Frank to an extent. The guy was a douche but over the last few days, he had been more kind to me than any of my previous friends. Raj and I were good friends but we never hung out outside of school. With Frank, it seemed like my entire life revolved around our friendship.

The Sixth Form Centre felt empty without him. He was the neutral friend between me, Wilfred, Haresh and Boris. So now, everything just felt awkward and so I went on my phone to distract myself, and there I saw an email from Mr Grove.

Hi Jason,

I hope you are feeling better now. Could you pop into my classroom for a quick chat after your Economics lesson.

Best wishes,

Mr G

At this rate, I would never get a free period to myself. However, he had saved me from a certain boredom.

After strolling to Mr Grove's room, I was greeted by a large smile.

"Jason, so good to see you."

"Am I in trouble?" I murmured.

"Of course not", he replied. "I have called you in here about a certain matter. Mr Ford, the Headmaster has instructed me to pass on a message." Mr Ford, wow! I had only ever met him once, for my interview to join the school. Since then I had never spoken to him.

"Mr Ford wants you to give a speech during assembly about your recent academic success and how you saved the school. He believes that a few words from a hero like you will inspire the pupils of Queen's to try harder."

Err, what? Me, in assembly? Every Tuesday, there is an Assembly held for the entire school where teachers give talks about certain things. Now they want me to talk. I can barely talk confidently in front of a small group of friends. Hundreds of people would kill me. Plus I would be talking about the my Gap-Self's success, not mine. This was a terrible idea.

"I am sorry sir, but that is not happening". The smile on Grove's face slowly dissolved into a look of perplexment. "You see, I get nervous in front of large crowds."

"Well," he replied, "you did win the prize for best monologue two weeks ago. You performed that in front of hundreds of pupils and teachers, not to mention your recent piano concert. There is no way that you get nervous in front of crowds."

Well, that excuse did not work. Was I actually an actor during 'The Gap'? I never expected that. So last month, I was the best at academics, music, sport and now drama. Plus I saved my classmates from death so of course Mr Ford would want me to give a speech. But then he would also want me to be the front and centre of the school.

'Meet Jason, our top pupil who is also a hero'. That did not work for me. I needed a new excuse.

"I have already told Mr Ford that you would be willing to do so. Oh and before I forget, he has asked to meet you personally". The lying snake. The teacher did not even give me an option and has already signed my life away without consent. And now I had to talk to the headmaster. I did not even know where his office was.

"When do I meet him?" I asked, needing some time to think through life and collect myself.

"He has requested to see you at 11." He glanced at his watch. "That gives you 10 minutes". This day could not get worse. Oh wait, I promised never to say that again because it most definitely could get worse. Next thing I know, Mr Ford could have been the one to have possessed me and had called me to his room to execute me after his bomb failed. How would he kill me? Poisoned drink or maybe a good old-fashioned suffocation. He could then throw me out the window and say that my death was suicidal. I really needed to be more optimistic.

I hurried to the Sixth Form Centre for advice. Haresh, Will and Boris were always so calm, they would know exactly what to do.

"Guys, the headmaster wants to see me," I cried.

"What are you doing here then?" Haresh uttered while eating a big bag of crisps. Will shoved his hand into the packet and took a big handful before scoffing it into his mouth.

"Mr Ford is not in this room." Will said.

"Yeah, I know that. I need your help regarding what to say to him".

"Just go with the flow," Haresh exclaimed. "Jason, you have never done anything wrong in your life. This can only be good news."

"I guess you are right. But what do I do about my nerves? The headmaster is a scary dude."

"I have the answer to all your problems," Boris said. He reached into his bag and passed me a cup of coffee. "This is the solution to any struggle I have."

After taking the cup, I took a quick sip. The thick liquid rolled out of the container and onto my tongue. It had such a foul taste that my tongue recoiled in disgust. It was plain, black coffee but it was so pure and powerful that I needed more. It poured itself into my body and down my throat. My heart had an overdrive of energy, as if new batteries had been installed. I rushed off to finally meet Mr Ford. I bounced out of the Centre but immediately realised that I did not know where to go.

"Erm guys, where exactly is Mr Ford's office?" Wilfred went on to give out the directions before I sped off.

I leapt up some stairs and threw myself through a set of double doors. Energy coursed through my veins. I was alive. Actually, I may have just taken some drugs? What did Boris put in that drink? Personally hot drinks were not my thing but this new sensation I felt made me desire more, a lust for a greater purpose.

Outside Mr Ford's office was a large waiting room. There was a receptionist there at a table. The room contained large sofas and huge coffee tables. This felt like the waiting room for a private healthcare specialist. It was like an expensive surgery where you would pay thousands to visit because you do not want to be on the NHS waiting list.

"Hello," I said to the receptionist, aware of the fact that I had never seen this member of staff before in my life. This entire wing of the school site was new to me.

"You must be Jason," she croaked, moving her glasses up her face, onto the bridge of her nose. "Take a seat, the Headmaster will be with you shortly." I pounced onto one of the sofas and was embraced by pure luxury as my posterior sank into a cushion of bliss. I hoped that Mr Ford would never call me, so I could spend an eternity here. Yet life still moved on.

The receptionist picked up a phone before pausing for a moment. The chorded phone she held looked like it had been pulled out of the 60s. In fact, her desk had a very vintage feel to it, bar the modern Apple computer.

"Hello Samuel, the boy is here to see you." There was a brief second of static before she placed the phone back down. "Mr Ford will see you now," she said. This all felt a bit too formal, like something out of the Apprentice. Surely the man could come out and greet me himself.

Reluctantly, I tore myself from the sofa and trudged out of the room. The entrance to Mr Ford's office was made up of two hefty double doors embroidered with silver lining. To the side stood a plaque with his name engraved. Mr S. Ford, Headmaster. With a gust of strength, I pushed open the doors and stepped inside. Even though my body was pumping with pure excitement, there was still an underlying dread to this whole situation. Something felt very off about all of this. This was not my success and so there was always a fear of my façade failing.

"Welcome Jason," came a voice, rich in texture and one that emulated power. The man stood from his throne and put his hand out. Mr Ford sat on a huge chair underneath a perfect portrait of himself in which he stood in front of the school gardens. His room was littered with small trinkets. Upon a shelf was a row of small statues from a spectrum of different cultures. One of the walls was taken up entirely by a painting of Jesus, standing tall with light emulating from himself. There was even a large statue of Jesus upon the cross within this room. It was as if this was some sort of shrine or mini-Church.

On his desk was another mini plaque saying: Mr Samuel Ford, Headmaster of 'The Queen's School'. To his right, was a glass case with dozens of trophies, beautifully polished to perfection. He could probably use them as a shaving mirror.

Mr Ford was of average height and his greying hair was neatly combed to the left with the slightest hint of gel. His forehead was completely ironed out of creases, hiding his old age. He had grey hair at roots, but a more of an artificial, reddish brown for the rest of his head. A few black streaks were littered throughout. Mr Ford's nose was long with a slight cleft at the end.

At that moment I realised that I was analysing him for too long and should shake his hand rather than leave him hanging.

"It is an honour to meet you, sir," I stated. Lies. I really could not care less about this elitist individual. He proceeded to smile in a celebrity manner where one performs a rehearsed grin that does not reflect their dread of meeting you. A 'two-faced smile' you could call it. Mr Ford could not care less about me as he only wanted me to be the forefront of his school to help encourage parents to send their kids to Queen's. Or for me to give out words of wisdom, guiding the pupils to become cleverer allowing the school to achieve greater A-level and GCSE grades, encouraging even more parents to enrol their kids. A simple, capitalist move.

That is the thing about elitist schools, they only care about the money and the fame. Before 'The Gap' I was just a mediocre student and the school could not care less about my well-being. On the other hand if Wilfred, a esteemed rugby player, had any signs of depression, the school would stick out their necks to make sure he got the best counselling. They could not afford for their star player to go off sick.

Another example, Raj would receive the absolute best extra free tuition from the school because he would compete in Maths competitions. The school would make sure that he was always at the best of his game because his success made it appear that the Queen's maths department was amazing. Which was not the case, as they would only give the good teachers to the smartest pupils. The vast majority would just get run of the mill university graduates teaching or retired bankers.

Mr Ford sat back down on his chair. "We have a lot to discuss my child." This man could easily be a supervillain. I could imagine him being the British bad guy in a spy film while he sits in a chair stroking a cat.

"Here at Queen's, we have taken great interest in your career." *Lies and deception.* "We have noticed your surge in grades and I am honestly impressed. And then all of a sudden you go onto become a great musician, sportsman and even an actor. Damn, you even made friends with the son of the Prime Minister and then went on to save his life by sacrificing your own." He chuckled to himself. "You really have become quite the celebrity. The thing is, Jason, the quality of students at this school has fallen. Every year, the number of pupils accepted into Oxford and Cambridge declines. These days Queen's boys spend all their time on social media and not enough time hitting the books. We need there to be a beacon of inspiration for them. And that beacon is you, boy. The last person to walk through these school gates with leadership qualities like you was indeed your brother Julian." Wow. I had gone several days without hearing his name and now here it was again. My streak just ended.

"Your brother, Julian, was hands down one of the greatest students and he has now gone on to do great things. I want you to be better than Julian. You have spent your whole life in his shadow, watching him win awards while you did nothing." *Nothing? Ouch* "Now, this last month you have grown out and it is remarkable. I can talk from experience. My dad was in fact a politician. My entire life was spent watching him give speeches and winning awards. When he found out that I wanted to be a teacher, he was enraged. But I proved him wrong when I became the headmaster of the best school in the country where the pupils are the children of CEOs and politicians. I know you have the same fire within you to be more like me and realise your true potential. That is why I want you to give the speech to the school tomorrow about how to become a better person. I've said my piece."

That was quite the speech and somehow I had to top that the next day in front of hundreds of angsty teenagers. This was a tough task especially since this was one big lie.

"Oh, I forgot to say," he added. "I am actually considering you as a top candidate for Head Boy next year. Keep up the good work and

129

you will be the forefront of The Queen's School. How does that sound?" I kept saying this day could not get any worse but fate continually found a way to bully me. *Me, head boy?* There was no way I was going to be Ford's lapdog.

"Thank you for the opportunity, Sir," I said. There were times when my tongue would say the complete opposite of what I wanted.

My watch stated that both my free period and the subsequent break time were now over and now it was time for Maths. My meeting with Mr Ford had overrun into my next lesson and so I was late.

The classroom was full and the teacher was talking through some questions on the board. I seriously needed to catch-up as I had no idea what all those numbers meant.

"Sorry I am late, I had a meeting with Mr Ford." There was a huge gasp of excitement within the class followed by hushed murmurs. They probably expected me to have been expelled. I sat down next to Yaseen and took out my exercise book in preparation for study.

"Is everything okay buddy?" he asked, compassionately.

"Sort of," I replied. "Ford wants me to do a speech in front of the entire school and he said something about making me Head Boy."

"That is great news," my friend said.

"That is where you are wrong. I struggle to talk in front of people. How am I supposed to give a motivational speech to hundreds of pupils?"

"Nonsense, you did that drama thing."

"That was a one off."

"Oh yeah. Well, here's the thing. Talking in front of crowds is not as bad as you may think. When God told Moses to go and confront the Pharaoh in front of a ton of people, he was able to pull through despite his stutter holding him back. If he can do it, then you can."

"I suppose that is true. I should probably write a speech then." But what words of mine could benefit the people of this school. I was an imposter living someone else's life.

Upon arriving at home, I told Mum the news and asked her to help me write a speech. She was happy for me, yet she said that the speech had come from my heart alone, else it would be a lie. Next, I decided to sit by my desk and brainstorm ideas.

Dear Queen's

That sounded too formal, this was not a letter.

Hello boys

Technically the teachers would be listening too.

Hello everyone. So far so good, now all I needed was some sort of quote from a famous person. Someone like Dwayne Johnson. *Oh wait, this was a private school. I should probably use a quote from a philosopher. Or maybe a Mathematician like Pythagoras.* Fun fact, Pythagoras was the leader of a cult and used to drown anyone who leaked any of his mathematical findings. That should go in the speech. People would like that. So far on my page I had.

Hello everyone,

Pythagoras-cult

This was going well but I needed to talk for 10 minutes. What else could I talk about. Oh yes, my success, which was not actually mine. What other success could I talk about. So let's talk about someone else's success, like Julian.

Julian – how he angers me

I can talk about my jealousy, people like that stuff, makes me sound 'human'. I can then explain how jealousy led me to try harder. This was going to be a great speech.

My success was split into 4 parts- Academic, Sport, Music and Theatre. The plan was to talk about each of them and lie about how I became so good.

Academic- Maths, Econ, Physics

Music-Piano

Sport-Rugby

Theatre-acting.

Another aspect of my life that fascinated Mr Ford was my heroism. So that needed to be discussed. *I could talk about what happened with the bomb and mention my thoughts at the time.* Nobody needed to know that indeed I was the one that planted it.

Bomb-heroism

That should be enough topic points, so to finish off, I should tell a joke, which I could think of on the spot. Now it was time for some video games followed by bed. Doing catch-up work was not a priority.

Chapter 8: The Speech

All night, I practised the speech in my head, delivering it to an imaginary audience. The only thing standing between me and victory were my nerves. Uncontrollable sweat, fidgeting and mumbling were all things that I feared.

"You have got this Jason," Mum said while I was eating my breakfast. "If only I could be there to watch my baby. Just remember to speak from your heart and you will be fine." Easier said than done.

On the bus to school, I flicked through my flashcards, going through each and every prompt. I had this, as long as my lie did not collapse.

There were 5 flashcards in total, each with one of the following:

Hello everyone

Pythagoras

Julian

Success

Heroism

As long as I kept to those topics I may actually have had a chance at not butchering the speech.

The school gates creaked open as I paced in. *Somebody should seriously oil those hinges. That should be in the speech. Maybe not actually.* All it would take to throw me off would be one person in the front row snoring.

There were now thirty minutes until the dreaded assembly. Going to the toilet now was essential as I did not want to wet myself in front of hundreds of pupils.

I found myself a quiet room where I walked in circles muttering the words. 'Hello everyone, my name is Jason and', upon checking my watch again, I saw that there were only 15 minutes left.

In the Sixth Form Centre, I looked for my friends in order to get advice.

"Focus on one guy in the audience," Boris exclaimed.

"Actually, you should look at several people, that makes you seem more confident." Wilfred added. "After every sentence change your gaze to another person."

"Just imagine everyone naked." interrupted Haresh. There was a moment of brief silence before Wilfred said

"Don't do that, that will only make things harder for you".

10 minutes left, I needed to go.

Next, I found myself standing in a small room outside the assembly hall anxiously wating. Mr Ford walked past and placed his hand on my shoulder. His firm hand clasped my shoulder squeezing out my nerves like an orange being juiced.

"I have every faith in you," he said. I did not believe him as sweat rolled down my face. My flashcards had gone damp from my clammy hands as my watch ticked down the final minutes before the show.

5 minutes left.

"Jason," came a familiar voice. My ears pricked up. The doors swung open and Frank burst in.

"Frank what are you d-"

"Shut up Jason. Now listen, I don't have much time". His face was beetroot red and he had huge dark bags beneath his eyes. He kept on panting, totally fumbled for words. "Listen buddy, I don't know what to do. My whole life has turned upside down. They are keeping me prisoner."

"Who are they?"

"The Government. They had me locked in a secure facility for my 'safety'. But that's not the strangest bit. It's my Dad." What could possibly be wrong with Ted Clifford? "He has been acting weird over the last week, even before the bomb."

"I am sure that is just the stress of the job," I stated.

"No, it's not that. He is different. Before he used to eat with his fork in his right hand and knife in left. Now he randomly eats with his fork in his left hand and then swaps mid meal. There are other things as well. His showers are much shorter, he adores classical music and hates pop which used to be his favourite." I could hear the hubbub of the assembly as all the pupils came pouring in. I glanced through the window and saw the pupils sit down on the chairs one by one, filling up the assembly hall.

"And several times now he has forgotten my name. Yesterday he called me Jason? What is up with that?" He put his hand directly below my neck, beginning to put pressure on my upper chest. "Do you have anything to do with this? He has only met you once and is now getting us confused."

He began applying more and more pressure onto me as I felt my ribs struggling under his weight.

"Jason, I don't want to sound crazy but I think my Dad has been abducted by aliens and replaced. He has suddenly become horrible and nasty, getting frustrated over the smallest things. He is not the same man."

Abducted by aliens? That sounded absurd. But so did having no memory of the previous month. Were these two events related? No, impossible. But maybe. Once the door to the supernatural had been opened, anything could happen.

"Frank, erm when did you say this strange behaviour started?"

"Last Monday. The 11th to be precise," he uttered. He released his hand from my chest. "The day after my party. At first I thought he was angry with me for trashing the house but it can't just be that."

The party? That must have been during 'The Gap'. From what I had gathered, there was a party on the final day of my 30 day slumber. So Ted started acting fishy the day of my reawakening. This was bad. Seriously bad.

The door creaked open and Mr Ford walked in, "Jason, they are ready to see you now." He paused for a moment. "Frank? Why are you here, go take a seat with the other students." I followed behind the Headmaster, leaving Frank behind. This was all going terribly.

As we approached the assembly doors, a boy opened the door for us as the headmaster marched in. The second that Mr Ford entered the hall, the entire school immediately shot up onto their feet out of respect. Everyone was standing as Mr Ford walked onto the stage.

"You may sit," he said into the microphone, with a sense of authority and leadership.

"Good Morning, Ladies and Gentlemen, I introduce you to this fine Tuesday morning with the pleasure of having one of our very own pupils talking. As you all know, this is Jason Clyde who is in the Lower Sixth and I have requested him to talk to you about his success and heroism performed recently." He gestured towards me and I quickly strode over.

In my mind I had envisioned myself walking proud across the stage, like a celebrity entering a talk show. But in reality I could feel the looks of everyone and it felt like small daggers being threaded into my skin. I scurried across the room and clambered onto the stage before looking upon the audience. Hundreds of boys looked at me with dead eyes. The impact of it pushed me back a little. I reached for the microphone. *Here goes.*

"Hello every-" There was a huge screech of feedback instantly. My face winced in disgust before I took a step back and tried again.

"Hello everyone," my voice bounced off the walls and echoed around. I had never been this loud before. I tried to focus on the speech but by head buzzed with questions.

So one day I come home from school and go to bed. Next thing I know a month has passed and I have no memories. Apparently that same day, Ted Clifford starts acting weird. What if he got possessed like me? The day before 'The Gap' ended was Sunday 10th November. That day I went to a party at Frank's house. What if I somehow transferred my possession to the Prime Minister and then I woke up as normal the next day. Ted Clifford is currently in his own 'Gap'. Okay, things were starting to get clearer.

At that moment I realised that the audience were looking at me, waiting for me to start.

"Hello everyone. I am Jason and erm today I want to talk to you about my success." Sweat slipped down my cheek. Looking to the crowd, I saw all my new friends sitting together on a row. At the back, Frank slipped in through a door and sat down on the final row. I needed the toilet again and both my hands and my head were sweating and *what was I talking about again?*

"So, erm Pythagoras said" *what was the quote again?* I simply could not remember. Was there even one? I needed to get rid of my nerves. *Nudity.*

I looked at Haresh. *Okay, he said imagine everyone naked.* I started to imagine but then quickly regretted it. Once more I flicked through my flashcards looking for something to say.

So I had been possessed and then passed on my possession to Frank's Dad. That meant somebody must have passed the possession onto me initially. The day before 'The Gap' started was Friday 11th November. *That day, who was in my house ready to possess me. Surely not Mum or Dad?* I kept on flicking through my flashcards until I say my answer right in front of me.

Julian.

No. *How could he possess me? That is totally ridiculous.* Julian was just a brain surgeon, not some wizard. *But maybe?* That would explain why Ted limped in the hospital. Julian always had a limp, so he must have limped by habit. That would explain why he quickly tried to hide it. Also, Julian was left-handed hence the swap of cutlery. And that would pray tell how he knew Mum and Dad's names in the hospital and why he called Frank Jason. But what was his motive and plan?

He took control of my body for a month so that I could make friends with Frank and hence get invited over to his house. When Julian went over to his house, he then possessed Ted Clifford, the Prime Minister. I woke up the next day with no memories of the previous month. *So Ted Clifford is actually Julian. What the hell?*

I swept my flashcards onto the floor and looked at Frank. He deserved to know the truth. About our friendship, about his dad, all of it. This all made too much sense with my conclusion clearer than it had ever been.

"Okay scrap that. Hello everyone, I am Jason and today I have an urgent message for all of you". Mr Ford smiled as I collected my nerves.

"My brother, Julian was the Head Boy here several years ago. A few of you may remember him. My entire life was spent in his shadow. My rare and minor successes were outweighed by his huge successes. And that is the why I am here. Julian did something impossible, in fact we both did something impossible.

This September was the first of my life at Sixth Form. I had just gotten my GCSE grades back and they were average. My one success which was a 9 in Maths which was deemed irrelevant when compared to Julian's big promotion to consultant the same day. My life of mediocrity meant nothing to anyone. But this speech is about what changed in my life.

You may call me crazy but I need to be honest with you. One day in October I went to bed and the next day I woke up. Pretty normal right? But my entire life had changed at that point. The reason is because an entire month had passed since I slept. I went to bed and woke up a month later with no memory of the last thirty days.

I was perplexed for a large period of time. How could I forget so much, maybe I had a mental condition? When I went to school I noticed that everything had changed. All my grades had significantly improved and my teachers now respected me. I had gained brand new friends and my best friend Raj now hated me. I was a musical genius, an actor and a sportsman but with no memory as to how I got there.

I am not your friend Frank, that was not me you made friends with. I am Jason, mediocre student, not high flying genius. In fact I should not even be up here because I am celebrating off of someone else's success. But this is the real reason is why I am here."

On the floor, lay the flashcard about Julian, staring me in the face. The words were on the tip of my tongue, ready to be released into the wild.

"The truth is that-"

"Nobody move!" a voice boomed. The door to the hall was smashed open and a man wearing a full black combat suit walked in. He slipped a pistol out of his pocket and shot up at the ceiling three times.

With each shot there were wails of shock from the audience. Sawdust rained down from the bullet holes in the ceiling. What was going on? A huge stampede of pupils rushed to the back door only for another military figure to block that exit. He wielded a large machine gun and behind him, a swarm of soldiers emerged, quickly surrounding the entire assembly. Every one of them wore black balaclavas and goggles concealing their faces. They had guns trained in on all of us. This was horrifying to watch.

The initial soldier that came in walked up onto the stage and shoved me to the side. This man was a literal giant, at least 6 foot 5. He was indeed a tank and had a utility belt around his waist which was filled with an array of knives and small guns. A grenade could even be seen amongst other gadgets.

"What the hell is going on, Mr Ford cried," his face beyond pale.

"Let me introduce myself," the soldier said with a thunderous voice. The entire school looked petrified. Even Haresh, the toughest person I knew, was streaming with tears.

"My name is Special Agent Achilles, and I mean no harm." the dead seriousness of his tone said otherwise. "I am here to collect fugitive Frank Clifford, who should be back in full quarantine."

This all seemed a bit too much. Why would Ted send a legion of fully armed soldiers just to retrieve his son? Why would he threaten an entire school with violence over such a small matter? This entire situation made no sense. But then I remembered that Ted was actually Julian. What would my evil brother want with the Prime Minister's son?

"This is a dangerous time Frank!" Achilles roared. "Now I need you to come with me before this situation gets any worse."

Frank simply stood up with his hands above his head. However, he kept his cool throughout, despite being in danger. A soldier barged in from behind him and rapidly cuffed his hands together. Frank was then aggressively lugged towards the exit.

Now with Frank removed, the assembly could go back to normal. Would the rest of the school day just go on as usual and we would forget that this had ever happened? What teased my mind was the fact that Frank was treated so harshly. Frank played a big role in Julian's plans and that puzzled me.

"One more thing", Agent Achilles added, "We will also be apprehending Jason Clyde." *What*? What had I done wrong?

"New evidence points to the fact that Jason was the one who planted the bomb in the school". There was a long pause of silence until the hall projector projected a small video of me placing the briefcase in Mr Griffin's classroom. This was from the school CCTV. How could I have been so stupid to not go back and wipe the CCTV?

"As you can see, Jason here is actually a criminal and is to be put on trial for his actions. Samuel Ford, you have been caring for a criminal and a murderer under the roof of your very school."

"Murderer?" I murmured, the words barely escaping my lips as my chest continued to tighten.

"You are a murderer Jason, responsible for the death of your brother Julian."

"You are lying!" I spat.

"Then explain this." The screen changed to a photo of me standing in a room. And in that very room, a knife was held in my hands, which had torn its way into Julian's torso."

"This was taken from the CCTV of your brother's apartment. The body was discovered in the River Thames this morning. Now, on behalf of British Homeland Security you are under arrest for the murder of Julian Clyde and the attempted bombing of this school."

At the exit, Frank had heard all of this. He spun backwards and looked at me. His face was pale and distraught.

"Take this piece of filth out of my school!" Mr Ford yelled, pushing me with brute force. Achilles seized my arms and held me in a headlock position. His oversized muscles dug into my neck, squeezing out all my energy.

I glanced to the audience. All my friends looked down at me as if I were bird poo on the street.

A pair of handcuffs were strung onto my wrist and securely fastened. The metal dug into my wrist like teeth. Two agents grabbed me, one arm each and dragged me away. The whole world had turned on me and now I was being taken away for crimes I did not commit.

Was Julian actually dead? If that was the case then my entire theory may have been wrong about Frank's dad. This made no sense whatsoever.

Being dragged out of school was like walking down the Hall of Shame. Teachers and pupils alike stood on either side of the path and watched me with their backs turned.

Mr Gideon had a look of disgust on his face. He spat in my direction and a blob of spit landed on my cheek. I was unable to wipe it away as my arms had been seized, so I had to endure the disgust.

"Get that traitor away from me!" Gideon screamed. I tried to slow down to talk to him, however the butt of a gun was slammed into my back. The pain shot up my spine, jolting me forwards.

At the front of this parade stood Frank with his two guards. Behind him was Achilles, who marched with pride. And then there was me, being hauled by two other men at least twice the size of me with three other agents there with guns trained in on me. The rest of the agents marched in single file behind. Outside of the school gates were three vehicles The first of which was a small black car. Frank was pushed into the back seat where two agents on either side. The vehicle behind was small truck with two seats at the front and a huge container hooked in at the back. Agent Achilles opened up the container to reveal two rows of chairs. It looked dingy inside as if it were a jail cell. This is where they would put me, caging me like an animal. I was innocent.

I had only one chance. With all my strength, I barged to the right, knocking an agent off guard before smashing my left shoulder into the jaw of the other agent. However, one of the soldiers cocked his gun and prepared to shoot, the nuzzle of the gun against the crown of my head.

"Don't make a scene of this," Achilles whispered into the agent's ear. He nodded and dropped his gun before thrusting his fist into my stomach with immense force. I tried to wiggle my hands free of the handcuffs but it was no use. Instead, I pulled my head back before smacking it into his nose. He recoiled back in pain, nose dripping with blood.

"Why you little," he grumbled before I felt a smack to the head from behind. Dazed, I looked around for some sort of weapon yet there was nothing. Before long, there were a series of punches and kicks in my direction. Whilst I dodged the first few, it was not long before I was on the ground, kissing the pavement. Each kick was like that baseball bat. My body roared out in pain but there was nothing I could do.

"Put him to sleep" came the muffled voice of Agent Achilles. I moaned back yet there was no response. My pain was brought to a halt by the incandescently sharp needle that pierced my neck. All pain seized as all I felt was the dagger. It was impossible to resist the effects as everything blurred together. The voices above fizzled into nothingness as I drifted off.

Part 2

Chapter 9: What Happens Next

I suppose my story had gotten to the point of no return. What started off as a simple 'Sixth Form Drama' had gotten to the position where I was now a wanted criminal on my way to prison or somewhere else. Perhaps I would be interrogated or even tortured? I had been through enough as it was and would happily tell the truth. These agents needed to know that the Prime Minister had potentially been possessed by my brother Julian. But I had no evidence. Before I could think any further, my face was slammed by a hard force, potentially crippling my nose.

"Good, you are awake". I recognised the deep timbre as that of Achilles. What did he want?

"What the hell is your problem!" I shouted at him. Blood poured out my nostrils and dribbled onto my lip. I rubbed my eyes, trying to clear my vision yet my ears were still ringing.

As my vision slowly came back, I saw that we were in some sort of forest. The trees towered over me, shielding me from any sort of sunlight. It was dark, perhaps close to midnight. *How long has it been since I was captured?* The occasional hoot of an owl could be heard in the distance. This area was truly melancholic.

Standing opposite me was Achilles. His balaclava and helmet were now off revealing his head. His skin was tanned bronze and he had a scar that ran between his left eye and his mouth. Achilles had long brown hair that was tied up in a bun. On the side of his neck was a small tattoo with some Japanese writing. He had a small amount of facial hair across his chin that was slightly longer than a stubble.

The rest of the agents were nowhere to be seen. I was stranded with Achilles. *Great.*

"What is going on?" I asked. "Where are we?"

"Our location is strictly classified," he said with a sickening smile. "You tried to kill the son of the Prime Minister and even murdered your brother. There is no prison that can hold scum like you."

"You have to understand this is a mistake," I pleaded. "Those acts were not done by me."

"Very funny. There is video footage. Now I am here to end your miserable life. People like you do not deserve to live."

"What about my parents" I cried. "You can't just kill me and throw my body into a river. They would be heartbroken."

"Trust me, your parents could not care less if you died. Remember you killed their other son." That was enough. This mockery needed to stop now. If I could defeat Achilles then I had a chance at survival. Nobody would find me in this forest. After a couple of months, I could come out of hiding, change my name, shave my hair, and live a whole new life. However, fate had other plans.

With a deep breath, I closed my eyes, relaxing my hectic mind. After opening them, I charged towards the enemy, ready to tear his head off and beat him to a pulp. Yet with a swift movement, he pulled out a pistol from his belt and held it out in front of my forehead. Instantly my body froze out of sheer terror as my heart skipped multiple beats.

"Turn around!" he screamed. Without complaint, his command was done. "Now look towards the ground and I will do this as quick as possible."

How had this happened? My life was going so well and now I was being illegally executed. Julian was truly a sick person, doing this horrible act to me. What would everyone at school think? Wilfred, Raj, Yaseen, Bruce, Haresh, Boris, Mr Grove, Griffin, Weaving, Ms Dawson, Mr Ford. I had not apologised to Raj yet. Mr Ford would probably erase my history from the school. This was a horrific situation. Furthermore, the whole world now believed that I had killed Julian. What would Mum and Dad think, thinking that they raised a murderer?

"3," he said, counting down

"2," I had a good run. I should just die in peace.

"1."

"Wait!" I cried, wisely choosing my final words. "You need to know the truth. My brother is not dead, he has some sort of special mind powers and has possessed Theodore Clifford. You have to believe me. This whole country is now at his mercy. I know it sounds ridiculous but you have to trust me. He possessed me first which is why I have no memory of doing all those crimes."

There was a pause of silence. Achilles had not shot me and I was still alive. For now. Slowly, I rotated to see the soldier who slowly lowered his gun. He had a look of confusion on his face as his face slowly lost its colour.

"Tell me more," he whispered.

"Last month I went to sleep and while I was sleeping, Julian possessed my body. He then used my body for a month in order to befriend Frank Clifford. Frank then invited him to his house, which is when he possessed Ted Clifford. Now Ted is actually Julian and he is planning something. I am not sure what, but he needs me out of the way which is why he sent you to kill me."

Achilles' blank face slowly transitioned into a smile. He reached into his pocket and pulled out a phone.

"Boss, he knows".

"Wait you know as well?" I asked. Achilles just kept on smiling as the following occurred.

The surrounding trees and forest slowly dissolved before my eyes. They slowly melted leaving behind just blank white space. The forest disappeared completely leaving behind four plain walls. I was now in a room with Agent Achilles opposite to me, still smiling. The gun was still in his hands and my face still had blood on it. Was this some sort of green-screen technology? Some sick interrogation technique? Would Achilles have shot me if I did not speak the truth? Surely it was a bluff? My perplexment was halted by the sound of slow clapping.

One of the four walls slid open revealing a door. Clapping slowly, entered Ted Clifford. He had the look on his face as if someone just told him a joke but he could not laugh because he was at a funeral.

"Hello Brother," he said, grinning.

Chapter 10: The Final Test

Of all the questions I had, there was one right at the top.

"What was that?" I asked. "How did the room suddenly change environment."

"You liked my trick" Ted (Julian) said. He sounded way too excited, as if he had just gotten the new PlayStation for Christmas.

"You see, Jason, I can do anything" Julian said, pulling a small fluffy rabbit out of his back pocket. It sat in his hands looking innocent before it disappeared with a snap of Julian's fingers.

"Molecular manipulation?" I queered. If Julian could seriously alter the atomic structure of atoms, then he would be unstoppable. Also he would be the richest man in the world, turning air into gold and would be able to end world hunger.

"It is all about the mind, brother". I am controlling your mind into thinking that there is a rabbit in my hand.

Julian clicked his fingers and the room turned into an exotic beach. I was shocked by the instant blast of heat and the bright sun blinding me, I bent down and ran my hand through the sand, feeling its hot, coarse texture slide through my hands. I grabbed a handful and watched it blow away in the wind. But we were inside? Where was this wind coming from? This all felt too real.

"I can manipulate and trick all of your senses," Julian exclaimed. "A month ago, I was able to capture your mind, allowing me to freely pass into your body and take over. And when I was done, you could not even tell that thirty days had passed."

150

"So, let me get this straight" I said, "Achilles knows that you are my brother".

"Yes, I do" Achilles chuckled. "Ted Clifford was the worst thing to happen to this country. That inefficient oaf let the pound rise out of control and allowed a huge rise in unemployment. That retard spent all his time living off his wealth rather than trying to help his country. I have pledged my allegiance to this country but never in a million years did I imagine working for that thing. He even raised the brat of a child."

"Do not get me started on Frank," Julian sighed. "Do you know how hard it was to be friends with him for a whole month? I would have to sit there and listen to him brag all day long about his holidays and fancy cars. And now I am stuck in his miserable father's body. The horrors of this body," he said grabbing onto the overhang. "Look how overweight I am, it will take months or even years to get back into my previous muscular, slender physique. If I did not step in, this man would have died from high cholesterol within the next couple of years."

"You're staying in that body?" I asked. Honestly, that may have been the strangest sentence ever uttered by my tongue. I could not believe any of this was happening and Julian and Achilles were just laughing this off as if it were a practical joke.

"Of course, well at least until this body turns told, then I shall find a younger body and keep on living. You could call it immortality." After he saw the look of disgust on my face, he spoke again; "We have a lot to discuss."

Julian signalled for Agent Achilles to leave the room. The wall slid open, revealing its sci-fi looking door. Moments later a man in a waistcoat with a thin black moustache entered bearing a piece of card. He put it out in front of me, gesturing for me to take it.

Starters:

Greek salad with feta cheese

Pimiento olives with hummus

"What is this?" I asked.

"I assume you are hungry," Julian said. "We have some of the finest chefs in the country here. Pick what you want and we will continue our conversation over lunch." Was this some sick prank? People's lives were at stake and all Julian could care about was some lunch.

Later on, that day, I found myself in another room with a small table in the middle alongside seats. Someone had given me a change of clothing, so I was out of my bloodied and torn school uniform and now was wearing plain black trousers and a T-shirt. It was November so my arms were freezing. When I asked for a jumper, I was ignored. Opposite me on the table sat Julian who was wearing a three piece black suit with a blue tie. He had a serviette tucked into his collar. It was strange eating in such a small room. There were no pictures on the walls or anything. Not even any windows. This room was plain white, like something out of an asylum.

"Your food, Master Jason," said the waiter holding a silver tray on his hand. I took the food from the tray, it was a salmon fillet, and on the side were some fries. It looked delicious, much better than the school food. Instantly I found myself digging into it. All that stress from the speech and being arrested had made me ravenous. After a couple of mouthfuls of the succulent food I realised that the silence needed to be broken.

"So erm what is happening with Frank?"

"Well, I suppose he knows the truth about me. So I will have to dispose of him. Either he remains imprisoned for now or Agent Achilles would gladly kill him."

"But he has done anything wrong?" I blurted out.

"Excuse me? Are you telling me that that abomination has done *nothing* wrong? Him and his father have worn this country to its bones." He proceeded to pull a piece of paper out of his pocket.

"Frank Clifford," he stated, reading off the perfectly square paper. "Involved in three car accidents, caught taking illegal drugs, underage drinking at fourteen and don't get me started on his school record. Three suspensions, about ten detentions. He even beat you up and smashed your phone. And now you are defending this person?"

He had a point. Frank was far from perfect. But in this situation, he was innocent.

"He is just a boy, he can learn."

"No, he is destined to become like his father. Eventually, through nepotism, he will end up at Oxford and will become a politician. He will get the people's vote and eventually make his way to the top of the ranks. The world is full of too many people like the Cliffords and I intend to bring a stop to that. Before leaders would have to fight each-other for power but now all they have to do is be more popular. There is no honour in that."

At this point I had had more than enough of games and mystery. Why was my body taken away from me for a month? Julian had become Prime Minister but now what? All that he had done was relish in his new wealth and joke around. He was already rich before this.

"Jason," he said, looking me directly in the eyes. The first time he had been serious all day. "I do not know how to put this, but your entire life had been a lie."

"How so?"

"Do you know who Jerry and Jemima are?"

Those names rung a bell. Where had I heard of them before? Then it occurred to me. Mum said something about promising Jerry and Jemima that she would keep me safe. But who were those two people? I even saw their names in a dream, carved into a headstone. They must have died but I had never heard of them.

"No idea," I uttered.

"Exactly. Everyone has been telling you a lie but I intend for you to learn the truth."

That statement could not have been more ambiguous. Julian cut a huge chunk of steak and placed it in his mouth. He chewed for a moment, gulped it down and then continued on.

"The thing about my abilities is that I intend to use them for good. This phrase may mean something to you. 'With Great Power Comes Great Responsibility'. I am the most powerful being on this planet so I have the responsibility of the world on my shoulders."

"But who gets to decide that?"

"Do you see anyone else with the power of a god?" Julian had always been different to everyone else, but now he was taking things to a whole new level and it terrified me to say the least.

"The world is being led by the weak rather than the strong. I intend to end suffering, injustice and oppression."

"How?"

"The only reason you are still alive is because I see potential in you. Initially I planted the bomb to kill you and Frank but you outsmarted me which was a first. I then placed you into the forest with Agent Achilles in order to see how much you really knew. It was a trial to see how well you could piece the puzzle. And hear this, if you got a single bit wrong, Achilles would have shot you there and then. His gun was indeed real and loaded. You survived my two tests which is why I want you by my side."

At this point, I was speechless. Julian was sadistic. He was prepared to kill me. Twice in fact. He stole my body, framed me for murder and now had taken the country for himself. The problem was, he was too powerful. If I joined him then I would be safe but if I was against him then he could very easily kill me.

"You have the brains to be by my side. You will be with me while we fix this world. I need you Jason. If you have a fraction of my intelligence then you are the second most powerful person on this Earth. Now, before you join me, I need to test you one last time."

Julian snapped his fingers and at that moment the waiter walked in a took our food away, snatching my plate from my hands. Julian jumped up, stretched his legs and walked around the room.

"The world does not come for free. You need to be willing to make a few sacrifices." he exclaimed.

All of a sudden, the door slid open and Agent Achilles burst in, dragging a body. He smacked the body onto the ground which had a bag around its head. Muffles could be heard from within. The agent ripped the bag off the body revealing the wounded body of Frank. His face was caked in blood and his left eye swollen. He moaned out in pain, trying to sound my name, but the agent slapped him with the back of his hand as if he were making a professional tennis shot. I flinched in pain at the disgusting sight before me.

"Now, you get to decide your fate," Julian said, taking a pistol out of his pocket and placing it into my hands.

"Kill him, and you will be by my side."

This was insane. I could not kill Frank. He may have been a jerk to me before but over the last few days he has been something else. He was the only one there from school when I was in hospital. And now here he was, battered and bruised at my mercy. This was an insanity to say the least. The gun felt cold in my hands. I actually had the power to end his life and it terrified me. Even though I was never going to do it, there was an itch to pull the trigger. My finger was drawn to it like an alcoholic to a glass of whisky.

"What will it be Jason? Join me and together we can change the world *or* you will die over this loser." He stepped over towards me and started shouting in my ear, his spit going down my canals. "Remember what he did to you! This boy is a threat to society. Do you want him to end up like his father?" His cold breath froze the sweat on my nape.

Frank looked over to Julian apologetically. Julian was using Ted Clifford's body, the body that Frank had looked up to his whole life and now it was being used to kill him. Tears streamed down his cheeks. My hands were sweating like anything. The gun was beginning to slip out of my hands. My breaths came out in quick succession as stress overwhelmed me.

"You have always been a disappointment Jason. Now is the time for you to finally come out of your shell. Break free and fulfil your destiny."

The gun felt like an anvil in my hands. It was far too heavy for what it was. The gun was pointed at Frank. It would be a quick death and would put him out of his misery. He had been suffering for long enough. I would be doing him a favour.

"Now I will count down from 5. When I get to 0, I expect that freak to be lifeless on the ground. 5!" his voice boomed.

I held the gun steady, preparing to take the shot. But then I simply lowered the gun. Killing someone was an instant no. There was nothing to think about. Nobody deserved to die. The eerie silence was more than it should have been. My brother looked at me, shaking his head in dismay before walking over.

"I expected nothing more from you." He snatched the gun out of my hand, cocked the pistol and shot Frank point blank. The blast screamed out causing my ears to ring. I glanced to the ground and what I saw was grotesque. Frank lay on the floor, motionless with his brains splattered on the ground. His eyes were white and completely lifeless. I fell to the ground and grabbed his body. It had gone stone cold.

"What have you done?" I whimpered.

"Doing the inevitable." Julian smiled. He was truly a psychopath. However at that moment, he clicked his fingers and the unthinkable happened.

The cold corpse in my arms began to feel lighter and lighter to the point where I was holding nothing as his body slowly faded in colour, disappearing entirely from the room. His blood on my hands dissolved leaving nothing.

"You failed the test". This was another one of his illusions, but it felt real. Too real. Frank was still alive but I felt absolutely no sense of relief. The whole experience had been far too dramatic. It could have taken years to forget that trauma. But I did not have years. Julian was about to execute me for failing his final test.

Before I could get up, Agent Achilles thrust a metal rod into my back, sending out electric volts into my body that shocked everything, numbing my limbs. I writhed on the floor in agony as blue sparks shot out. The two of them walked out and slammed the door behind them. I struggled to get up but the electricity burned through me. My muscles went into spasm as I fell to the ground. My lungs had frozen and I was starved of air. Once the door was sealed shut behind them, the lights went out. Leaving me in pitch black as I lay there totally useless. The shock went on for several minutes but by no mean did it get easier with time as it continued to tear ruptures in my skin and boil my blood.

After what felt like a year, the energy stopped and my body was relieved of the torture. My lungs regained minimal strength and sucked air back into my body as if I were breathing through a straw. However my muscles were still in extreme agony. A weapon like that should not ever have to be used on a human. Not even the worst humans deserved something like that. *Was this Hell?* Yaseen told me that Hell involved the body being burnt alive only for it to constantly regenerate forever. My thoughts kept on rolling until eventually my drowsiness consumed me.

"So, does anybody know the formula to calculate Aggregate Demand?" Mr Griffin asked. Before the man had finished speaking, Raj's hand had instantly shot up.

"C+I+G+X-M," he stated.

"Correct, now, what affects consumption. Raj's hand shot up again. "Jason, what do you think?"

I was so tired. I did not want to answer the question. In fact my thoughts were on home. It was only mid-afternoon and I was desperate to be back in the comforts of my bedroom. Economics was the last of my concerns.

"Jason, we are wating". At that moment something hard hit my head. I turned to see that Frank had thrown a scrunched piece of paper in my direction.

"Hurry up Jason. Are you too dumb to understand the question?"

"Answer Jason!" Raj shouted. My classmates began to stand up one by one and started circling around me.

"Dumb student,"

"False friend,"

"Traitor,"

"Disappointment."

The last one hit harder than it should have. School was not for me. I never tried because I never wanted to succeed. Most people had their lives plans laid out from the start. I never had any idea of what I wanted to do in life. In fact at that moment I felt more alone than ever in my entire life. Just me and my thoughts. Did you know that loneliness is cold? I never knew that an emotion could have a temperature. But at that moment, I felt colder than I had in my entire life.

A certain creaking sound awoke me from my slumber. I listened as the door slowly crept open and light peaked in, strangling the darkness. With the darkness defeated, I glanced up to see a shadowed figure who put out his arm and called out to me.

"We have to leave now." I gingerly raised my sore arm and felt his palm in my grasp. His skin was soft and his hand was warm. So warm. He clasped his hand around mine, maintaining a strong connection and yanked me up to my feet. The light stung my eyes whilst I took in the surroundings. The figure standing in the doorway was none other than Frank. Even though I knew Julian's trial was fake, I could not help myself from swinging my arms around my friend and pulling him into a hug. His chest was against mine while those chills from before slowly died out.

"You okay buddy?" he asked. I had never felt more relieved. It was time to get out of this hellish landscape. Watching an image of Frank dying in front of me had haunted me. Even the thought of it made me want to puke.

Frank wore a hood that obscured his face yet his swagger was still the same. He signalled for me to follow behind him and I did exactly that, watching as he crept around the corridors. These corridors were like the room I had just come from, plain white with no windows. This place was a labyrinth, with us having to take turns every couple of seconds. At this point, my trust was put entirely into him and I begged with every atom of my heart that this was not another one of Julian's mind games.

"Stop there," he murmured, as we reached a corner. I peered around to see that there was a man patrolling the halls. He bore a long rifle in his arms, looking like it could take me out with a single shot. The man was decked out in plain black combat uniform which made him stick out in the white corridors. Like Achilles, he had a belt around his waist, home to an array of gadgets, weapons and other murder devices.

Frank picked up a small stone and tossed it along the corridor, as if he were skimming stones on the sea. The agent instantly looked up and ran in our direction. As he came around the corner, his face met the mighty fist of the Clifford. The Agent was knocked back a bit. His hand sped towards his belt however Frank swung his leg into the agent's balls. He was completely winded and collapsed to the ground. Before he could get back to his feet, Clifford had him in a headlock, squeezing the agent for a couple of seconds until he eventually slipped away. Since when did this boy become such a skilled fighter?

"He'll live," he said reassuringly.

We paced onwards, leaving the agent unconscious on the ground. Within a couple of seconds, we had reached some elevator doors which were just ordinary, nothing special. Frank pressed a button to go up and we waited.

"Why up?" I asked. There were no windows so I had no idea as to where we were. We could have been in Antarctica for all I knew.

"We are currently underground," he replied. The doors scratched open and we stepped inside. To my shock, there were dozens of buttons. We were on floor B2, the floors went all the way down to B9 and all the way up to 12. The B floors were all the floors underground with B9 being the lowest. There must have been some serious Government secrets on that floor. Perhaps the cure to cancer was being developed down there or maybe a formula that could start a zombie apocalypse. Who knew?

The elevator crept up the shaft until we had reached the ground floor. When that happened, the doors itched open, rustic in sound. On the other side was a reception but here was the catch. It was just like a normal office building. No militia, no high personnel, just people going about their daily lives. There was a hubbub of people swiftly walking up and down. Through the spinning doors a man rushed in, sipping some coffee. He was dressed in a suit but his tie was not on. Instead it was in his hand as he rushed. The coffee cup was chucked into the bin and he ran to an elevator where he started doing up his tie.

The large floor had the main reception desk. There was a single elevator on the left side of the room, where we found ourselves. A sign stated 'No entry'. There was an array of elevators on the right side of the room which is where the man with the tie went. The floor was sparkling clean and was gleaming with polish. A majestic chandelier was placed in the centre of the ceiling where it glistened. This office building felt more like a 5-star hotel than a place of work. There was even classical music playing, and it helped create an ambience of peace. But our situation was far from bliss.

Frank hurried me across the room as I stumbled behind him. We dodged all the workers walking up and down and headed to the spinning doors. For Government headquarters, this place was surprisingly lacking in security.

However, at that moment, the elevator doors behind us reopened and a man popped out. Like the other security guards, he was tall and muscular. On the contrary to the rest, this man had some sort of emotion on his face. In fact, he looked incredibly angry.

"STOP THOSE TWO!" he yelled with saliva globules bursting from the orifice. The sound of the hubbub instantly dissipated and everyone looked directly at us. Frank shoved the closest person to us towards the security man and ran. I followed behind, speeding out of the building. It was as if we were on an assault course, dodging people and jumping over the occasional mop. At one point, I ended up knocking a man's coffee into his face. He screamed out in pain as his face melted but there was nothing I could do.

"Sorry," I cried before running off. The security man was fumbling behind us yet he was still incredibly fast. Once we got outside we sprinted as if we were in the Olympics. A stitch began to form in my chest but I ignored it as I felt the adrenaline pumping inside of me, my muscles booming with energy as if they were high on caffeine. We were on some road in the middle of London. I did not know the surroundings, but Frank clearly knew his way as he traversed through the streets, turning left and right around corners. He knew the map of this place like the back of his hand. And all I had to do was trust him.

The problem was that the security guard was built differently. While we were doing a 100-metre sprint, he was doing a Formula 1 race on the same track. The man was a literal machine. *What kind of gym workout turns you into that?* Whatever it was, I could have benefited from a few sessions. His eyes were dead set on us as he leapt huge strides. The look of determination on his face was horrifying.

After some time in the Labyrinth of the city of London, we found ourselves in an empty street where there was a lone car parked on the side of the pavement. It was a black Mini, looking almost brand new from its impeccable shine and dirt-free windows. We walked closer to the car and saw that there was a young lady sitting in the driver's seat. She was dressed in a suit and so probably worked in one of the office buildings. When we saw her, she had a mirror in front of her and was touching up her lipstick, completely oblivious to the two teenagers running towards her. Frank gently knocked on her window.

"We need your car," he stated, bluntly. She completely ignored him. If we were to shake off that security guard, we would need a car. As horrible as it sounded, our lives depended on grand theft.

Suddenly, Frank pulled a gun out of his pocket and held it up to the car window.

"Don't make me repeat myself," he groaned. Where did that come from? When she saw the gun, she let out a scream and jumped out. At the end of the street, I could see the guard coming towards us. He knew what we were doing and sprinted even faster, as impossible as that may have seemed. A predator would never let his prey get away. Frank snatched the keys out of the girl's hand and shoved her to the side before jumping into the car.

"I am so sorry," I said to her, apologetically before getting into the passenger seat. The guard was now getting closer and closer, and somehow he was getting even faster. This guy could have honestly given Usain Bolt a run for his money.

Frank revved up the engine before stomping on the pedal. The guard was close now but we were able to zoom off in the nick of time. He would not give up so easily though, as he whipped a gun out of his pocket and started shooting the car. I bent down and watched as the back window exploded into tiny fragments. The guard had shot three bullets. One grazed the side of the car, one shattered the back window and the third one supposedly missed.

That was when Frank wailed out in pain. I turned and saw that the bullet had lodged itself into the dashboard. However, its trajectory was via Frank's arm. There was a large cut on the side of his arm and blood was gushing out. Even though he was in extreme pain, the boy still kept his cool and remained focused on the road.

Frank lifted up one of his hands and held it to his arm, putting pressure on the wound, while he had the hand from the wounded arm still on the wheel.

"I am gonna need you to put pressure here," he winced. In one of the cup holders were a packet of tissues. I ripped one out and pushed it onto the wound, soaking up in blood immediately.

"We need to go to a hospital," I stated. The blood would not stop no matter how much I tried patching it. Frank needed proper stitches and full medical attention.

"Jason," he said calmly, "My father and the entire country will now be looking for us. A hospital is a definite no."

"Then what do you suggest? I can't just let you bleed to death."

"There is one person who can help us."

Chapter 11: Sanctuary

"He'll be okay," Wilfred said reassuringly.

"Thank you for helping us. I understand that helping out two fugitives is not ideal."

"No worries mate. Anything for one of the boys". This situation was truly horrible. After Frank got shot, we ditched the car and hobbled to Wilfred's house which happened to be nearby. His parents were away on holiday, so it was a perfect hiding spot for now.

I switched on the TV and the first thing that popped up was the news.

"Police are still looking for fugitive Jason Clyde who has kidnapped Frank Clifford, the son of the Prime Minister, Ted Clifford. While his intentions are still unclear, Jason is to be considered a high threat individual. We now move on to our correspondent."

This was absurd, I did not kidnap Frank. Frank was being relentlessly hunted by Julian and I helped rescue him. In fact, he rescued me.

The screen showed an ariel shot of school where the site had been deserted. "Right now, I am outside 'The Queen's School' which is where Frank and Jason both attended. It was here where Jason saved the lives of his classmates from a bomb. However, through recent evidence, we have discovered that Jason was indeed the one who planted the bomb. Jason was also found to be guilty of murder of his older brother Julian Clyde. Julian was a world renowned brain surgeon and his work in medicine will always be treasured. The headmaster, Mr Ford announced that the rest of the school week should be cancelled to help aid police investigations."

A photo of Julian was projected on to the screen. He was smiling in the photo revealing his perfectly white teeth. He wore a suit that was perfectly ironed, as always. In his left hand was his signature cane. The photo made him out to seem like a great individual, but I knew he was a psychopath. He had brainwashed the world into thinking that I was the villain when in reality it was him.

"We now go live to Downing Street where Ted Clifford will comment on the situation at hand".

The screen cut to outside of Downing Street where Ted / Julian stood. His hair was dishevelled and he had huge bags under his eyes. Even his suit was creased and his tie was lopsided. He was really putting on the act that he was stressed over his son. The man seemed fine last time I saw him which was only a few hours ago. How much make-up was he wearing?

"I cannot believe what has happened. I sent my son to one of the top schools in the country in hopes that he would be surrounded by good company who would keep him safe. I did not expect one of his classmates to be a psycho and to kidnap him from a secure Government location. The thing is", he paused for a second while a tear rolled down his face. "The thing is, I miss my son dearly and hope that he is okay."

Julian was a good actor and it showed. He could not care less about Frank, all that mattered was his big plan which I was yet to uncover.

167

"Now here is where you all come in, my people. Jason Clyde is to be considered an extremely dangerous individual and is now the most wanted person in the country. If any of you were to find and locate him or my son, there will be a one million pound prize waiting for you. Jason is a threat to our lives so you must look out. Any tips as to where he may be will also result in a prize. On the contrary, any attempts in assisting Jason or any relevant information withheld from the Government will result in a minimum of 10 years imprisonment".

I quickly grabbed the TV remote and switched it off. This was a lot to take in. Rather than escape from the government, we now had to worry about an angry British mob desperate for money. I glanced across the room to Wilfred. By concealing us, he would end up in prison.

"1 mill, that's a lot of money. I would not even have to go to uni with that sort of cash and could be set for life." He then seized the scalpel he used on Frank. Blood dripped off of it and trickled down his wrist as she approached me.

"I now have the choice, make all that money or risk a life in prison. It was dumb of me to let you two in. My life plans have been ruined."

"Will, please, I understand it was unfair for us to turn up like this, but you need to let us go. The world is in grave danger. My brother is controlling the Prime Minister. He controlled my body as well and made me plant that bomb. It sounds crazy but it is the truth. Julian has plans to take over the world and by taking me in, you would be sealing the fate of millions if not billions."

There was a brief second after I made my plea of pure silence. His scalpel still dripped blood and it creeped me out. I took in my surroundings, looking for a potential weapon. There was a metal rod right outside of the fireplace. That would make a could spear.

"Of course I wouldn't sell you guys out" he laughed. "That really is some cover up story. You should work on that excuse though. That's gonna fool no-one."

"You see," I laughed nervously. That was the truth. There was nothing more to add.

"Now, let's make a plan." He led me to another room where Frank lay on a bed. His arm was all bandaged up. The room on the other hand was covered in tissues and blood.

"I can't believe I was able to stitch you up after watching a YouTube video," Wilfred laughed, aware of his shoddy work. "But seriously, you need to go to a legit hospital."

"That's not happening," Frank said, sitting up. His face was slightly pale and his trousers were stained in blood. His chest on the other hand was on full display. He winced in pain as he cradled his arm. The fact that he was able to drive with a bullet wound was remarkable. He was now sitting on a bed in the middle of a kitchen. The kitchen was overly clean, as if nobody had ever used it. There was a complete lack of food, with near empty cupboard. This family most likely got all their food through delivery. When we initially arrived, I carried Frank into the kitchen and lay him on a table and then Wilfred and I brought down a random bed. Will did most of the lifting, claiming that he needed to work his biceps.

169

For a couple of seconds, there was an awkward silence, while nobody knew what to say. What was there to say? We were all as confused about this situation as each other. Frank had almost been shot to death, and my life was now worth over a million pounds. The awkward silence ended when Wilfred looked at me. He gazed for a couple of seconds, before saying.

"Buddy, we need to do something about you "You are on the front cover of every newspaper and sprinkled on billboards all over the country. Half of England will have memorised your face"

"What are you suggesting?"

"You are gonna need a Wilfred Campbell costume change."

Some time later, I found myself in Will's bedroom. He had a huge wardrobe that stretched along his entire wall. His desk was also massive. On top of it were a couple of papers but mainly there was a large, curved monitor. It was switched on, with a wallpaper of a New York Skyline. His keyboard had green lights peeking out from underneath each key. To the side of the desk was his PS4 standing tall, with an array of wires coming out.

I took a seat on Will's awesome gaming recliner chair. Its cushions hugged my muscles as I sat down, releasing all sorts of happy emotions. Meanwhile, Wilfred slid open his wardrobe, revealing a multitude of different outfits. He had about five different tuxedos and seven different coloured suits. They were light grey, charcoal grey, black, navy blue, light blue, brown and purple. *Why does he have a purple suit?* I thought to myself.

From within his wardrobe of wonders, the boy pulled out a pair ripped jeans and a hoodie before hurling them in my direction.

"Hopefully these should fit you," he said.

It was nice to wear something warm after running around the streets of London mid-November, wearing a T-Shirt. The hoodie was plain black. Next I pulled a woolly beanie over my hair. Wilfred's jeans were a bit too skinny for me, especially in the posterior area, but they were better than nothing.

"Here you go" Wilfred said, handing both Frank and I a backpack. They weighed a ton, but it was essential. These contained enough food to last us a week, as well as first aid equipment such as replacement bandages for Frank. "And here is a spare iPhone with sims for each of you," he exclaimed, handing us both brand new iPhone 11s. Where had these come from?

"How can I repay you?" Frank asked.

"Just don't die," he said bluntly.

The plan for the next week was as follows. Survive and get the truth out. The exact truth behind Julian's plans were unclear however I needed to get my name cleared. Wilfred's cousin, Charlie Driver was a renowned news editor, so we planned to meet him first. At this moment, we were in South Kensington, and this guy lived in New Malden so a short train and bus journey would do the trick. The time right now was 15:30. At 17:00 we would leave so that the rush hour traffic would help us blend in. Once I got to the news editor, I would tell him the truth, and Frank would explain that he had not been kidnapped. Then the editor should publish it and the world would

171

know about the truth behind Julian and Ted Clifford, so he could be arrested for his crimes.

Out of nowhere, the sound of a car pierced the silence, alerting me. Through the window, I saw a freshly waxed, black Mercedes pull up outside of Will's driveway. It gently slowed down and halted, when a man stepped out, wearing a black suit and tie. His hair was light brown and combed to the side, with his gel shining in the sunlight. He had put in a tad too much. The man walked towards the front door with slightly hunched shoulders whilst twiddling his thumbs behind his back. Upon reaching the door, he paused for a moment, adjusted his tie and cleared his throat before knocking on the door.

"Okay, you two need to hide in that wardrobe," Wilfred said. This guy, although he did not look like it, was most likely a government agent on patrol. He then headed to the door. I hid in a cupboard filled to the brim with his mum's dresses. There was a fat stench of perfume whilst I hid. From my position, I could just about see what was going on outside as there was a small crack through the door, big enough for me to see through.

When he opened the door, the man cleared his throat again.

"Good afternoon, sir, my name is Kenny Peterson. I work under Her Majesty's Service, and I am here to check if the wanted individual Jason Clyde has come your way. We have been told by erm your school that you are close with him and er Frank Clifford. Have you heard anything about their location and if you have, please could you erm let us know?" This was followed by an artificial smile. *Did he rehearse that?* "We may have evidence that Frank and Jason are with you?"

"Do you have a warrant?" Wilfred said, somewhat aggressively.

"Well erm no. Thank you Sir. I shall be on my way." He then turned around and scurried back to the car to whence he came. However, when he was approaching the car, the sound of a door opening could be heard before it was slammed shut again.

"The boy is lying," came the familiar voice of Achilles. How could I hear his deep and thunderous voice all the way from inside? He left the car and marched towards the house, his boots clumping on the ground as he marched.

"Jason is here. I can smell him," he growled. He shoved Wilfred to the side and stormed in. From what I could tell, Achilles had never failed a mission and today that streak was not going to end.

"Hey, you cannot just barge into my house like that!"

"I can do whatever I want. If you are found hiding Jason, you will be accountable for treason, so I suggest you shut it."

'We need to go', Frank mouthed. The bus would arrive in 7 minutes, giving us time to get to the bus stop. The only way out was to climb out of the window upstairs and then we could traverse to the end of the street by rooftop, Assassin's Creed style.

"Where are they?" Achilles grumbled, smashing all furniture in the way.

"I have no idea what you are talking about," Will mumbled.

The agent continued on his rampage, looking under every piece of furniture. Currently, Frank and I were crumpled in a cupboard in the living room which was also where Achilles was. If we got out, he would see us and that would be the end of that. He inched closer and closer to us, looking side to side with an eagle's vision.

My heart rate began to pick up, as the predator approached us. His hands were giant, big enough to tear my head off. All of a sudden, he locked gaze with our cupboard. *Shoot.* His strides began to increase in magnitude as he stormed over, a true force of nature. He thrust his hand onto the handle and began to pull it open. My heart was leaping out of my chest and my hushed breaths we short and rapid. The only way out of the situation would be to fight him. But my hands were sweating and shaking. This would be the equivalent of a mouse fighting a sabre-toothed tiger. Even Frank was dwarfed by this man.

"Excuse me sir," came the whimpering voice of Kenny.

"Not right now!"

"You are going to want to see something next door."

"Can't you see I am busy." His voice was so tremendously close. Within inches.

"Yes but it is urgent." He said, building up the courage.

"If this is a waste of my time, I will personally make sure that you are revoked of your duties and sent back to office work. Is that clear Peterson?"

"Yes-sir."

Achilles released the handle and trudged off into the neighbouring room.

The relief I felt was beyond anything. The puke building up in my chest was sent back down. Frank gave me the nod, and while they were distracted, I ever so slightly pushed the door open before crawling to the stairs. Clifford followed behind.

"WHAT!" the noise threw me off focus causing me to almost jump.

"Whose blood is this?" His voice shook the building and echoed through my bones, rattling them.

"That is my dad's. He cut himself shaving."

"Boy, this is fresh blood, so I will ask you again, whose blood is this?"

"My Dad shaved an hour ago, that was when he cut himself. The cut was so bad that he rushed off to the hospital. I think he cut an artery or something."

After clambering up the stairs, whilst avoiding any potentially creaky floorboards, we entered the bathroom, where there was a huge window, big enough for us to escape the chaos.

"Peterson, analyse this blood. If this belongs to who I think it does then they must be nearby. This blood is an hour old at most."

Frank pushed open the window and stepped outside before gesturing for me to follow. Gingerly, I raised my leg and stuck it out of the window onto the ledge. The ledge felt weak under my strength. Once I was outside, a huge gust of wind came in my direction. The cold wrapped itself around me and jogged my footing. Above, Frank had successfully made his way onto the roof. He was a pro. The conversation could be heard from inside. After a brief pause, Achilles broke the silence.

"You are so full of crap. Now tell me, who's blood is this?"

Rock climbing was not my forte. Now my life depended on it. The wind slapped me on the back and egged me on to fall. I resisted and proceeded to climb up. My hand moved up to another ledge and I used it as leverage. My bicep pumped as I clambered up using all my strength. Whilst Julian had used my body, I had gained a little bit of muscle which was finally coming in useful. If I ever got out of this mess, I would go to the gym more often. It had done miracles for my body.

"Sir, we have identified this blood as being Frank Clifford's." That was followed by more screaming, yelling and even some crashing.

"This is Special Agent Achilles; I need you to send in backup as well as drones to scout my area. We have found Jason and Frank. Block off roads, do whatever you need to do. Do not rest until the Prime Minister's son is returned to him safely." He paused for a second. "Peterson, take Mr Campbell in for further questioning."

Achilles was onto us. I sped up my climbing to the top of the house. There was now only a small distance left to cover, yet there were no more ledges to use. I would have to jump the last bit. After taking in a deep breath, I pushed off with my leg and prepared to grab the top. Whilst in the air, another gust of wind came and blew me off course. My hands slipped and I found myself falling. All of a sudden, Frank seized my arm, holding me from the top of the building, careful not to let me drag him down. He hauled me up and I got onto the top of the building where the wind was powerful and free. I walked with such caution, as if I were on a mountain, watching my footing with close intent.

"Wilfred Campbell, you are under arrest for the assisted kidnapping and potential murder of Frank Clifford."

Shoot. I had landed someone else into my affairs. This was between me and Julian and now Wilfred and Frank were suffering because of it. Who would be next? Raj, Yaseen, Boris or even Haresh? In fact the entirety of Queen's was being affected because of me. The truth needed to be out there as soon as possible before this got any worse.

On the roof, I could see the rest of the street. There were about fifteen houses between us and the bus-stop. Frank began to run and expertly jump between the detached houses. It was as if he was a professional street runner. Was there anything this guy could not do?

In the distance, Wilfred was handcuffed and taken into a car by Agent Peterson. Achilles on the other hand was scouring the area for us. I could see the bus approaching the bus stop which we needed to get onto.

After summersaulting onto the final building, Frank slid down the side and jumped onto the main ground with a gymnast's precision. I on the other hand was clumsily hopping over chimneys, hoping not to fall in. The bus was only a few metres away so I needed to be quick. Sirens began to howl in the distance as police cars rolled into the area. I leapt onto the final building and began to climb down. The bus had now stopped and passengers began to leave.

How was I to climb down this structure? These Kensington buildings were rather large and this Daredevilish activity was a first for me. First, I lowered my leg down, placing my foot onto a narrow window ledge. Each of my limbs followed, one by one. But this ledge felt like it could break any second. My toes were tingling like anything and my head was feeling nauseous.

The final passengers had left the bus and new passengers began to board. Frank looked at me, unsure whether or not to get on the bus. Meanwhile I crawled down the house, holding to every bit of leverage for dear life.

The bus doors were about to close and I was still one storey away from the ground. There was only one way to get out of here in time, to freefall. After closing my eyes, I released myself from the house and let myself fall. Instantly I plummeted to the ground, my leg crumbling under my weight. The force from the hard concrete slaughtered my knees. However, Frank was there to pull me up and I hobbled over to the bus where I got in, the second before the doors closed. Unfortunately for me, things only seemed to go from bad to worse.

Out of nowhere, dots began to appear in the sky. These black dots got bigger until I could make out what they were. A huge swarm of drones descended from the sky and dispersed into different directions, moving like bugs looking for a meal. They were each small in size, sporting four sets of rotating blades. They had huge cameras at the front, bulging out like a mosquito's eye. Before long, a multitude of police cars pulled up on the road, with officers patrolling the area.

On the bus, I scanned the pass Will had given me and sat down at the back, keeping my head low at all times. Frank sat on the upper deck to keep us apart, lowering suspicions. This bus was packed full of people as we had expected from London rush hour traffic. However, being near so many people at once could result in somebody seeing past my disguise. People would see my face and not think twice about me being Jason. At least that was what I expected.

A few moments later, someone tapped on my shoulder. I turned around to see an old lady sitting behind me. She wore large glasses and had pale and wrinkly skin. She looked frightened by the bug like creatures that were hovering past the bus, scanning each and every one for potential threats.

"Excuse me, young man, do you know what is going on?"

Luckily, she had not clocked who I was. How would I respond to her without giving away my identity? In fact, did anybody know what I sounded like?

"I believe the Government are doing checks, looking for that Jason person. I have heard that he is the most wanted person in the entire country."

"Nonsense. He is just a boy and nobody that age can be truly evil. If you ask me, that Ted Clifford is hiding something. I have never trusted him. When you live as long as me, you can tell apart the good and bad ones. He is a bad one, and you are a good one," she said before mouthing 'Jason'.

Wait she knew? Was my disguise that poor that she could see straight through. I was shocked for a second since if she could figure it out, then highly trained soldiers would definitely recognise me.

"Don't worry, your secret is safe with me," she smiled reassuringly.

The stationary traffic was terrifying. Police patrolled the streets up and down, and any one of them may spot me. I just kept my head down and hoped for the best.

Eventually the traffic passed, and the bus moaned back into action. We had left the ruckus behind before things got too bad. They would probably close the roads and seal off anyone inside but luckily we escaped that.

The next part of the plan involved getting onto a train that would get us near to Charlie's house. Frank and I both got off the bus at the same time and headed towards the train station. However, when we got near, we ran into a problem. The station was barricaded by police officers. There were four of them ushering in people and checking their bags. As well as the police officers, there were drones circling above like vultures. Trying to get into the station would be suicide.

The alternative would be taking a taxi or an Uber. But that would risk getting ratted on. There was a bounty of one million pounds on my head. A taxi driver would happily take me out and use that money to quit their job. And with police patrolling the streets, walking would be useless.

We just had to take the risk so I pulled my hood over my head and walked in. We had to queue first in order to be checked. The queue was heaving with people pushing and shoving. Rush hour traffic now had an extra step to it, and everyone was not happy. The stench of sweat was thick and tensions were as high as ever. Everybody just wanted to get home from a long day of work. This queue very much reminded me of the lunch queues back at school. Everyone would charge in just to get some food. A much simpler time.

Eventually, I fed my way towards the guard, who took a small look at me before wrenching my bag off me. He aggressively zipped open my bag and flicked through all my stuff. Nothing too suspicious. Some plasters, a spare set of clothes, an electric toothbrush. How much tech did Wilfred have? White teeth were not my priority at the moment. In fact I would be fortunate to get out of this whole mess without Achilles knocking out a tooth or two.

"Next," he mumbled. He barely noticed who I was and could not care less. I popped out of the swarm of people and was followed by Frank shortly afterwards.

Soon, we had hopped on the train where we found seats. I was careful not to make any eye contact with anyone. When the train doors slid shut, I felt a sense of impending doom. If anybody recognised me, there would be a huge fight. 1 million pounds was a lot of money. Some would gladly kill for even a fraction of that. If 10 passengers teamed up to beat me up, then they would each receive £100,000 which could potentially mean early retirements all round.

Within a few moments, the train grinded into action and sped off. My surroundings outside slowly blurred away. I watched as the entirety of South Kensington was riddled with police, security and drones. The streets were filled with police cars, guard dogs and a ton of sirens. It was a miracle I was able to escape unscathed.

The train carriage had been cleaned thoroughly as if it were a hotel. The floor shone with polish which was most unexpected from London transport. On the contrary, the walls had been splatter-gunned with posters ranging from all sorts of strange things. Posters about Snickers, the RAF and Shampoo. 'Shave your head in 90 seconds'. That was what one of the posters read. It displayed a man holding some contraption over his head that looked like something from the 'Alien' movies.

The carriage was filled with ten other people. There was a mother with one of those double decker pushchairs. I wonder how she would choose who to put on the bottom deck. Clearly one of the children would get a better view, while the other would be stuck looking underneath the other. Honestly, if Julian and I were twin babies, I would be on the bottom deck. That was guaranteed.

The man to my right was standing up and held the bar above his head. His armpit was exposed, resulting in a cheesy stench being wafted in my direction. In his other hand, was a large briefcase, similar in size to the bomb I found before. In fact, it looked too similar. A sense of unease built in my stomach.

One by one, at each stop, each passenger got off, leaving Frank and I alone. This was our first opportunity to talk in a long time.

"It has been a manic few days," I said, cutting the silence between us. After a short pause, Frank began to open up.

"I can't get over what is happening to my dad," the boy groaned at a barely audible voice.

"I am sure he will be fine."

"That is where you are wrong. With my Mum dead, I can't get over the fact that I may be an orphan soon. My Dad is in serious trouble and I know it," he paused for a moment before speaking again. "I am sorry to hear about your brother. I never really knew the guy but he sounded great. I figured it wasn't actually you who killed him. You wouldn't do something like that."

"Of course I wouldn't. Somebody has framed me for murder".

"I just really hope the same person that killed your brother is not also after my father. The thing about me and my dad is that I was always in his shadow. I was always Clifford Jr or Ted's son or the Prime Minister's brat of a son. I never had my own identity."

"Same with me," I said, my eyes beginning to heat up. "My whole life I have just been a 'mini-Julian', never just Jason." There was another pause for a minute or so, before Frank spoke again.

"If you knew anything about what is going on with my Dad, you would tell me," he said.

However, just as I was about to reply, the train halted and Frank had already gotten up to leave.

"Let's bounce," he exclaimed.

Chapter 12: The Message

The train station was moderately busy however it was filled with even more police officers than before. There was roughly a ratio of two police officers for every person in the station. The usual noise was instead silenced by fear. Upon reaching the exit, Frank and I were approached by four officers.

One of them was shorter than me. She took my bag off me before inspecting it. She had an impeccably ironed uniform and her hair was in an austere bun. She must have been someone of high authority. Another officer started searching Frank's bag. Whilst our bags were being rummaged through, one of the policemen began a full body search on me and my friend. The man placed his hands up and down my body with a sense of force. He had done this so much today that he was fed up. This was very apparent from his restlessness.

He checked all my pockets but in the end found nothing suspicious. Without warning the female officer pulled the hood off my head and gazed at me for a second.

"He matches the height" she groaned. The officer seized my jaw and opened my mouth before looking at my teeth. I was getting increasingly worried. They would figure out who I was and that would be the end of it.

"What is your name?" she asked aggressively. How would I respond. There were four superior fighters surrounding me, a completely unbalanced fight.

However, before I could answer there was a scream. The shrill cry came from the other side of the station.

"There's a gun," wailed a voice. The four officers pushed me to the side and ran towards the noise. Before we knew it, we were alone once again and made a run for it.

"What was that?" I said to Frank.

"Remember that gun I stole earlier. I dropped it in the station on purpose to create a distraction and it worked." Frank then pointed to a bus approaching before sprinting ahead. This bus was what we needed to get to the editor's house. The final step of our journey. I leapt onto the bus before it drove off and then we were safe once again.

The next part of the journey was action-free. The bus ride took about 20 minutes. There were little to no people riding along with us. When I got off, a huge block of flats faced me. This was the place.

The man we were visiting was Charlie Driver. He was Wilfred's older cousin who worked for the Mirror. He was a news editor and one of their best at that. He was our man for the situation. We would tell him the truth about Julian and everything. Hopefully he would publish that so the world could know the truth. Then the police should take care of the rest by arresting Julian and his accomplices. A solid plan.

The time was six, so Charlie should have gotten back from work. We headed towards the building which was battered from age with vines growing out of the walls. On one of the floors, the window had been smashed. Most likely smashed by a football from the playground nearby. There was graffiti all over the nearby area and the ground was cracked and uneven. This had to be his second home. This man was loaded for life, with some of his reports being ground-breaking. Charlie lived on flat 38, so I rang that number. It bleeped and bleeped but there was no response. He was most likely still at work, working on the latest headline. Probably a story regarding Frank and I.

I looked over to Frank, but he was playing with a basketball on the hard play. He dribbled it before tossing it into a hoop. He had the height of a basketball player, but never got into the sport. That did not stop him from being a complete natural.

"Go away, I'm busy" came a static voice through the speaker. The quality of the sound was so poor that I could barely make out what he was saying.

"I need your help" I shouted back into the machine, unsure if he could hear me.

"I am not buying anything," came the gruff voice.

"My name is Jason Clyde, I am here to make a confession."

"Do I look like a priest. You're the one that got my cousin arrested. There is no way I am letting you in."

"I am with Frank Clifford. We need to tell you everything." After that, there was a pause for a minute. There was just static coming out of the speaker. Frank still played basketball, majestically dribbling the ball before making a slam dunk. The hoop was so worn out that there was no longer a net. Clifford wiped the sweat from his brow and continued to play.

"Come in, quickly." Charlie whispered.

I signalled for Frank to come over. The door to the apartment buzzed open as if it were a prison cell door. We walked into an eerily dark corridor. The walls had river-like cracks meandering across them. Chipped paint was scattered all over. The elevator looked incredibly unsafe, so we took the stairs.

That was a mistake. Each stair creaked under pressure. There was a point where I saw a missing stair and nearly fell down. This building was largely unsafe and was in desperate need of refurbishment. What was such an esteemed reporter doing in a dump like this?

Charlie's flat was on the third floor. The stairs continued to spiral on forever once we got off them. I gently knocked on Charlie's door only to hear crashing on the other side. Metal clanked and there were a few grunts. When he went to open the door, it would not budge, so he had to kick it. The door wobbled open and popped off of one of its hinges. Through the doorway was an unruly mess of all sorts. Firstly, the tiny kitchen was littered with dirty dishes. A swarm of flies hovered above, licking off scrapes of mouldy ketchup. I looked down to see Charlie bent down, trying to fix the hinge. He jumped up to his feet and put out his hand.

"Come in," he grumbled. Charlie was a skinny man with relatively long, unkempt hair. It shone from the sheer quantity of grease. His face had little colour and his cheeks were devoid of flesh. He wore a wonky pair of thin rimmed glasses and had the early stages of a neck beard forming. The man wore a sleeveless white T-Shirt that struggled to fit over his stomach and had large stains all across.

Gazing at his hand, I was astonished by how bony it was. Any trace of muscle was now gone. The man wiped his face with the back of his hand before leading us in. At this moment, he had not even acknowledged Frank's presence.

Charlie kicked some clothes to the side, making a path as we followed behind. He took us to a large sofa where he gestured for us to sit. Before we did, he threw some empty pizza boxes onto the floor. He grabbed a slice from one and started chewing.

"Make yourselves at home." he smiled, while eating. The living room was covered in papers. There was a board on the wall full of photos and newspaper articles, all connected by red tape. Kind of like in the movies.

"Do you want something to drink?" he asked. He pulled out a bottle of grape juice and poured some for Frank before giving it to him. He then began to start pouring for me.

"No, thank you," I said. From the ill state of this apartment, I would not be surprised if there was mould growing in the juice. It would be at least a year past its sell by date. I sat down in the chair and Frank next to me. Charlie sat on one of his armchairs before he started talking. The one he sat on had several tears and a large wet patch, perhaps spilt water or maybe even urine.

"So, tell me everything. Right from the beginning." He pulled out a crumpled piece of paper from under the chair. He then started feeling around his body for a pen. After a pause, he pulled out a chewed up pen from his back pocket. Was this guy for real? I though Wilfred's cousin was supposed to be some famous reporter, not whatever this was. There had to have been some serious miscommunication. *Oh well*. There was no other option.

188

I proceeded to tell Charlie everything, from my weird dream to becoming top of my school. I then explained Julian's plan. How he used my body to get close to Frank only to use him to take over Ted Clifford and seize control of the country.

"Wait," Frank said. Up to this point he had been very silent, sipping away at his juice. "So, you are saying our entire friendship was so you could get close to my father". He spoke slowly with a hint of anger.

"Well sort of. My brother used my body to do that. It was his plan.?"

Frank stood up all of a sudden, took a giant sip from his drink, wiped his lips and said, "My whole life I struggle to fit in. Everyone compared me to my father and so I could never escape his shadow. I was never Frank, I was always Ted Clifford's failure of a son. You were the first person to understand that Jason. You stuck with me, no matter what. And now you are saying that was just some lie for your dead brother to possess my Dad. Our friendship meant nothing then?"

"Do you think I would willingly become your friend?" I shouted. "You sent me to the Nurse's office twice, not to mention smashing my phone. And don't get me started on the years of teasing before that. You are the last person I would befriend. You and your looney friends have only caused me problems at that stupid school." I started to feel hot and sweat trickled down my back.

Frank tightened his fist, blinded by fury and paced towards me. He swung his hand into my stomach. His signature move. It hurt but over time I had become accustomed to pain and so I retaliated with a kick to his shin.

189

"Stop this!" Charlie yelled, shoving me back onto the sofa. "This country's future is at stake and you two are arguing about your friendship. Now Jason, hurry up and finish your story." I was seething with anger and so I gave a long hard stare at Frank before telling Charlie the rest.

"Ok, so the Prime Minister is being possessed by your psychopathic-telepathic brother. You say he has some big plans but you don't know what they are. And what evidence do you have supporting this whole story?"

"None", I murmured.

"None?" he scoffed. "That is the dumbest story I have ever heard. There are no such thing as telepaths. Are you saying your brother is one of the X-Men?" he began to laugh hysterically, slapping the sofa. But his laughter was halted by a sudden thud.

I looked to my left and to my dismay, Frank had collapsed onto the floor. His face was kissing the ground and his body lay there, limp.

"Frank, are you okay?" I whispered. There was no response. I kept on shaking him, willing for him to awake. Blurting out before was an accident. It was wrong of me to do that. Next to Frank, I noticed his grape juice spilt on the floor. He drank so much of it. It must have been-

Before I could finish my thought, I spun around to see Charlie in the mid swing of a baseball bat. I rolled out of the way and the bat smashed into a wall.

190

"Don't make this harder than this needs to be," he growled. He spun the bat in his hand, building up momentum. I clambered around the room, yet found myself in a corner. He raised the bat above his head and swung at me. I had no time to dodge, so my arms became my shield. The bat smacked into my forearm, sending shrills of pain through me. My shoulder wobbled out of weakness. It hurt like hell. Before he could prepare the bat again, I swept my right leg into his ankle, tripping him over. Charlie stumbled to the ground where he grunted.

"What are you doing?" I cried out. The man regained his footing. The bat was held firmly as he prepared for Round 2.

"Do you know what happened to me?" he asked. I was in too much pain to focus on what he was saying. I noticed a red patch starting to form on my top's shoulder and winced in pain while he rabbited on.

"My life was perfect. I lived in a glorious house with my dream job. I had married the girl of my dreams. Everything was perfect. Until it wasn't". He had a sombre look on his face, and his stance weakened. I took the opportunity to grab his wrist and pry the bat from him. However, he kneed me in the balls, winding me, before jolting the bat into my stomach. I flew across the room and landed into a pile of pizza boxes and dirty, stinking underwear. My stomach screamed out in pain as Charlie stood over me.

"My life was pure bliss until I found out the truth," he said with a sadistic sadness in his eyes. "I uncovered a secret military mission in Cuba that resulted in the massacring of a village. Many children were killed and the world needed to know the truth. I was a news editor, a messenger to the people and so wrote the perfect article, uncovering the entire mission. And do you know what happened next?" While he was talking, I tried to crawl across the floor for safety but it was no use. A strike from the bat hit my back, obliterating my body. Something had broken, hopefully not my spine.

"Do you know what happened next?" he shouted. "Not only did I lose my job. My wife dumped me and I lost everything. My house was raided and burnt down, destroying all my evidence. In the end, I was thrown into this absolute dump, with no job and no family. That is what happened to me!"

"I don't care," I groaned. A kick from his foot went into my stomach. Blood spluttered out of my mouth. Instantly, another kick connected with my chest.

"You should care!" Do you know why? Because I am going to claim my million-pound prize by handing you in. And then I will finally be able to start a new life, somewhere else. Across the globe if I have to. Nowhere near this disgusting, filthy country." Greed had driven this man crazy. I lay on the floor, caked in blood. This man was so sadistic that he could not see the effect of his actions. Why would he beat a 16-year-old kid to death?

Using the last of my strength, I reached out only to face another kick. Hot blood built up in my chest and burst all over the floor. Everything was red and filled with pain. My muscles ached and my bones squealed in agony. Blood dripped from all corners of my body and it felt horrific. I used my hand to rub the blood out of my eyes. They stung as I tried to take in my surroundings. Charlie stood there grinning while Frank remain collapsed on the other side of the room.

"One more ought to do it", Charlie said with a sinister smile whilst he prepped the bat. He spun the bat in his hands in a windmill fashion, flicking blood across the room. My blood. He rose the bat above his head and I prepared for the worst. The pain would be over soon.

The man swung the bat, knocking me clean in the jaw as one of my front teeth shot out across the room doused in blood. However, before I could feel the pain, out of nowhere the blood flew in the reverse direction and my tooth returned to its original place while my body was pulled across the room and the bat returned to its original position. *What was that?* I thought, remembering that something similar had happened in the school rugby game.

Charlie prepared to make the exact same swing again, but this time, just before I closed my eyes, I noticed something shiny under a pizza box, reflecting light in my eyes. Before I could comprehend, my hand had shot out and unearthed the item. To my astonishment, it was a pair of scissors. The bat was now moments away from making contact and so I squeezed the scissors and jammed them into Charlie's leg, roaring out in rage as a newfound energy took control of my body.

"Argh!" screamed Charlie. The scissors were wedged deep into his left calf. Blood spat out of the wound. At that moment, he fell to the ground, screaming and swearing.

"Why would you do that!" followed by cusses. I had never hurt somebody in my life and now I had just stabbed someone. He deserved it yet it still felt uncomfortable. He writhed and screamed on the floor and I just watched. That was not enough. This man did not deserve to live, it was time to finish the job.

I scrambled onto my feet with great difficulty. My arms alone felt like anvils, pulling me down. The pain all seemed to blend together and I channelled it into red hot fury. Charlie had dropped the bat to the floor whilst he was screaming. I took a glance at my right hand, tightened my grip and thrust it into his face. His glasses flung to the side and shattered. Sharp pain shot through my fist but it felt good. Usually when I would punch something, my hand would slow down before impact but this time it just sped up. I flung my right hand into his face, then left. Another right. His disgusting face needed to go. Right. Left. Right Left. *More. More. MORE!* my conscience yelled at me.

At that moment I noticed a mirror across the room. It had been cracked from our fight. But in the crooked reflection, I saw the face of a killer. A man drenched in blood, teeth clenched and fists glowing with fury. That was me, Jason.

What had I done? Charlie lay below me, potentially dead. The man just wanted some money and I had gone ape on him. He groaned a bit before his lips itched into a grin. What was I to do? Should I have just left him. This man needed medical attention but so did I. My red vision faded as the world came back into perspective. The sound of my rage dissipated revealing the heavy breaths of Charlie and I. Long, heavy breaths. But no other noise.

The silence was broken by the sound of the door crashing down. Soldiers in black uniforms flocked the room surrounding Charlie and I. From amongst the agents emerged Achilles, his hair down and his face darkened. Instead of talking, he just picked a gun out of his pocket and shot me.

Before I could react, a sharp syringe short out and pierced my shoulder. I tried pulling it out but my whole body was so sore. My arms were much heavier than before, being yanked down by chains.

Eventually my legs gave way and my body slumped to the ground. My entire muscular system had turned off. I was aware of my surroundings yet could not move, totally paralyzed.

Charlie thrashed around before standing up. He wiped blood off his face and began talking.

"I present to you your prize. Frank and Jason, as requested. I will now take my one million pounds." Achilles looked around suspiciously before making some hand signals. Two agents proceeded to pick up Frank and carry him out of the room. Two more agents came my way before grabbing my arms and pulling me up.

"Leave him," Achilles muttered. "Everyone leave now, I will take care of these two." In a highly organised fashion, they marched out leaving Achilles, Charlie and I in the room. Once again, I tried to move, yet my muscles remained limp.

"Where's my money?" Charlie said impatiently. He took a tissue and started cleaning his face. His nose was warped out of position and he was squinting without his glasses.

"Jason told you everything right?"

"Yeah, he made up some crap about Ted Clifford being possessed. That weasel would do anything to get out of jail." he sniggered.

"Everything he told you was true," Achilles said, looking at me. A sorrowful look, as if he felt sorry for me for being in this situation. It was as if he wished things could have gone differently. What was he about to do?

"You are telling me that was real. No way. You have got to be joking."

"Do I look like I am joking". At that moment he pulled another pistol from his belt and held it to Charlie's forehead, pressing it against his bleeding skin. Charlie dropped the tissues he were holding and clumsily raised his hands above his head.

"Please, I promise I can keep a secret," he said desperately, beginning to get emotional. The aggressive beast had gone leaving a frail old man. I tried to call out, but my body repelled my commands.

"You know too much," Achilles said before pulling the trigger. The blast shook the whole flat as Charlie's head whipped back and brains scattered across the room. A blob of blood splatted on my face and started dripping down. The man crumpled to the ground, deceased, with a pool of crimson forming underneath his head.

Achilles pulled the gun away and walked over to me. He was wearing thick gloves and grabbed my hand. He proceeded to wipe my hand all over the handle of the gun before tossing it to the side. I tried to scream out, but instead only tears rolled down my face, stinging my cuts and bruises.

Having heard the shots, several agents burst in with distraught looks on their faces.

"Jason broke free and shot him in the head. Get that gun to forensics, his fingerprints are all over it." He then signalled to the masked agents who aggressively grabbed my arms and hauled me up. I tried to break free, but it was no use.

"Take him to my car, I will take him to the boss myself."

Achilles' car was a small black Audi. It looked brand new and was free of dirt. For a special agent, I was surprised from the lack of dents. He probably got into car chases on a regular basis. However, I could not stop thinking about Charlie. That man died because of me. If Frank and I did not visit him, he would still be alive. Too many people were getting sucked into my affairs. The agents opened the passenger seat and chucked me in. Achilles sat next to me in the driver's seat.

"The drugs will wear off in several hours. Don't think about moving, it will not work." I glanced in the wing mirror and saw that my face was still caked in blood. The stench of it toxified my nostrils.

Achilles revved the engine and we drove off. Due to my lack of muscles, the speed slammed me into my chair. It felt like I was experiencing the G-Force of a rocket. He sped off into the distance and pressed a few buttons. Immediately, the car started flashing blue and blaring out sirens. The agent then started overtaking cars like it were a go-kart race.

"Now you probably have a lot of questions," the man said. "Your brother will happily answer all of them. He has been so eager to see you again." He paused for a moment. "Once he tells you his plans, you won't keep running away. He will tell you, like he told me."

I was unsure of what to make of that statement. Julian did not want me dead. He needed me for some big plan. But what could I give to him that would be so important? Was it worth the death of Charlie?

197

The journey went by in a blur with only my thoughts to occupy. The agent made no sound throughout, focusing solely on his driving.

All of a sudden, Achilles braked, and my head flung forward before swinging back and smacking the chair. I tried to move but it was still impossible.

"We are here." This was not the same place as before. In fact we were in a completely different area. We were just in the middle of some high street. People walked up and down the streets as normal, doing their shopping and having fun. I would do anything to get my old life back.

Before I could say anything else, Achilles grabbed a cloth and placed it over my mouth. Some strange odours entered my mouth. In fact, it felt strange, kind of loopy. Like if somebody mixed perfume with deodorant. *Oh wait, isn't that already a thing?* My thoughts trailed on as I drifted off to sleep.

Chapter 13: New World Order

I may have dreamt. Who knew? That was the curse of dreams; either you remember them or you do not.

My eyes opened to a dimly lit room. To my right was a small bedside table with a glass of water on top. Overhead was a heartbeat monitor and some sort of drip contraction that led towards a needle that pierced into my left hand. I was wearing a white gown and my arms and legs had been bandaged like a mummy. Someone had patched me up after my encounter with Charlie. The bed I was in was large, much larger than my one at home. It was comfortable all over which was strange for a hospital bed. This was obviously not a hospital, most likely another Government facility and Achilles was probably not too far.

The door to the room crept open and in came a man dressed smartly from head to toe. From his immaculately polished shoes to his impeccable tie knot, I knew it to be Julian. But in Ted Clifford's body. It was going to take time to get used to that.

"Jason, little bro, how you doing?" he said in a friendly manner. But this man was far from amicable, being the literal devil. Framing me for murder, attempted terrorism and now the death of a journalist.

"Release Frank and Will, they have done nothing wrong". I muttered, my lungs still crying out in agony.

"We have been through this; Frank is a bad person. Wilfred on the other hand is innocent. I will be sure to release him once you cooperate. Now, we have a lot to discuss, which is why I want to show you this."

The ceiling above me rumbled and two of the panels slid to the side. A small box then emerged from the darkness and turned on, projecting an image onto the wall opposite. Displayed was BBC News. The reporter was sitting in the studio and then started talking.

"Today, for your Thursday morning news, we bring you the latest on the disappearance of Frank Clifford. Frank went missing this Monday after fellow pupil Jason Clyde kidnapped him. There was little knowledge on the location of the Prime Minister's son until some evidence was found. Frank's blood was found in the house of another classmate Wilfred Campbell. After further investigation, it was discovered that Wilfred aided Mr Clyde in the kidnapping before he was taken into custody for further questioning.

Frank and Jason were found in the house of ex-journalist and news editor Charlie Driver who was unfortunately dead when the two boys were found. He had been killed by Jason. Frank has now been safely reunited with his father and Jason will now be facing dire consequences. We now go to Downing Street where Ted Clifford will comment on his son's reappearance."

The recording then moved to Downing Street where Julian / Ted was surrounded by press.

"I have been enthralled by the founding of my son. Ever since my wife died, he has been all I have. He is now resting and should be back to full speed by tomorrow. We then hope that he can explain exactly what happened to him. Jason and Wilfred are now being interrogated as to why they tried to take my son from me. And I promise that they will be severely punished."

And the tape ended there. The screen went completely blank and I felt the silence of the room swallow me. My hands were sweating like anything and my heart rate on the machine was spiking.

"Easy" Julian said reassuringly. Hearing my brother talking with the voice of Ted sounded wrong. He was a liar and a manipulator. Somehow I needed to set Ted free from Julian's control but all this psychic stuff was confusing as hell. Julian glanced at his watch for a second before he started talking.

"I have one more thing to show you". He pressed a button on some remote and the projector changed to show some room. In the room was sitting a boy who had his face in his palm. It was Frank. He was surrounded by guards on all sides, all of which bore guns.

A flash of anger rolled through me and I tried to jump up. My muscles were no longer paralyzed by drugs. I did not care if I died, Julian needed to die. My hands were thirsty for murder. Immediately after leaping up, I was pulled back, like a dog on a leash. There had to be some invisible chains or something holding me back. This was the telepathy again, convincing me that there was a chain.

"Easy, easy" Julian said condescendingly. He instantly turned off the projector and walked over to me. "Right now, we are in my mind. This place is called 'The Mind Emporium' and I control everything here. I need you to listen to me. Your old life is destroyed and so you have no choice but to work with me. Either you work by my side or spend the rest of your life in prison? I need you. In fact the entire world needs you. Now, will you help me."

"No."

Julian sighed and looked at his watch. "Your entire life has been a lie. Let's sort that out. Do you know how I got Achilles on my side? I showed him. Everything." And then he snapped his fingers. The chains around my wrists popped open and I was free. I slipped out of bed and charged towards Julian. Before I knew it, my arms had reached for his neck. But when I strangled, there was nothing there. Ted Clifford's body disappeared into smoke. The room then began to blend away. Strange colours trickled in from all directions and the wall in front of me formed a pattern, a kaleidoscope of many colours. And from within that pattern, a door formed. My hand found itself on the door knob and before I knew it, I had stepped inside.

"Welcome to my mind!" boomed Julian's voice. "Here, anything is possible". The darkness around me faded away like a smog revealing bright lights. My eyes ached as I adjusted to my new surroundings. A huge Ferris wheel loomed over me, whizzing around. To my left was a giant roller coaster featuring all sorts of dips and spins. The track featured a giant loop followed by a spiral. A car zoomed across it with intense speed. Next I found myself looking at a bumper car ride. Pretty standard so far. This place was a haven of different colours, with a smell of bubble gum haze.

I wandered around the place, taking in my surroundings. This whole place felt off though, like it was too good to be true.

Next, a limo pulled up next to me out of nowhere. I was taken aback by the surprise by its sheer length. It went on and on and on, able to seat maybe hundreds. The limo drove all the way, leaving the back door in front of me. Before long, a man popped out of the vehicle sporting aviators, a freshly ironed suit and a cane. This cane was made of pure gold, glistening in the light. From his neat blonde hair to his large square jaw, it was obvious who this was. Julian. Not in Ted Clifford's body but the actual Julian. My brother.

"Did you miss me," he laughed. His voice now sounded much younger, still innocent with youth and less gravelly. He still spoke with sophistication yet now it felt so much purer, from the source. "I thought I would talk to you in my true form."

"How did you do it?" I asked. The only words I could muster up regarding all this madness.

"You need to be more specific" he smiled.

"How did you become a telepath. That should be physically impossible. This whole place is impossible. What drugs have you injected into me?"

"Slow down, brother. Your whole life you have been looking at reality through a keyhole. Now it is time we opened that door and revealed the treasures of our lives."

"Just get to the point. I am tired of your games. Enough people have suffered, just get to the chase." It was at that moment, that I noticed that I was walking around freely. My hospital gown had transformed into plain trousers and T-shirt. However, my cuts and bruises still covered my body.

"You're no fun," he said, tossing his cane to the side before walking over to me. However now, he had no limp. "I am not sure exactly what happened but there was this substance that was exposed to our parents before they gave birth to us, I developed some sort of new abilities that manifested when I was about eight. Now I can read minds, project images and possess others."

203

This was absurd. Surely Julian was joking? This had to be some sort of dream. Why did Mum and Dad never tell me that Julian was special? Did they even know?

"From my extensive research, there appears to be some sort of Dark Matter in my blood. Not the usual kind, this is something different, very different. Ominous, I know. It is laced into my bloodstream and your bloodstream too. Yes Jason, you have gifts too."

He had to be lying. Dark matter? He was crazy. I must have been dreaming. This had to be some psychedelic dream. Maybe it was still October and the whole Gap and everything after was just some weird dream. It was time to finally wake up back in my bed. Back in October, before everything went all wrong. When I was still the loser at school with the world's nerdiest friends. Why did this have to happen to me? I had been kind to everyone my whole life. This all had to be fake.

"The powers will manifest when you have fully developed your personality. At the age of eight, I was a child genius and knew exactly what I wanted in life. The powers manifested then. But you, you have no idea of what you want in life. You have little to no personality and are just cruising through life, one day at a time. No wonder you have no abilities yet."

"You lie," I said softly

"Does this look like a lie" he cried. The fairground suddenly got more hectic. The Ferris wheel spun faster and faster. The roller coaster carriage began to undergo a loop. It now travelled fully upside down whilst the passengers wailed with joy.

Suddenly Julian snapped his fingers and everyone just paused what they were doing. The Ferris wheel froze and the roller coaster as well. The carriage was upside down yet the passengers did not fall. Their faces of joy were stuck on, mid smiles. Gravity had paused as well. Impossible

This is just virtual reality.

"It is most certainly not the work of technology," Julian said, butting in. "I can read your mind remember."

Surely, he can't read my mind.

"Surely he can't read my mind. Yes he can".

This was impo-

"Impossible?. I am always one step ahead of you." I needed something to throw him off. If I picked a number between 1 and 100 it would be impossible for him to figure it out.

88 sounds good.

You are about to ask me to pick a number that you are thinking of between 1 and 100. You pick 88?

How did he know?

"How do I know? Telepath, remember?"

This was getting ridiculous. I charged forward, right hand in front. I thought that somehow beating him up would end this. Before I would punch him, my left leg would sweep him over. Adrenaline pumped through me as I braced for the attack. Julian caught my right hand as expected. I then thrust my left leg into him, however he jumped over my sweep. It was as if he could see it coming, throwing

205

me to the ground. I glanced up at him, defeated. There was no way he could be defeated. My hand stung from the attack and my knees had grazed against the ground. All of a sudden, Julian stuck out his hand for me.

"I know this is a lot to take in. Once you finally develop your powers, you will be such a useful asset to me. It is time that I told you everything, from the very beginning". The fairground setting dissolved away leaving us in pitch black. I still could not believe what he was saying. There was no way that I had special abilities hidden for all these years. What would my powers be? Super strength, invisibility, flight? Maybe I would get one of those trash powers. Like the ability to shoot glue or swim fast. Also if my powers had not manifested in 16 years, then they probably would never come. Julian had to be mistaken. It is like how brothers do not necessarily have to have the same hair colour.

The darkness then faded and we were in an empty white room. Julian then paced across the room. It was refreshing to hear him talk in his own body again, rather than Ted's.

"Jerry and Jemimah. Names ring a bell?" he exclaimed. They were the people Mum and Dad mentioned when I was in hospital. I also saw their names on a gravestone in one of my dreams. That felt like years ago at this point.

"Jerry and Jemimah were lovers in the 80s. They met at school and became close together pretty quickly. At some point in their lives, they got exposed to a form of Dark Energy. To this day I am still not sure of the details. In 1994 the two finally married and in 96 they had a son. That boy grew on to do remarkable things. Jerry and Jemima loved their son so much that they had another child 7 years later. Sadly when the boys were 8 and 1 respectively, their parents died in a car crash. And here is the piece de resistance." He paused for a second.

"Jerry and Jemimah are our real parents. They died when I was 8 and you were 1. The same car crash that gave me my limp was the same that killed our real parents. A week after that, the trauma of it all helped me to forge my powers. We were adopted by close family friends Graham and Sarah Clyde. They are the parents you remember. They do not know about our powers, which is why you were never told."

I clenched my fists. Tight. Too tight. This was too much to take in. I felt sick, all over. My lungs contracted and I took short breaths. My real parents? I was inclined to laugh at the fact but then I remembered. Whilst in hospital, Mum said that she promised Jerry and Jemima that she would look after me. I was not even hers? Did they even love me? I was someone else's baby and was more a burden than anything to 'Mum' and 'Dad'.

In a fit of rage, I punched the wall next to me. It hurt. Not enough. Again. I punched and punched, feeling all the pain. An entire life of lies. My right hand was thrust into the wall. When I pulled it back, I saw blood trickle down from my knuckles.

"Is this blood even real?" I cried. Tears streamed down my face, stinging me as they went down.

"No more illusions" Julian whispered. His body then changed back into the Prime Minister. His lean jaw became a double chin and his stomach plumped out. His hair then went from blond to brown. My hands were still covered in blood and the wall was cracked from my punches.

"Why did you never tell me?" I roared, my cheeks wet with tears. Julian had been keeping this secret from me all my life. He should have told me.

"Trust me, the truth would have ruined your life. You never would have fit in. You would grow to resent Graham and Sarah like I did. I did what was best for you."

"You don't get to decide for me" I shouted. Rage poured through me. Julian was a monster. Imprisoning Frank, mentally torturing me and making me a wanted criminal. I had had enough. I then noticed the cracks on the walls shaking. They started to shrink in magnitude and faded away. The blood on my knuckles disappeared completely and my skin was completely healed. The smile on Julian's face then dropped.

"Trust me, the truth would have ruined your life. You never would have fit in. You would grow to resent Graham and Sarah like I did. I did what was best for you" Julian said.

"You literally just said that," I asked, puzzled. Julian looked even more confused. "And did you use your powers to remove the cracks on the wall?"

"What are you talking about?" Julian said. "What cracks?" I glanced back at the wall, now devoid of any damage. Another one of Julian's tricks no doubt. Yet I still needed answers. Julian's confused look had not gone away while there was an awkward silence. This person, my brother, was responsible for all the suffering in my life. He needed to go. I wanted to get back to my normal life at school.

Julian broke the silence with another snap of his fingers. "So, back to my story".

"That's enough bombshells for one day", I said, preparing to fight Julian. All of a sudden, he gave me an angered look. With a wave of his hands, a metal pipe ripped out of the wall and it bent itself around me. A chair formed at the back of the room and I was thrown onto it, before being handcuffed.

"You will listen to every word I have to say!" he said intimidatingly. I tried to pull myself from the chair but it was no use. The setting then changed, taking us into a theatre. There were huge rings of seats behind me. Audience members flocked the seats. On the front row, and in front of me were huge red curtains. They were truly colossal in size. To my left was Julian, clapping giddily. To my right was another Julian, clapping giddily. The entire audience were just Julians, clapping. Their claps echoed around the theatre, creating a thunderous ruse. This theatre felt huge, like an arena. The seats just kept on going and going, for infinity. Once again I tried to wriggle free yet my hands were still cuffed.

After a few seconds, the curtains began to slide away. I could hear the gears turning, moving such an enormous structure. Once the curtains had fully slid away, Julian was revealed to be standing on the stage, in his own body. The entire audience immediately erupted into applause and cheering. The audience, even though it was fake, felt truly alive as Julian waved his hands, embracing the screams of excitement. The grin on his face was unlike any other. He enjoyed torturing me. He was enthralled by it.

"Good Evening, my comrades". The applause got even louder and more erratic. The sound started to ache my ears. "Today I reveal our great plan". The applause only got louder and louder. Julian paced across the stage before holding his hand up, gesturing for the audience to hush. And they did, without hesitation.

209

"When I was a boy, I was unlike the other kids. While everyone was outside playing, I was inside, teaching myself Algebra at the age of 5 and so never fit in. For the first 5 years at school I was bullied relentlessly. The other kids, you see. They were jealous of my superior intellect."

Suddenly, on the wall behind him, a shadow formed. It was a silhouette that danced across the wall. The shadow was of a small boy, surrounded by taller ones, all pointing their fingers at him. The boy ducked, in sheer fear of everyone else.

"What kept me together though was my love of my parents." The shadow of a man and a woman walked onto the screen and brushed away all the bullies before embracing the boy. "However, at the age of 8, my parents passed away." The 2 adults faded away. "Earlier that year I heard a noise in my head. While I was walking down the street, I saw a girl walking with her mother. She screamed out to me for help. When I approached her, I soon found out that the woman she was with was not her mother, but in fact a kidnapper. After getting the woman arrested, I spoke to the girl. The girl asked me why I helped her when she did not ask for help. I told her that I heard her cry out. I soon figured out that she never said anything, and it was my imagination.

"The next day I saw two men walking together. One of them said, 'I can't believe I slept with my best friend's wife'. He said this without even opening his mouth. After investigation, I found out that the man had had an affair with the other's wife. Later on, I discovered that I could read the minds of individuals. However, things only got worse. Every day there were voices, whispers."

The halls began to fill with whispers.

"Come closer"

"Leave me alone." Followed by screams.

"Where's mummy?" came the voice of a small child. She then started sobbing.

"I can't believe she dumped me"

"So much pain. This knee is killing me"

"Money. Someone give me some goddamn money!"

The whispers started to come faster and faster.

"Drugs"

"Booze"

"Babes"

"So much blood"

They came quicker and quicker.

"I could hear and feel the suffering of the entire world!" Julian screamed. "I could not walk along the street without hearing the demented thoughts of someone. And the voices never stopped. The idea of having powers seemed awesome yet it ended up being a curse. Later I decided to use my abilities for my benefits. I discovered that I could make people see things. The next day at school. I went up to the school bully and made him see the ghost of his dead father. It drove him insane, and after a few days, he was moved to a psychiatric hospital. I soon discovered that the pain and suffering I heard around me would never end. The only way I could make the suffering stop would be to end suffering. And that is my plan, to end suffering in this country."

His statement caused the crowd to go mental. It was like a goal had just been scored in the World Cup Finals. All the Julians around me started dancing in their seats. The person next to me was crying. He wailed loudly and was wiping away tears with a tissue.

"I am so happy" he cried. What were these bots?

This whole fiasco was preposterous to say the least. Thousands of Julians watching a performance from my brother who had pledged to end suffering on a national scale. An impossible feat to say the least. How would he even begin to accomplish such a great task without causing major political disarray. Julian danced around in the applause before holding his hand up to quieten the crowds again. They followed soon.

"First, I took the body of the Prime Minister." Julian pulled a remote out of his pocket and pressed a button. A cage was gently lowered from the ceiling. As it descended, the crowds booed and jeered aggressively. In a cartoonish manner, someone picked up a tomato and chucked it onto the stage, hitting the man in the cage. A groan followed.

Ted Clifford was locked up in the cage, looking completely exhausted. His face was decrepit and withered whilst his arms were looking frail. He was wearing a simple T-shirt with white underwear. His stomach hung from his top. The Prime Minister had always maintained a good image yet here he looked dreadful.

"Kill him!" someone screamed violently before throwing another tomato.

"Patience", Julian whispered, rubbing his hands together. "I need to keep him alive so he can give me information. Information that I can use for my plans."

"Please, let me go," Ted mumbled. Julian looked at him, with anger in his eyes.

"This country has been under your terror for long enough. Once my plan is fully in place, you and your brat of a son can reunite in Hell."

"Please, leave Frank out of this. He has done nothing wrong". Ted's plea was interrupted by Julian breaking into maniacal laughter. He then pressed another button on the remote. Ted's cage then began to rustle before being hurled upwards. The crowd continued to jeer as he was pulled back into the ceiling. The old man screamed until he was once again hidden from the eye. Once the Prime Minister was gone, I realised that there was still hope. In this moment, Julian's body was dead and now he lived in Ted Clifford's body. However, I had just learnt that Ted was still alive within Julian's subconscious or 'The Mind Emporium as he called it. If I could somehow release Ted from his cage, he could retake his body, eliminating my brother for good. My thoughts were suddenly interrupted.

"Thank you for your patience everyone, now we have got business to tend to. First I will become this country's best ever leader. Before long, when my time has come to a close, I will have to campaign for the vote of the people. After they see the work I am about to do, they will have no choice but to vote for me. And if I lose, I will just possess the winner. Bit by bit, I will embed my presence into the country and fix all the socio-economic problems. And that is just the beginning."

For Julian, this whole thing did not sound so messed up. It was bad, but he had good intentions which was conflicting to say the least. As long as nobody got hurt.

"And now, this is how I will end suffering. Personally, I will further subsidize farmers to increase the national produce of food. From there, national healthcare will be increased, ensuring that no injury, big or small gets overlooked."

Was this Julian's plan all along, to make this country a better place?

"And now, for my favourite bit. So unemployment and homelessness are things. Well. My plan is to at least triple the police force across the country. Every unemployed person will be offered the job to train as a policeman or woman and serve my cause. To help fund this, tax rates will be raised exponentially for the rich. This wealth tax will result in me having more money to fund my so-called 'army'. And then, the final step is to raise capital punishment. It is time for the 'Death Sentence' to return to this country. For too long, people have gotten away with murder, violence among others. With my new increased police force, anyone who steps out of line will be imprisoned or even worse, executed."

"You can't do that" I mumbled. The smile on Julian's face vanquished and he looked at me, dead in my eyes. Before he could say anything, two audience members had picked up my chair and they started walking to the stage. Like a king, I was carried onto the stage. It was a weird feeling to say the least. Soon afterwards, they placed me opposite to Julian, who created a sofa for himself to sit on whilst the setting turned to that of a Breakfast Show. The stage behind him evolved into a calm, almost zen environment with light bluish colours and a large abstract painting formed full of multicoloured lines all in different directions.

"What is wrong with my plan?" Julian asked. He said it in a confused way as if he was in the right. He was astounded by the fact that genocide was horrific.

"You can't kill all those people. It is not right. And not to mention this 'police-state' you want to enforce".

"Jason, you are so naïve. I am only killing criminals that have no chance in this world and so am ending their suffering. Do you know how many people die due to the recklessness of the law? Every day, dozens die from knife crime, drunk driving and poverty. It is time that the elitist structure of society ends and we start helping the people at the bottom. If we dispose of the criminals, we will have more money to spend on those who actually need it. And then once the rich are taxed, all their money will be redistributed to the poor. An extra 2% income tax for a millionaire would hardly be noticeable and that money could help a plethora of poverty stricken men and women. You of all people should know. Your school is literally a hive of rich kids who end up inheriting their parents' wealth without having to work an inch. Now what are you telling me, you support nepotism and elitism?"

The entire crowd roared with excitement. I looked out to the hoards of audience members. Even though they all looked the same, there was a huge sense of dread. One Julian was terrifying. Thousands though, that could be detrimental. A nervousness clouded my body as I felt the pressure of everyone looking at me. Julian and his army of cronies were hell bent on bringing this country to its knees and I wanted the complete opposite. This entire situation was fake, just some big illusion, yet sweat still gushed down my spine.

"So, are you some sort of sadistic Robin Hood?" I said, my voice shaking. "Things desperately need to change but there are easier ways to do it. We shouldn't have to bankrupt the rich just to help out the poor."

"Then what do you suggest?" There were times at school, especially in Economics when I was put to the spot. The same question every time, 'what would you do differently?' How was I supposed to know? I was only a kid. These politicians had spent years studying politics and real-life matters. They would know what to do in order to make things change. But me on the other hand...

"I don't know," I muttered.

"He doesn't know!" Julian shouted. He stood up, out of his chair and looked to the audience. "I present to you my little brother". The entire audience was laughing, with the occasional boo and jeer. A random audience member chucked a tomato in my direction. Before I could react, it had smacked my head. It erupted upon impact and splattered me with disgusting juices. The tomato was not even fresh as it reeked of mould. As I was freaking out, the curtains slowly began to close. The embarrassment that flooded my body could finally be put to ease. After a short while, the curtains sealed shut, leaving me and Julian on the stage, now darkened. His show biz smile faded while he looked at me.

"I am disappointed in you brother. Honestly, I expected you to understand my plan. Even your powers did not manifest after so many efforts. I literally let you escape last time so that you could finally find your foot in life and develop your powers. I even sent Achilles to kill that journalist to help motivate you. Wilfred and Frank are literally being tortured in prison because of you. I had such big plans for you, but it appears you are much worse than I expected and dead weight for my big plan." Before I could react, the background changed back to the white room. Julian looked at me, now as Ted Clifford. "I have a meeting now and so Achilles will deal with you. It is finally time to fix this country." He got up and headed to the door. He clicked it open and disappeared into the vastness of the Earth before locking me in.

I sat on my bed, feeling truly defeated. Julian was about to begin a despicable plot to change this country and there was nothing I could do. Absolutely nothing. This was the biggest loss of my life. The death of everyone would lie on my shoulders. And then I remembered the truth about my parents. Sarah and Graham were never my parents so now I had no family. Julian was the last of my family but now he was going for national dominion. The pure insanity of that statement. Not as insane as me potentially having powers though. What kind of a weird fantasy story was this? But if anything, I needed to develop my powers and fight Julian, rescue my friends and prevent the end of this country.

Easier said than done.

Chapter 14: The Alignment of Fates

After what felt like years of waiting, the door to the room pulsed open and from the doorway emerged Achilles looking exhausted. His face was darkened by fatigue yet his eyes remained focused. As usual, he was kitted out to the teeth with assortments of weaponry. Guns, knives, grenades, he had them all. I would not have even been surprised if he was concealing a bow and arrow or even a sword. His heavy military boots whacked the ground with each step and upon entering the room, he cocked a pistol and pointed it at my head. He did so with such carelessness, as if he had done this deed many times. He had become desensitized to death at this point, which was probably why he was assisting my madman of a brother.

"This is it kid," he whispered.

My muscles still ached all over, making it near impossible to move. The gun was pressed against my forehead and there was nothing I could do. The cold metal tickled my skin as it prepared to end me.

"Why are you doing this?" I asked.

"Clearing our tracks."

"Why are *you* doing this. You have spent your whole life serving this country, why would you turn on it?"

"Who said anything about turning on this country? I am helping it."

As he spoke, I took a giant risk and thwacked my head forwards, knocking the pistol away and my head connected with his nose. The crunch sound that it made was disgusting to say the least. The soldier cried out in agony before seizing control of his firearm again. There was no way that I could beat this man in a fight, so I fled. The elevator was up ahead, acting as my safe zone.

"You're dead kid!" he yelled, wiping blood from his nostrils.

The corridor felt so long as I paced through it. The elevator was mere metres ahead, my light at the end of the tunnel. All of a sudden, three gunshots could be heard. My body was thrown upwards in surprise. The first bullet glided past me and lodged itself into the elevator door. I waited to see whether the second one missed or not however my thoughts were silenced by a sharp pain. An explosion of pain filled my body and my leg screamed in agony.

As I fell, the third bullet raced above my head. If I had not fallen, then that would have destroyed my brain. Collapsing to the floor, blood leaked out of my leg. It hurt like anything. Achilles ran across the corridor, gun in hand, ready to fire. Using all my will power and strength, I tried to get up, yet it was too hard. This was the end. My body was in indescribable pain, as if kidney stones were passing through. It felt horrific as I watched the blood gush out the wound. The agent was now so close, within firing range. But then the strangest thing happened.

Rather than run forward, Achilles halted and ran backwards, still facing me. Then the bullet that went over my head flew back into the barrel as Achilles' gun made a suction noise. In confusion, I tried to do something. All of a sudden, I was back on my feet as if pulled up by some invisible hand. The bullet in my leg rushed out and went back to the barrel, resulting in my leg healing instantaneously. The wound was completely gone and the pain a distant memory. Finally, the first bullet was released from the elevator door and went back into Achilles' gun. The dent on the door was completely gone, as if nothing had happened.

"You're dead, kid," Achilles yelled again. I turned around and looked at him, puzzled. He literally just said that. The man then shot three bullets again, and they were headed the same way as before. The first one missed naturally and hit the elevator. The second one came for my leg. I knew exactly what to do this time and so raised my leg. The bullet missed and the third one came for my head. I simply ducked and dodged it yet again. Achilles looked at me, baffled. How could a trained marksman like him miss such a big target three consecutive times?

"What was that?" I shouted.

"You just dodged 3 bullets perfectly. How is that even possible?" Rather than question the impossible, I paced towards the door and pressed the button. Achilles tried shooting again but now his gun was empty. In a fit of rage he tossed it to the side, as if he were an ungrateful toddler on Christmas day. From his back, he pulled out a huge machine gun. I had never seen of those in real life, only in video games and movies. The elevator doors flicked open and I jumped in. There were so many buttons, so I just pressed 0. The ground floor should be a way out of this place. Achilles loaded his toys with ammunition, readying to fire. The doors slid shut, and as they did, he shot a spray of bullets. Fortunately, the elevator shielded me as the sound of metal clanking came for me while small dents formed on the door.

The elevator blasted up, getting me away from the madman who could be heard cussing in the distance. The elevator itself was nothing short of elegant. There was a mirror that stood from top to bottom allowing me to see my dishevelled self. My face was still bruised and wounded from my encounter with Charlie. But something did not feel right. This was the first time seeing myself since finding out the truth. Jason was adopted. I was looking at the face of someone else, someone born to a life of pain who potentially had powers. Before my thoughts could get too deep, the doors pinged open.

I noticed that this was the exact same reception as previously, the same Government facility, yet this time escaping would prove to be much more difficult. Standing outside the lift were three agents who were wearing black suits with sunglasses as if they were bouncers at a nightclub. Upon seeing them, I tried to close the elevator again, but was punched in the face by a strong hand. Blood splattered from my face across the mirror. The man prepared for another strike but as his hand moved forwards, the blood on the mirror flew back into my face as he flew backwards. Once more he swung his hand for the exact same punch as before but this time I knew it was coming, so I dodged it.

The man's arm was exposed for that moment, so I yanked him into the elevator and kicked a button, closing the doors. The man looked at me, completely dazed. He probably wondered how his jab had missed. Now that the group of three was split up, I took on the one man. He chucked his glasses off before rolling up his sleeve, preparing to fight. As we were in an elevator, the space was very compact, so landing a punch would have been very difficult. Rather than fight hand to hand, the agent pulled out a pistol and shot me. The bullet split through my shoulder, knocking me into the mirror. My head smacked backwards against it, creating a spider-web of cracks. A whole world of pain was dropped onto me but before I could wince, the following happened.

Once again, the cracks disappeared and my body was thrust forward, with the bullet flying back into his gun. He pressed the trigger and this time I ducked, and punched his elbow upwards, potentially breaking his arm. While he screamed out in pain, I pried his gun from his hands before shooting him in the leg. The sound rung, taking me back a little. A moment later, I re-opened the elevator doors to see the two agents still standing there. With a Marksman's aim I shot two bullets. However, both bullets flew way above their heads. My terrible aim was followed by 2 gunshots in my direction. One landed in my stomach and one my shoulder. Before the pain could kick in, the bullets returned to their respective guns giving me another chance to shoot. This time I aimed a bit lower and successfully landed a shot on each soldier's shoulder respectively, but high enough to be recoverable. Whilst the agents were crying out, I ran out of the building feeling a burst of excitement. My powers had manifested.

It appeared that I had the ability to reverse time. So far, I could reverse time by 2 seconds at most and then live out that instant again. There was still a lot of testing required, but for now this was my best opportunity at defeating Julian. This felt good. Too good.

Ahead, a bus was slowing down, preparing to stop. My getaway vehicle. When the door opened, I leapt into it, not sparing a second. I took a quick moment to take in my surroundings. This bus was moderately busy with plenty of seats available. However, before I could walk on,

"No entry without a pass" grumbled the driver. He was a relatively old man, with little to no hair. His bus driver uniform was creased, and he had huge sweat patches at his armpits. Despite the cold weather, the heat of his little booth was enough to make him sweat like an animal. Now that he was barring me entry, I needed an excuse.

"Please," I said smiling. In my peripheral vision, a figure resembling Achilles had exited the Government building and was now racing towards the bus, like a cheetah after its lunch. Clasped within his hand was his machine gun. The entire public looked at him, more confused than scared. The man looked more like some cosplayer rather than an actual soldier.

"No pass, no entry," he growled once again. Miserable man. It was time to put my powers to test. Achilles was now dangerously close to the bus and would kill me if I did nothing. I held my breath, closed my eyes and pushed. Pushed as if I were about to break wind, squeezing my hands tight. I then looked out the bus and could see Achilles running backwards, whilst my body was pulled off the bus.

Once more, I stepped on and looked at the driver. It was time to do something a little naughty. The person in front of me was about to scan their card, but I snatched it off them and scanned it myself, giving me entrance.

"Hey!" he shouted out.

"No pass, no entry" the driver said to him. Feeling smug, I moved on through the bus and took a seat on the bottom deck. The chair was hard, worn from years of use but it felt like Paradise. For once, the stresses of my life could dial down. Within a few minutes I would hopefully be far enough away to hide. Out of my window, Achilles was sprinting, slapping the window as he got closer to the door.

Fortunately for me, they swung closed, barring the lunatic from entry. Moments later, the vehicle drove off, leaving him behind to rage at his failure.

But instead of stopping, the man only ran faster, like an unstoppable force. Eventually when the bus was too fast to catch up with, he froze where he stood. Twisting my neck to watch, the man seized his gun with both hands, gazing through the scope before he pulled the trigger. Instantly, I ducked down, and listened as the glass behind completely shattered. To my left, the shoulder of a passenger exploded, blood splattering everywhere and screams ensued. A huge splash of blood slapped onto my face, before rolling down. It was hot and thick and wriggled down my face. But I knew what to do.

A tight squeeze later, the blood on my face returned to the shoulder of the passenger and the bullets were sent back out the bus whilst the glass reconstructed itself.

Achilles shot his gun again. This time I pushed the head down of the person next to me, allowing the bullet to fly past him, lodging into a seat ahead. Every single shot had missed as the passengers around me looked at Achilles in sheer terror. A man had just attempted to kill some innocent bystanders. A lady looked at me and pointed.

"You. You are the one on the news!" More screams and shouts followed. The man on my left, rather than thanking me for saving his life, decided to shove me off my seat.

"1 million is a lot of money," he smiled. The driver was still driving the bus despite the shots, completely oblivious to what was going on. Before I could grab a hold of myself, a heavy boot connected with my ribs. Wincing in pain, I was kicked again, and again.

"Kill that piece of filth". The situation was getting out of hand, so I reversed time.

"1 million is a lot of money" the man said as he pushed me off my seat. My head was dazed from the jump, ears ringing, eyes blurry. I was probably using my powers too much. I reached for the gun in my pocket and pointed it at the man who squealed in fear. In fact, a puddle formed in between his legs.

"I am not the threat here. I was framed. The man out there is the real threat, you have to help me defeat hi-". Before I could finish, the bus froze to a halt at some traffic lights. Achilles had now caught up, gun still in hand. Sweat dripped down my neck as he walked past my window, staring deep into my soul as he did so. The passengers just looked at him, as he kicked down the main door and entered.

"Get off my bus!" the driver shouted when he saw the gun. Instead, Achilles lifted a pistol to the door of the driver's booth and pulled the trigger. The sound of blood splattering filled the air. The shot barely made me flinch as I knew exactly what to do. It was time to save him.

"Get off my bus!" the driver shouted when he saw Achilles' gun. This time, I clambered to the front to try and stop the agent. However, it was too late. He lifted the gun again and pulled the trigger. Once more, the man's head exploded with blood splattering in all directions. I tried again. The blood flew back to his head as it reformed whilst the bullet returned to Achilles' gun.

"Get off my bus!" he said. The bus felt so long. No matter how fast I ran, there was no stopping the inevitable. The gun fired again, and my ears rang in pain. My eyes were now completely blurred and the ringing of the gun only got louder. I needed to turn back time again and save his life. My hands made a fist and pulled in, but nothing happened. My limbs felt numb as I tried again to loop time but nothing was happening. Instead, my body was crying out in pain. It was no use; the driver was dead.

"Hello Jason," Achilles said as I writhed on the floor in pain, coughing up blood. My abilities were limited and thus had used up every bit of my energy. Every last drop. After seeing Achilles murder the driver, the passengers started to believe my story. One of them, a man in his mid-thirties, wearing a suit and tie placed his briefcase onto the floor before walking up to the bully. His shoes were freshly polished as he stood before Achilles, who towered over him. The man looked up, completely devoid of fear.

"Leave him alone." Achilles scoffed at his attempts of heroism before holding up his gun. Before the man could react, a bullet-sized whole formed in his head and blood squirted across the ground. I moaned as his lifeless body fell beside me. Once again, I tried to turn back time, but nothing was happening. Achilles looked me down, like a bear, ready to kill its prey.

"Everyone out now!" he roared. The public just did as he said as they flocked to the bus door before pouring out into the streets running around like headless chickens. The agent then got his pistol, cocked it and held it to my head, whilst his finger wrapped around the trigger.

This man was on the verge of killing me and I could do nothing. My powers were failing me and my body was worn to bits. The best thing I could do would be to stall for time to allow me to rejuvenate my energy. What could I possibly say to distract the beast? And then it hit me. Julian wanted me alive for my unique abilities. Because I did not develop them, he sent Achilles to kill me. Now that I had powers, Julian had no choice but to keep me around for his plans. Achilles would never be allowed to lay a finger on me. Now I just needed to prove my powers.

"Achilles," I scoffed.

"What is it?" he growled.

"I have finally developed my powers. Julian would not want you to kill me." The man did not flinch in the slightest. Instead, he gripped the gun even tighter to the point where his veins were bulging from his muscular hands.

"Prove it then." I needed to think quickly. *How can I prove my time skills? I know.*

"Pick a number between 1 and 1000". Achilles looked at me, truly baffled. His finger was still caressing the gun trigger, ready to execute me.

"Now tell me that number," I smiled

"What kind of a trick is that." The agent said, getting impatient, now pushing the barrel against my forehead.

"Tell me," I said with a stern expression. The man gave a sigh before revealing his number.

"832". I had what was needed. Now everything just depended on my powers. Once again I held my hands tight and wished to go back and it worked.

"Prove it then." Achilles said.

"Pick a number between 1 and 1000." I paused for a second. "You selected 832, right?" The agent looked shocked. He scratched his head and thought to himself. The perfect opportunity for me.

I swiped my leg and kicked his tree trunks of legs, knocking him over. It hurt me more than him. Whilst he was falling, I brought my knee up to his face and connected to it in a truly satisfying way. Rather than land on the floor, the agent used his elite military training to spin around, seize a knife from his belt and plunge it into my stomach. The dagger ripped through my skin like butter and blood burst out.

"I don't care if your brother wants you alive. I will kill you!" It hurt bad. Beyond bad. I tried to hold back my reaction but it was impossible as I screamed out in pain. The deranged man proceeded to push the knife in even further as I shook in pain. *One last push and the pain will stop*. I thought as the knife left my stomach and my skin healed.

The connection of my knee to his face was utterly satisfying as his nose crunched on my knee. Using his advanced training, he spun around and grabbed a hold of a knife. This time, I punched his hand away from me before he could make contact. The knife clattered onto the floor and Achilles looked at me, enraged.

"I don't care if your brother wants you alive. I will kill you!" he screamed before shooting me with his pistol. The bullets ripped through my chest and blood emerged out like ants under a log.

After smashing my knee into his face, he spun around and tried to stab me with his knife. I punched it out of his hands, and it hit the ground.

"I don't care if your brother wants you alive. I will kill you!" he yelled before opening fire with his pistol. He shot 6 bullets which were dodged with precision. The man looked at his gun, perplexed. Before he could do anything, I flung my left leg and swung a perfect arc to the point where my toes connected with his testicular area. After a faint crunch, his face was revolted as he fell down. However, the agent had one last trick up his sleeve. Literally.

He pulled a grenade out of his belt and yanked the loop out of it before hurling it in my direction. Before it had even reached me, it blew up and fire blazed out of it, scorching my legs. The heat crawled up me like a giant tarantula, ready to rip off my head.

This time when he threw the grenade, I jumped to the side. The agent crawled behind a chair as the explosion ripped open the back of the bus. A large chunk of metal was headed towards me and with a twist of my head, I was able to avoid a certain decapitation. *Too close.* The entire bus shook in that moment as bits of metal and shards of glass sprayed everywhere. The grenade Achilles used was one of small impact else I would have been decimated at that instant. This fight between the two of us was coming close to an end as blood dripped from my face onto the floor. Every muscle in my body scorned, including my fingers. I just wanted to collapse in my bed and sleep. However, my vision was blurred and my skin reeked of a mix between fresh and dried blood. My opponent on the other hand was barely injured at all. The most damage he had taken was that his hair had come undone, allowing it to rest on his shoulders. Even Achilles knew that this would be an easy match for him as he slowly stood back up while brushing his hand across his belt, searching for a method to end me.

At that moment, I noticed that the bus was on top of a hill, that went down for ages. The engine was still on with the driver deceased in his seat. However, the impact of the blast pushed everything forwards and I watched as his corpse slumped down and pushed the acceleration pedal. Within moments, the bus roared into action and flew over the hill and started speeding down. *Shoot.*

Achilles and I were both pulsed backwards, towards the end of the bus where the complete back was missing, revealing a large gap encased by jagged metal teeth. Bright orange sparks could be seen flickering off the back.

The vehicle continued to drive ahead toward an impending doom. There were no other vehicles in the way so it went truly haywire and despite this roller coaster of a ride, Achilles was still hell bent on killing me. He charged in my direction but I remembered my gun. There was one bullet left in it so I had to be careful. Any attempt at using my powers could have proven fatal so I had only one shot. Literally. Clutching the gun in my hand, I prepared to shoot, whilst attempting to keep my hands steady. The man swung his leg at an almost impossible angle and kicked the weapon out of my hand, ninja style and it flew out of the window and disappeared into the street. The agent then went full boxer and started pounding my chest with his giant hands. Each punch felt like a wrecking ball being swung at me. He then landed a cross on my face as blood, saliva and a tooth splattered across the bus. It was impossible to dodge his attacks while also trying to remain steady on this rampant bus.

While he was punching me, I noticed a small black box in his belt and so yanked it free with a stretch of my arm and pressed the button on it. A taser. I jammed it straight into his chest, shocking him. However, rather than collapse, he clutched the taser and ripped it out of my hands before swinging his right leg. It twirled in the air before smacking my chest, knocking the wind out of me. In agony, my body collided with the wall behind me, before being pulled to the back of the bus by G-force.

The vehicle was now getting faster and faster. It went through traffic lights and miraculously nobody crashed into it. At the end of the hill was a large, brick, office building. If I failed to break the vehicle, then it would smash front first into the building, killing both me, Achilles and many civilians. Fighting the unstoppable agent was no longer a problem, now I had to be a hero. The agent thought otherwise.

He seized his knife on the floor from earlier. He stood at the front of the bus and ventured towards me, which was uphill. He held the top of the chairs and clambered across the bus. When he was close, Achilles plunged the weapon towards me. Luckily, I ducked and it wedged itself into a chair. The forces of nature were pushing me towards the gaping hole at the back of the bus but I had to resist as I held onto a seat with dear life. If Achilles could somehow fall through that hole then I would have the opening needed to stop the bus.

The beast plucked the knife from the chair, flipped it in his hands and proceeded to attack again. His first attack was a swipe to the chest which I easily dodged by bending backwards. His next move was a twist of the hand, bringing the knife back and he welted it into my arm.

I roared out in pain as the knife penetrated my skin. It hurt like anything and this time I could not loop time so would actually have to live through the pain. Out of pure survival instincts my right fist was thrusted into Achilles' chest, knocking him back. He was now inches from the tear in the bus. My left arm was still squealing, with blood gushing out. I took the opportunity to smash my elbow into his face. He was hardly phased by the attack yet I was able to rip the knife out of my arm. As I did so, the pain worsened ten-fold but I did not let that stop me.

It hurt like hell. I thought it would be badass, ripping a knife out of me yet it stung like anything. Blood pumped out of my body and pain replaced it. However, I was driven by so much will. The urge to defeat Achilles, defeat my brother and save Frank and his father. I thought of all the pain I had gone through in the last few days; Charlie's death, finding out I was adopted, gaining powers. The pain of the knife was minimal when compared to that. In fact the pain drove me. It fuelled me to fight back, to not be overthrown by a bully, to have my say.

I clasped the knife in my hand, smothered in blood. My blood. Within seconds my hand steadied. I then pulsed my hand forwards and pushed the weapon into Achilles' chest. However, the agent grabbed a hold of my arm and resisted me. While the knife was going in, he was pushing it away with such great force that it barely pierced his skin. His strength was incandescent when compared to mine and the man showed absolutely no fear or pain whatsoever. I pushed and pushed but he would not budge.

At that moment, I kicked at his knee, twisting it into an awkward position as he growled in agony, losing his concentration. That gave me the chance to plunge the knife into the dead centre of his chest. It punctured his unbreakable skin, gliding through muscle to the point where the blade could no longer be seen. Achilles' eyes widened in pure agony as he roared.

I took the opportunity to punch him in the face. As my knuckles connected with his forehead, he began to wobble and his heels lay on the edge of the bus. He tried to push forwards but instead, the force of the bus pushed the man out of the moving vehicle and into the street.

As he fell out, Achilles was frantically waving his hands trying to grab onto anything. I realised that the man had been condemned to a death sentence. The man tumbled backwards, with blood gushing out of his chest and was met by the bonnet of a car. A Land Rover had swerved to the side to avoid the tumbling bus but in doing so had crashed into a rogue Government Agent. But I could not look at the wreckage for too long, as the bus continued to zoom down the hill.

My surroundings slowly came back into focus. The bus was now seconds away from crashing. The entire street had been cleared of passengers and vehicles. Some people stood on the pavement and watched as I pounced across the ground, leaping forwards into the driver's booth. Before everything was over, I tossed the body of the driver to the side and slammed my foot on the break pedal. The bus started to slow down yet the impending doom was incredibly close. The bus skidded and slid down. It was too fast at this point. Within seconds, I had lifted my foot off the break and jumped out of the front door. There was no hope in halting this bus.

My body flew out and collided with the hard tarmac. I rolled against the ground, my skin being torn at. The bus then smashed into the building. It was slower now so it did not completely obliterate the tower as it wedged into the building while bricks tumbled from above and glass smashed.

As I tried to muster up the strength to move, I noticed all of my blood on the floor. It was utterly painful considering my arm was still screaming from being stabbed. So much blood. It scattered the street like paint. I gazed into the distance and watched as several police cars circled around me like wolves surrounding an injured deer. Officers flocked around me, guns in hand, ready to fire. There was no way I could fight all of these people simultaneously.

A man came out of the door of one of the cars. He had a fat moustache, like a caterpillar on his lip. His hair was tousled and rough. The police officer wore a bullet proof vest and looked incredibly angry.

"Jason Clyde, you are under arrest. Do not try and resist," he said in a gruff voice, hardened by most likely years of service. Soon he was followed by dozens of other officers. His finger itched on the trigger. Killing me would be the highlight of his career. There was no point fighting back. With no powers, I would be shredded by hundreds of bullets and my death would make the front page of all the newspapers. The only way I could get out of here was with the truth, which they would never believe.

"You have to trust me," I said, unable to hear myself from the continuous ringing in my ear canals. "Ted Clifford has been possessed and I need to get to Downing Street now to save his life before our country is turned on its head."

The aged officer glanced at his watch before clearing his throat. "Just be quiet, you have caused enough damage already. Now then, you are under arrest for the murder of your brother, attempted murder of Frank Clifford and now under charges for millions of pounds worth of street damage and the murder of Special Agent Achilles." Did *I just kill a man? Achilles' death was not my fault*. The guilt of murder began to fill me as an uneasy blanket of ice formed over my body, causing me to shudder.

"Please, you have to believe me. I was framed. My brother Julian is behind all of this. This man has taken control of the secret service and is extremely dangerous. I need to get to Downing Street to stop all of this". These words sounded insane.

"There is no way I am falling for that crap," he said, gun still in hand.

"He is right", came a voice from afar. He spoke briefly and swiftly as he ran to my location. Behind him, a group of about ten others flocked. It was the man who sat next to me on the bus. His clothes were doused in sweat and his face was bright red and his hair was now matted and greasy. "Jason saved my life on the bus. He saved all of our lives," he said pointing at the entire cohort of my fellow bus passengers. They all simply nodded in agreement.

"The agent with the long hair ambushed us and tried to kill all of us. He shot the driver and Jason saved us all from his wrath. Surely there is some truth in what he has to say?"

The officer looked around. He lowered his gun and put his hand to his face. Running his hand through his hair, he glanced at the bus passengers standing before him. In the background, fire engines soared across the street and started putting out some small fires. There were ambulances as well, but no bodies were found, because there had been no casualties.

"I put my life on the line by braking the bus and preventing an even bigger explosion. Surely that is not the behaviour of a killer?"

The stern expression of the officer softened as his pursed his lips and relaxed his eyebrows. "That's quite the story kid", he said, raising an eyebrow. After a brief pause, he signalled for all the policemen to lower their guns and they followed ensue.

"Let's go," he said, gesturing for me to follow him. He gently opened the passenger seat of his car. "I can get you to Downing Street, but once we are there, you are on your own." I was so relieved and enthralled that the pain from the bleeding seemed a distant memory. In fact, my face and hands were still doused in blood, to the point where my eyes were stinging from exposure but I could not care less. This was my chance. My shot.

"You are not going like that," he added. "You would not last one minute in such condition." The officer signalled for a paramedic to come over from the ambulance and she followed. When the paramedic got closer, she was startled and looked over to the officer, perplexed. Before she could say anything, he stepped in.

"Oh yeah, he's most likely innocent. Patch him up and give him some painkillers." The paramedic simply nodded and got to work. In her hand was a medical kit, full of bandages, wipes, stitches and even scissors. She started off by wiping my face of blood and seriously, there was a lot of it. 5 wipes were required just to polish up my face just so that I would not look like something out of a Horror movie. My forearms and elbows were all grazed and scratched up from landing on the tarmac. And don't get me started on the knife wound on my arm.

While my arm was being stitched up, all I could think about was Julian. The pain of stitches meant nothing to me. Right now he was orchestrating something diabolical. He did not know that I had powers at this moment, so that would be my advantage. In fact he probably thought me dead. But then again he had eyes everywhere. Someone must have reported to him about Achilles' death. Currently my new abilities were still acting up. They worked on and off especially during the 'bus brawl'. If they failed while fighting Julian then I would be toast. And would they work against his mind powers?

After being bandaged like a mummy, I finally got into the Police Officer's car. He turned on the engine and started driving, zooming off into action.

The roads ahead were all full of traffic. However, we were in a police car. The officer put on his sirens and I watched in awe as the entire traffic parted for us like the Red Sea did for Moses.

The inside of the car was quite messy. An empty cigarette box was on the floor and all the cupholders were taken up with coffee cups. Boris would have loved this place. Remember Boris? Those were simpler days.

"I am Chief Inspector Evans," the old man said in his gruff voice. "Don't bother introducing yourself, I know all about you." Due to the loud nature of the sirens, he spoke in a raised tone. Not quite shouting. It was more like talking while wearing headphones.

"You must be hungry. Here, have a Snickers." He handed over a bar of Snickers that was crushed and perhaps completely melted. But I was famished at that point so eating it was a no-brainer. I peeled open the wrapper like a banana and ate the goo of what was left of the chocolate. The nuts crunched in my mouth and the sugar revitalised my senses. It felt too good. Who knew how long it had been since I had had a proper meal? Now the school lunches seemed like eating at the Ritz.

While I was licking the delicate chocolate, I was totally oblivious to the surrounding houses. We were now entering the richest part of London, driving past landmarks and structures of exquisite decor. Eventually, Evans started talking again.

"You should be in prison right now. The entire country is after you and if we are seen together, I would not only lose my job but could end up imprisoned. You have to understand that what I am doing is insanely dangerous and reckless to say the least. The only reason I am helping you is for my 7 year old son." He paused for a second. "I have always wanted to be a hero, someone for him to look up to, but my career has been far from great. Turning you in would make me famous. But on the contrary, helping you save the Prime Minister's life would make me more than famous. It would make me a hero. Someone who is cool. That's all fathers want, for their kids to look at them as a role model. And now with me and my wife divorced, who knows what kind of an opinion he has of me. Hopefully you will understand someday. I've said my piece," he said.

Everything I knew about family was a lie. I used to think that my parents raised me out of love. But learning that it was an adoption, some *favour* to dead friends. It completely shattered my idea of love and belonging. But what Evans was doing seemed noble and I respected that.

Evans soon parked the car at a point near Downing Street where the entire road had been gated off with many police officers standing outside. There was security just to get to the road. To my right, Evans was rummaging around the car before he found a small black box. He handed it to me.

"I noticed that your magnum is out of ammo. Take this and reload it." I looked at the gun, confused at its inner workings. I tried slotting the box of bullets in but nothing happened. Evans then put out his hand and took the gun off me. After some turns and slotting noises, he handed the gun back.

"This goes without saying, but what we are doing is extremely illegal. A police officer should not be giving a teenager a gun to go and waltz into Downing Street. Now tell me, what is your plan?"

A plan? I had not really thought of that. My plan was to fight Julian and safely return Ted Clifford's body to him. There was not much else to it. But seeing the multitude of officers and guards, let alone the fact that the gate to the street was truly colossal with its razor-sharp piked gates, this would be impossible. Climbing over it would be a feat in itself, not to mention the multitude of people watching. I held the gun in my hand, not knowing what to do with it.

Along with the dozens of officers, there were also many members of the public eagerly watching. There were even news presenters speaking about the issue. One of which stood right in front of the large gates, wearing a bright red dress that impeccably matched her lipstick.

"Today, we are outside Downing Street where Prime Minister Clifford is having an important cabinet meeting. At this moment we are not sure exactly as to what they are discussing however, the Prime Minister has teased some big changes for our country." This was not good. There were way too many people here at one of the most guarded locations in the country.

After a couple of seconds, I had jumped out of the car and was looking at the crowds. Chief Inspector Evans followed afterwards. He opened the boot of his car and brought out some clothes.

"I know you don't have a plan Jason. So here is mine". He threw the clothes in my direction. From amongst the clothes, there was a black sleeveless jacket alongside a shirt and tie with some trousers. He also gave me a high visibility jacket and a tall hat.

"I need you to go undercover as a police officer," he smiled.

Chapter 15: The Mind Emporium

Glancing into the mirror of the car, I could see myself as a true police officer. From the tall hat to the painfully bright jacket, I looked like a true defender of the law. Within my belt my gun rested still, fully loaded. My hat was slightly pulled over my eyes to conceal my identity. Nobody would expect a criminal to be dressed up as a police officer. But maybe the baggy trousers would give it away.

"Let's do this kid," Chief Inspector Evans said, adjusting his tie before itching his moustache.

He led me through the crowds, pushing past people. There were dozens of people packed like sardines. With security guards surrounding them, guns in hand. There was one man in a hoodie who was in my way. So I simply shoved him to the side. When he turned around, he was enraged, ready to kill somebody. But upon seeing that I was a police officer, he backed down and raised his hands in a form of surrender. I continued to mow through the masses, smelling all sorts of horrid body odour and deodorants.

At one point, a microphone was shoved in my face. "Officer, how would you like to comment on the current political situation? First about the whole thing with Jason Clyde and now Ted's promise of a brighter future." Next to the lady was a man with a giant camera on his shoulder. His left eye was squinted, and he was grinning, eagerly waiting to hear my response. I was about to reply when I realised that this was being broadcasted live to the entire country. If I spoke, then somebody would pick up on my true identity. Sweat started to crawl down my back as thoughts raced through my head. Being put on the spot like this was not ideal. The reporter's smile slowly dropped as she lost her patience. She opened her mouth to speak but before words could leave her mouth, the microphone was pushed to the side.

"Please do not distract my partner," entered Evans. The reporter nodded gently and moved along. The camera man trudged behind her solemnly. Evans waved his hand at me, signalling for me to follow. Once we approached the gates, there were a few security guards. One of them put out a hand to prevent us from moving in any further. Evans swiftly pulled out his shiny police badge and waved it in front of him.

"I am Chief Inspector Evans" he said, "and this is"

"Chief Inspector Smith" I said confidently. Evans slapped me on the back and laughed.

"Don't get too cocky, *Constable* Smith," he smiled.

The security guard looked at me, confused, before moving to the side. He whispered something into his walkie talkie and then opened the gates. He opened them by such a small gap to the extent that it was near impossible to squeeze through. Luckily, I was able to do so with ease. I had now made it to Downing Street.

The street was magnificent with tall architectural wonders that screamed wealth and royalty. The buildings were geometrically satisfying with octagonal bends and gorgeous pillars. The road itself felt narrow with the two sides of buildings looming over you like the walls of a tunnel. At the end of the road could be seen number 10 where the current meeting was taking place. The problem was that the sides of the road were all filled with security guards. From police officers to general security. Somehow, I had to break in. This disguise would not last much longer.

We slowly trudged through the streets, aware of the hawk eyes watching our every move. Slowly, I gently lowered my hat over my face.

"Stop there, you two" came a voice from afar. Evans opened his mouth to talk but was immediately interrupted. "Police have no jurisdiction beyond this point. Now turn around and leave." The man had barely made eye contact with us when talking, trying to usher us away. He was moderately obese with his shirt popping around his belly. The man had a pistol in his belt and looked unafraid to use it. After he said that, several more security members surrounded.

"I am afraid I cannot do that," Evans said, before puffing his chest out a bit. He reached into his pocket and pulled out a badge, different from before. "My name is Special Agent Achilles and I report directly to the Prime Minister. Alert him of my arrival." What was he thinking, posing as Achilles? Did he seriously steal the Agent's badge? It was as if he planned for this moment.

"What kind of a name is Achilles?" the man sniggered. "There is no way in Hell that I am letting you anywhere near that meeting."

"Well then," Evans said, clearing his throat. "I am here to report that Jason Clyde has escaped from custody and is heading straight here to massacre the entire cabinet. Now you had better get off your fat arse and do something about it."

"Bloody hell," he muttered. The guard looked angered before he whispered into his walkie talkie. Several moments later he put it down and lifted up a megaphone.

"Everyone, Jason Clyde is on his way. We all need to triple security. This is an emergency. Protecting Mr Clifford is our absolute

243

priority." The entire force of security immediately looked about themselves, grabbing their guns before preparing for action.

"Allow me through, I must personally protect Mr Clifford," Evans exclaimed.

"Fine" mumbled the man, "but the rookie must stay." *Rookie? Was my acting that bad?*

"Do you know who this is?" Evans said. "This is Special Agent Smith, my *partner*. His name is legendary. This fine young man will be entering with me. Either you let us both in or none of us."

"Fine" he said begrudgingly. The man then led the two of us through the entire force of security. He led us right to 10 Downing Street where dozens of officers stood solemnly, guns in hand. The house had its famous black door at the front, surrounded by the elegant white porch. Gates stood tall and guarded the house. The building was built with beautiful black brickwork that made it look truly astounding. The guard was about to open the front door when he was stopped by someone. And that someone was a familiar face.

The man wore a black suit with black sunglasses. He barred the entry for Evans and I, whilst his other hands crawled to his pocket where his gun lay. This was the MI5 agent who came to visit me in hospital alongside Julian. If anybody were to recognise me, it would be him. The overweight security guard was taken aback by this man's behaviour and thus spoke.

"I present to you Special Agent Achilles and his partner *Agent Smith*. They have been specially sent to protect Ted Clifford."

The MI5 agent scoffed before lowering his sunglasses a titch and gazing at Evans and me. He then proceeded to readjust his glasses.

244

"That is not Agent Achilles. I have worked with the man myself. And if I know Achilles, he would never have a sidekick. Definitely not a boy. The man then slapped the hat off my head. "You've landed yourself into quite the predicament. Jason".

I stepped back, astonished. Hundreds of officials and security surrounded me. This was the worst place to be caught. The guard we had tricked looked absolutely shocked. Immediately he reached into his belt to grab his gun. However, before he could shoot, a bullet ripped through his shoulder as he fell back, blood spurting out of the wound. Everybody stared at Evans, who stood there, gun in hand.

"Jason, run!" he screamed before bullets started flying in all directions. I took the opportunity to tumble forward and push the MI5 agent aside and smash the door open. I ran in before anyone could do anything.

Usually, I would take a moment to take in the marvellous surroundings but this time I was in a rush. Outside, the sound of guns blazed and along the corridor, up a flight of stairs was a room, and inside I could hear an array of old British voices. The stairs were glorious with patterned carpet, surrounded by yellow walls. These stairs appeared to be never ending as I vaulted up them, taking in the line of portraits that stretched along the walls.

The next floor was a wooden wonder, with its varnished ground that both screamed modern and dated. But before I could catch my breath, I hurried to the conference room to finally end this one and for all. The final boss of this sick game. And if this were to be any harder than Achilles then I would be screwed to say the least.

The room was extravagant in its glory, with a huge table, longer than my house. Around the table sat a plethora of people. These were

Clifford's cabinet, who were totally oblivious to the supernatural powers of Julian. The room had a beautiful rug that was placed under the table and an exquisite chandelier hung from the ceiling, glistening with its millions of tiny crystals.

Upon opening the door, the sound of discussion faded away, as Julian looked at me from the other side of the table. From the distance, it was hard to gauge his thoughts. Rather than overreact, he stood up, whilst the entire cabinet began to look at me, with shocked faces. Several opened their mouths as if about to speak, but Julian interjected.

"Everybody, I would kindly appreciate it if you could leave. We shall continue this meeting tomorrow. Jason here and I have a few things to discuss." The politicians followed the orders directly, flocking to the door where I stood, giving me all sorts of looks. As they flocked to the door, I quickly took the opportunity to pull out a phone. This was lent to me by Evans in case of emergency. My fourth phone this story. And so, relying totally on its storage, I propped it up at the side of the room, recording everything. But I did it discretely to prevent my brother from seeing. Meanwhile, I cocked the pistol in my belt preparing to shoot Julian. If I shot him then this would all be over. But suddenly the unthinkable happened.

After the final person had left, the door swung shut, leaving Julian and I alone.

"Good to see you, Jason. I knew a simple prison would not be able to contain my brother." I had had enough of his witty remarks, his hidden evil and most certainly his manipulation. Immediately I tore my gun from my belt, aimed it at him before shooting with marksman's aim. The bullet rippled through his body but left the man unscathed. My brother smiled before vanishing. Behind me, two more copies of him spawned and walked in my direction. With precise aim, I shot both of them, at point blank, yet they just vanished. More Julians appeared and I shot all of them until a voice came.

"What is *real,* brother?" his voice surrounded me. Not coming from a specific corner of the room but from multiple points at the same time. All of a sudden, he appeared directly in front of me. I seized the gun, ready to end his miserable life when suddenly the gun started to feel light. The smooth sturdiness of the handle became rough and grainy. Small granules of sand started pouring out of the weapon, leaking onto the floor. At that moment, the entire gun blew away in a gust of wind, leaving my hands totally empty.

Julian walked towards me before clicking his fingers as his face transformed back into his own with his blond hair and wide jaw.

"We are in your mind, aren't we?" I moaned, realising that this battle would be next to impossible to win.

"Why are you here, *brother*?" he said with spite in his tongue.

"To stop you," I growled. My gun was now gone but Julian was still unaware of my powers so I could use that to my advantage.

"I am afraid I have no use for you" he said, looking at his watch. While he said that, a coolish silver gleamed in his hands. Like jelly, it wobbled and rippled before stretching out. It reached out and became a long staff with a point at the top. He held the javelin in his hands, exercised it, and then hurled it in my direction. The spear tore through my chest, shredding several major organs.

"Now here's the thing. Dying in the 'Mind Emporium' will kill you in real life. Your mind will be destroyed and your body will just become an empty vessel", Julian laughed, watching his younger brother die. However, before the pain kicked in, my powers came into play giving me a second chance. The javelin flew backwards, into Julian's hand and my chest healed back. Like ice melting, the spear returned into the man's hand as a liquid ball again.

"I am afraid I have no use for you," Julian said while a javelin manifested in his hand. He hurled it at me, as if he were an Olympic athlete. This time I side-stepped and the weapon lodged itself into the wall behind me. My older brother smiled.

"I see you have finally developed some combat skills. No wonder you were able to dispose of Achilles so easily." He said before waving his hand. A sharp metal embedded itself into my back. The spear had flung backwards, like a boomerang, impaling me again. Once more I used my powers, but it hurt so badly. My body tried to resist as blood oozed out of me.

"I see you have finally developed some combat skills". He waved his hands and this time crouching did the trick as the weapon billowed above me, causing a near miss. Rather than look impressed, Julian's smile had gone.

"Very well then," he murmured. The javelin returned to him and within a blink of an eye, it glowed white before transforming into a shotgun. My brother wielded it with great strength and pulled the trigger. A spray of bullets burst out, knocking me back.

"Very well then" I summersaulted to the left and dodged the attack. Julian was getting more and more impatient. From his perspective, I was just dodging all his attacks, he still did not know about the time reversing.

248

"Just die already!" he shouted as the room began to rumble. The stones on the floor began to dance as a loud noise approached. Suddenly the wall to the left exploded from impact and a large train sped through, blaring as its wheels ground against the floor. Before it could hit me, I reversed time again.

"Just die already!" he yelled as the room began to rumble. I dived forward, narrowly missing the train as it smashed through the room. It then collided with the opposite wall and kept on driving off into the sunset. The walls of the room suddenly fell down, like the set of a sitcom, revealing the surroundings. We were now in a darkish setting, with purple skies and a melancholic background. We were in the fairground that Julian had shown me before but now it was abandoned. The rides were all rusted and dusty. The trees surrounding us were withered and broken. The floor beneath me was covered in mud, making it difficult to move. Dodging was now going to be even harder.

"This is my world, my rules!" Julian screamed. "Hurry up and die you squirt". He stomped out of rage and at that moment, the ground cracked and began to split beneath me. Before I could get to one the sides, the two parts of the earth flew apart like magnets repelling. The gap in the ground was so large that it swallowed me whole, leading me into a lava pit.

"This is my world. My rules!" As he stomped, I jumped to the left, so that the split in the ground did not envelop me. The ground ruptured so that now Julian and I were looking at one another from opposite parts of the ground. But that loop was painful. A small cough of blood burst out my mouth whilst my lungs took short, sharp breaths. My do-overs were running out. With a stream of lava running between us. Even though this was just Julian's imagination, the atmosphere felt so real. The hot lava was so hot, that my face began to sweat endlessly and the thick smell of ash was abundant.

After dodging so many of his attacks, Julian had a huge temper tantrum of trying to kill me. Thunder, poisonous snakes, shadow demons. Even a swarm of bees. Julian then prepared himself for his next attack, a shot from his pistol. I had foreseen this attack. He was going to shoot me in the stomach. So a sidestep to the right should work. And it did. In a fit of rage, my brother hurled the gun to the ground, shattering it into tiny fragments of glass. He then clenched his fists as he squatted down. His face started to darken and his veins popped out, notably on his neck. He then pointed his finger at me, shaking.

"Y-You! You have powers. What are they? I demand to know!" he said, closing his eyes and trying to focus. But before he could read my mind, I came up with the perfect response.

"I am a telepath, like you. I can read your mind and avoid your attacks before you do them. Don't bother trying to read my mind, I am blocking my real thoughts and giving you fake ones". Julian started pacing up and down before snapping his fingers. The rift in the ground was removed and the purplish skies morphed away, returning us to Downing Street.

"Prove it!" he spat.

"Pick a number between 1 and 1000" I said. After a second he replied to me.

"I have".

"You picked 245, didn't you?" Upon saying that, Julian was enraged. He punched the wall with his hand and shouted.

"You little snot! That was just a basic trick, there is no way you can actually read my impenetrable mind".

"You wanted me to have powers, right?" I asked, boastfully as a drop of blood leaked from my nose, splashing on the immaculate floor beneath.

"I can sense your deceit, your lies. You cannot hide from me forever. You are untrained and naïve. Even your body is beginning to give up on you," he said as the putrid taste of blood formed in my mouth. "Your powers will falter long before mine. So I suggest the following. Either you join me or I let your body destroy itself," and as he said that, the walls of the room erupted into flames. The fire tore through the entire room scorching me. As the heat approached Julian, he simply surrounded himself in a bubble. The fire was agonisingly hot, and I watched as the hair on my arms burnt off within nano seconds. In response, I quickly formed a time loop but it would not do me much good.

The left wall burst into flames, the same as before. This time, I knew it was coming but there was nothing more I could do. I tried running out of the room but it scorched me again.

And again.

And again.

There was no escaping this move. *Did Julian just checkmate me?* I thought as my body erupted in flames once again.

"Either you join me or I let your body destroy itself,"

"Wait!" I yelled. I could not bare to be scorched again. It was horrific, like having your hand strapped to a boiling hot kettle, leaving you unable to flinch away.

This time there was no explosion.

"I am waiting", Julian groaned.

"No more," I whimpered, fumbling to the ground in exhaustion, blood seeping out of numerous cuts. Both nostrils seeped blood and my hands were soaked in the same crimson violence. My vision began to blur as more and more blood pooled to the ground. "I will join you," the words feeling alien in my mouth.

"That is glorious to hear. You see, all these tests were to help you develop your powers. The bomb in your school, the forest encounter with Achilles. And then I added even more variables to help you; letting you run free from my prison, ordering the execution of Charlie Driver right in front of your eyes. And then there was the final variable. Telling you the truth about our parents. The thing is, we need trauma for our abilities to manifest. For me, it was the death of my parents. Watching them die in that car crash whilst my leg was crippled gave me the momentum needed to awaken my talents. And now, after so much work, I have done the same to you."

Julian was walking closer and closer and me, to the point where he had me in a corner, looking down at me. The man had no sense of emotion left within, only harsh beliefs.

When the opportunity was right, I slammed my foot onto his toe and thrust my fist into his stomach. However, he barely flinched as he retaliated, smashing his rock hard shoe into my face.

"Your stamina is running low," he laughed before clasping his muscular hands around my neck, both squeezing and pulling me up to his eye level. Whilst I squirmed, trying to break his grip, he continued to squeeze.

Out of nowhere, he lessened his grip. Only slightly, but enough to keep me alive. The villain then closed his eyes and relaxed as if listening to meditative music.

"Interesting," he smiled. What was he on about? "So, you can turn back time. Only by small increments. And it appears that it has a major toll on your body," he said, wiping the blood from my forehead. "This power is most useful. With some proper training, you will be a real asset. But the thing is, we can't have you running rampant and trying to overthrow me. But some conditioning will do the trick." This was enough. I was not going to be this psycho's puppet. These powers were for my use, not *his*. Unfortunately, his hand was still around my trachea, ready to snap it at any time.

Julian was right. My body would not be able to use much more power. And so, before he could do anything, I bolted out the door. I whipped open the door and walked outside, under the purple skies of Julian's mind. The man made no effort to chase after me. As I hurried past a stand, a small speaker started to sound, cackling as it did so.

"There is nowhere you can hide in my mind. I control everything."

Straight ahead of me was a building. It was a historical one in fact, with a huge dome at the top. The brickwork was ancient with the walls beginning to yellow. I took the opportunity to race through the front door. There had to be an exit to this place. If not, then perhaps I could find Ted Clifford and release him from captivity and boot Julian out of his body.

As I walked into the building, my right calf immediately went into spasm. The muscle twinged and it hurt like anything whilst my body slumped to the ground as I crawled forward. Using so much power had its side effects. At this point, my stamina was pathetic. I tried stretching out my foot, allowing the pain to lessen. The building was filled with all sorts of winding corridors. There was little to no time to spare as Julian could approach at any moment, so I sprinted into the labyrinth, turning around corners left and right with no real aim of where to go.

At one point, there was a long corridor with a doorway at the end, shrouded in darkness. I hurried along, careful not to trip. However, my foot stepped on a small button. I paused at that moment, careful not to move. Suddenly, a small hatch opened in the wall and a brown spear jolted out and impaled my heart.

I was back at the start of the corridor. This entire stretch was filled to the brim with booby traps which was not ideal. Since my body was aching from time looping, I turned around. There had to be another route through this maze. However, as I began to head outside, the doors sealed shut, locking me in, amongst the multitude of death-traps.

Out of nowhere, a voice began to echo through the walls, slightly static in nature but clear enough to make out.

"It appears you have stumbled upon my Death Tunnel. Cheesy name, you are right. This bad boy was designed by me at the age of 15 after having seen one too many adventure movies."

What was this place? Had Julian planned for someone to come here? Too many questions but not enough time. The 'Death Tunnel' was my only way out of this place if there was a way out. There was no option other than to run through it. However, my ears still rang and my body still ached from the constant danger. Did I have enough power to make it through here?

This time, when traversing the area, I avoided that button, but ended up stepping on another mechanism, a flamethrower.

After avoiding spikes, axes, spears and even a saw, my body was exhausted. Using up so much power had its cons as I limped out of the corridor, feeling my life slipping away. Who knew how many cuts and bruises I had endured? The long, booby-trapped corridor led to a huge gate, red in colour and metallic. In fact, there were aspects of it that reminded me of the dreaded school gates. Perhaps Julian had used that for his inspiration.

It required quite the pulse of energy to push through, especially considering my exhaustion. On the other side, there was nothing but darkness. A big, black, empty void. I decided that passing through would be best. What was the worst that could happen?

After walking through the dark void for what felt like ages, the area lit up entirely. The sudden burst of light was intimidating at first but it gave me a full view of my surroundings. Opposite me stood endless rows of seats that stretched on for what could have been miles. They just kept on going, all the way up into the sky. At that moment, I realised where I was. My body was placed in the centre of a stage of a giant theatre. The spotlight was focused on me, aching my eyes. Apart from the central seat of the front row, the entire audience was empty. Julian had led me to the same stage where he had done his speech before. This had to have been where Ted Clifford was being held captive.

255

"The traps I placed should have used up all your powers," Julian said, standing up from his seat and walking over onto the stage. His pace was slow and reserved, while his body was totally calm. It was as if he had all the time in the world. "Do not try and attack me."

However, as soon as he placed his first foot on stage, I jumped towards him, ready to beat the life out of him. Yet he just waved his hand, swinging me back by some sort of invisible hand. It pushed me with a firm punch, knocking the wind out of me. Dazed, I readied myself to attack again, but Julian was one step ahead.

Out of nowhere, my feet were thrusted upwards, off the ground and into the air. I waved my arms frantically, trying to get a hold of the situation. But it was no use. I was flying.

"How are you doing this?" I asked, getting queasy from the height as my toes tingled.

"I was holding back before. Now I will completely and utterly destroy you." The man was serious as he raised his hand before lowering it.

My body was flung to the ground, face first. My nose crumpling before the marble floor. I tried to scream out in pain, but my mouth was held shut. It hurt like anything. Julian then raised his hand and I was tossed into the air again. As if he were swatting a fly, he slapped his hand to the right and in response, my body was smacked against a pillar potentially shattering my spine.

Before I had a chance to heal, he swiped his hand to the left and I was hurled at another pillar. I was being thrown around like a ragdoll and could feel my bones break, one by one. And Julian, he had never looked more intent. He was so focused and driven by hatred. It was scary how much built-up rage he kept behind that immaculate face. Like a conductor mid-symphony, he waved his hands up and down, left and right, and my body continued to be tossed around.

After about a minute of senseless violence, he drew his hand to a halt. Now my body was held in the centre of the stage, blood gushing out of all corners. He still held me in suspension, maintaining his look of intent. Slithers of force were then applied to each of my limbs, as if they were pulling me apart. All of a sudden, Julian clenched his fist and I felt a huge gust of force around my neck, crushing my trachea and blocking off any oxygen. As he squeezed I counted the last seconds of my life. My body was battered and bruised so surely this would be the end? I tried to summon my powers but my efforts were useless as I felt blood ooze down my face. My powers relied on energy, and I had none of that. The pain was beyond immense as I wanted to scream out. There was no hope, none whatsoever. Julian would kill me right here in his mind, on a huge stage in front of an empty audience. *An empty audience?* I thought, as the fragments of an idea came together.

Doing my best to hold back my anguish, I opened my eyes and glanced at Julian. My vision was blurred yet I could just about make out the fact that his face was cut and bruised, as if he had taken a beating. I had not landed a finger on him, so why was he so wounded? That was when it hit me.

His powers acted in a similar fashion to mine. The more we used our powers, the more our bodies would suffer. It was as if we were spending our life just to use a bit of dark energy. Julian was hurting himself just to use his powers and the more he used it, the weaker he would become.

The entire theatre was empty. The entire amusement park was empty, devoid of anyone else. Last time he brought me here, the place was overflowing with joy and excitement from an army of mindless Julians. The 'Julians' were people that lived in his mind. A made up audience. The more people in the Mind Emporium, the more energy that Julian uses. He was focusing all of his power on killing me, so he needed to scrap this place to its bare essentials. It was like having tabs open on a computer. The more you have open, the slower the machine. Julian removed all his tabs just so he could focus entirely on slaughtering me.

"Pathetic", I groaned as blood burst out of my mouth. At first Julian did not look bothered but then he gradually got more and more agitated, to the point that he lessened the force on my neck ever so slightly, buying me some more time.

"Speak!" he said, sharply.

"You have all this power" I said before coughing out dots of blood. "You have all this power and yet you choose to kill me in such a boring way." I paused for a moment, summoning more air into my chest. "You can do better. You have this immaculate plan yet you are going to kill me in such an uninteresting way. Where is the excitement in that?"

Immediately, Julian clenched his fists again, harder this time. It hurt so much as he just kept on squeezing, intent on completely obliterating me. I felt pressure building up in my chest, as if the air was going to tear out of it. My head was heating up like anything and my eyes were bulging. Any second now my life would end. *Any second now.*

"You are right," he said, begrudgingly. After one last squeeze, he let me go and my body slumped to the ground. "I am gifted with all this power, yet I choose to kill you in such a simple way. This death needs to be the most glorious moment in human history." he said with a Shakespearean tremor. Meanwhile, I was choking on the floor, feeling the air circulate into my body and rejuvenating my cells. I wiped the blood covering my eyes and looked up at the madman, who was now hovering in the air, arms raised as if he were exciting a crowd of people. And all of a sudden, the ground grumbled with great energy, as if the Earth was terraforming. The stage was pulled off the ground and in its place was a huge sea of lava that spread off into the distance. The intense heat gnawed at my face while huge rocks emerged from the pools of fire. The entire area quaked whilst the immense changes to the surroundings continued. The thick magma rolled around the boulders that surfaced, forming large podiums.

Now, a huge crowd had formed on the rocks, cheering at Julian, who was now hovering above me like some sort of ring master. The crowd was made up of hundreds if not thousands of Julians. They shouted and screamed in pure excitement at the feet of what was yet to come. Their entire concentration was focused solely on me who was lying on the stage which was now a circular arena surrounded by an ocean of flames. My plan had to work or else a painful death.

Above me, Julian was waving his hands around, as if he were conjuring the dead or doing some sort of majestic voodoo. He shot his hands up towards the purple sky and a swarm of particles formed overhead. They spun around and interacted before manifesting into a giant ring laced in silver. The shape was like a doughnut with a thick outer circle and a hole in the middle. This hole was cyan in colour and glimmered in the night. As if he were enlarging an image, he swiped his fingers and the doughnut appeared to bloat in size. It whirred and creaked whilst it began to grow to inhumane levels. Before long, the ring now shadowed the entire crowd, with its centre directly above my head. The centre of the ring was continuing to manifest into some liquid like material. A thin sheet of cyan water spread all around this 'death-ring'.

"My Friends!" Julian roared, immediately followed by thunderous applause. "Today I show you the execution of my brother Jason in the most spectacular fashion." As he said that, thick metallic chains ripped out of the ground and shackled themselves around my wrists, holding me firmly to the ground. They were cold around my arms and seemed to be laced in some sort of gold. These chains were both imperialistic in strength as well as being elegant in design.

"My brother is currently chained to the ground" he shouted, which was followed by boos and jeering. "When the time is right, the ring above him will fire a singular laser that will incinerate him. By killing his conscience in the Mind Emporium, his physical body on Earth will no doubt die."

The crowd squealed in excitement.

"Kill him!" they roared.

"Kill him!" they came once again. It was as if I was being publicly executed for treason in the 1600s. A public hanging of a traitor, however in this instance, I had done nothing wrong.

"KILL HIM!!!" they yelled, even more violently. And that was when I noticed it. The entire crowd was made up of Julians yet one of their faces went blank. Entirely blank, just a plain sheet of skin. No eyes, ears, or nose. It was quite a disturbing site to behold. And then

260

the same happened to another one, and another. I glanced up to Julian who was sweating like anything and his face was dripping blood. Red violence poured from his eyes and nose, yet he was too excited to notice. The man was so engrossed in the spectacle that he did not notice that his powers were barely holding together. Small details on the audience members kept disappearing. There was one that was yelling but was just a floating head. Even the rocks were beginning to lose their texture and shape. They went from authentic designs to a more basic shape. Just cubes of rock.

However, the ring above me still posed a threat as the thin sheet of liquid within began to glow bright, blinding the audience. The liquid, as if it had a life of its own, rippled, and began to churn. Within a few moments, it was moving in a circular motion around the centre, directly above my head.

"10!" Julian shouted, as the liquid swirled faster.

"9,8," the purply liquid began to move out of the ring, forming a conical shape which stretched out from the device, looking like a large V. The bottom of this V was sharp and began to glow brighter than the rest.

"7,6," The liquid had now become a perfect cone of a tornado of purple that was truly rampant.

"5," the audience joined in. I gave a yank at my chains hoping to break through but they were still tough as nails.

"4," I pulled again and could hear the whirring of the machine above, getting louder and louder, whilst the whirlwind continued to accelerate beyond proportion.

"3," the metal was cutting at my wrists however I noticed something else. I could no longer feel the heat of the lava on my face. Julian was losing more and more control of the environment. In fact, the sound of the audience had slowly declined.

"2," with one final hurl I pulled the chains but rather than break, they ripped off the ground, with chunks of rock attached to the ends, like a mace.

"1" I barely had any time left. The ring of rock I was on was surrounded by lava. Perhaps cold lava? There was only one way to find out.

"0," jeered Julian as the tornado moved down incredibly fast. It twisted through the air towards me and I summersaulted into the lava. I did it right at the last moment to disguise my fall. The lava felt like water as it soaked my body. The whirlwind blasted through the rock, obliterating it within milliseconds, sending rocks and pebbles flying in all directions. The audience went hectic with excitement and screamed the place down. My plan had worked. Now to defeat Julian.

"Thank you and goodnight" he called out before clasping his hands together. At that moment, the crowd crumbled into thin air leaving the psychopath alone. He had a large grin on his face as he had finally killed his brother. Now was my chance.

When the time was right, I dove out of the magma and clasped my hands around Julian's neck, feeling his real flesh within my grasp. I remembered how he strangled me and tried to crush my body and so exacted my revenge. The man growled out in anger and flew to the side, crashing onto a rock. Now I faced him, one on one. His face was completely battered and bruised, with a multitude of cuts.

"You!" he shouted. He revealed his right hand and winced through some pain. He shook his hand but nothing happened. The man looked at his arm, confused, and shook it again. A bright light appeared before manifesting into the shape of a sword. The force of the manifestation pushed me back, freeing his neck. He then winced some more and the blade began to grow. I took the opportunity to dash towards him, dodging his first swipe at me. Julian shook his hand more and the blade grew ever so slightly. He wiped the blood from his nose using the back of his hand and set his eyes on me.

Like a fencer, he lunged forward, hoping to strike me, yet I sidestepped to the right. From all my time loops before, I had slowly become able to predict his moves. Julian was a very aggressive fighter, putting attack before defence. While his sword was forward, I took the opportunity to swing my leg at his open chest. It connected with a crack, pushing him back.

"Why won't you just die" he spat with blood oozing out his mouth. His teeth were now coated in red gore as he blindly struck at me again. Out of instinct, I raised my arm to protect my face but the sword just slid through it like butter. Blood burst out of my arm yet I felt no pain. My body was driven entirely by pain so an extra cut did absolutely nothing. Once again, I charged at him, this time going for a rugby tackle knocking him clean off his feet. That move was from Frank. He fell back, head smacking to the ground and then I took the opportunity to snatch the sword knife off him and plunged it deep into his chest. But as the blade pierced his skin, it morphed into a load of bubbles before my very eyes and then floated off into the eerie surrounding.

Julian was now on the floor, underneath me, at my mercy and so I did not hold back. First I summoned a right jab to his face and watched as his nose cracked to the side. I then smashed him with a left cross as a tooth blasted out of his bloodied mouth. At that moment, he choked on blood and began to talk,

"Jason" he gargled but I did not give him an opportunity to continue. My right hand was too feisty, so it thrust itself back into his horrific face. With each punch, I was forced to remember every horrible thing he did to me; lying about the death of my parents, being rude and condescending to me all my life, stealing my body for a month, trying to kill me multiple times, framing me for murder and now he wanted to take over this country like some Dictator. Not to mention the horrors he had inflicted on Frank and his father. This monster had done enough to ruin my life and that of others.

As I beat him, I lay witness to the complete collapse of the Mind Emporium. First the lava began to evaporate, leaving only concrete and rock. Entire buildings just turned to dust or crumbled like sand. Watching all this destruction was not enough to stop me as I landed another fist on his once perfect jaw. Each punch was harder than the last and I saw as my knuckles were bloodied with the blood of both us brothers. The Ferris wheel in the distance blew away in a puff of smoke and the entire theatre fell apart like a Jenga tower. The sky burnt away like paper and the cold air soon disappeared. The surrounding completely vanished, leaving us in an empty, black void, placed on some rock. Again, I hit him and watched as his eyes puffed while his face was mangled.

However, the tides changed at that moment as I suddenly felt a sharp pierce to the side of my stomach. I squealed out in agony and watched as Julian had formed a small dagger in his palm that had found its way above my pelvis.

Instantly the black void disappeared, and we were back in the meeting room. I woke up, having been lying on the floor for several minutes now. I rubbed my eyes and noticed that my body was still subject to all the injuries. My arm was still cut and there was still a knife wound in the side of my belly. I placed my knackered hand to the wound, trying to prevent the blood loss. We were back in the real world. Opposite me was Julian, in Ted's body, covered in blood with his face unrecognisable. He gradually clambered up as if he were a boxer escaping a knockout. He got to his feet before lingering over to me and whacking his leg into my face. The blast knocked me back, dazing me. Both of us had exhausted our powers. This final scramble would just be a match of wits and brawn. However, Julian had the advantage, as my gun from earlier was conveniently placed to his right. Before I could move a muscle, he bent over and clasped the murder weapon before aiming it at me. His wounded hand shook and wobbled but from this distance it would be impossible for him to miss. He held the gun firm, with his index finger on the trigger.

"This is the end, *brother*." The final word stubbornly stumbled from his mouth, having been said with great distaste. The gun was held pointing between my eyes. One bullet was all it would take to kill me. And then he pulled the trigger.

First, I heard the gun fire and soon the pain shot through. My eyes were held shut as the bullet pierced through my head, killing me. And that was that.

However, after a moment, I opened my eyes to see that the bullet had only grazed the side of my cheek. How was that even possible? Julian held the gun right in front of my head, there was no way that a bullet could swerve that much and completely avoid my brain.

Opposite me was Julian who was struggling to hold the gun straight. His hand was shaking tremendously whilst he was sweating like an animal. It was as if he had seen a ghost. With a look of utter petrification, he opened his mouth to talk yet no sound came out. Once again, my brother aimed the gun at me, but his hand was being pushed away from me. The gun was held in his right hand but was slowly swerving to his left. He took his left hand and tried to support the weapon but it was not enough. Sweat rolled down his head as he looked totally baffled.

"Get out of my body," he whispered under his breath, just loud enough for me to hear. The words, forceful and pungent. Julian pushed the gun further to his left to the point that his was now perpendicular to both me and him.

"This is for what you did to Frank" he said again, getting angrier. The gun was now inches away from facing Ted's chest.

"Jason, he is too strong. I have to do this" he said, the gun now pointing at his own chest. With the Mind Emporium destroyed, Ted Clifford was finally set free and able to reclaim his own body but Julian was resisting him.

"Wait! There must be another way."

Suddenly, his face tightened, and a look of despair appeared. "What are you doing you filthy scumbag. You are ruining my plan."

Ted now held the gun, firmly at his chest.

"Go to hell!" he said and pulled the trigger. The bullet erupted through his stomach, blood splattering everywhere, while the gun slipped from his hands to the ground. Mr Clifford collapsed to the ground and winced in pain yet remained calm as his life slowly escaped. Julian on the other hand was quite the opposite.

"What have you done! NO! Years of planning! I will have my revenge. This is not the last you shall hear from me Jason! I will, I will," but his voice was cut off. His spirit had been destroyed, allowing Ted to fully reclaim his own body in his last moments.

There was nothing I could do. I tried to loop time, to prevent him from shooting himself, but nothing happened. I watched helplessly as my brother finally died for good and the Prime Minister of England bled to death.

The back door to the room blasted open. I was so tired, so drained that it was next to impossible to look up.

"No!" came a familiar voice. It was distressed in its tone. "What happened?" he shouted. "Father!" his voice now sorrowful. Frank knelt to see his father. Where had the boy been all this time? I had no idea, but it was heart-breaking to watch him now.

"Frank," Ted smiled weakly, "I am so proud of the man you have become. It was wrong of me to ignore you all the time with my work. In the end, I would give anything to spend another day with you."

"Father please," Frank sobbed. Ted placed his hand on his son's face, showing him one final moment of affection. His hand gently stroked Frank's face, wiping a tear from his pale cheek.

"I love you son," he whimpered as his arm lost its strength and collapsed by his side while his eyes lost their light. In a truly touching manner, Frank gently closed the eyes of his father.

"Say hello to mother for me," Frank said, while a tear splashed onto the face of the deceased Prime Minister. The boy then locked his eyes on me and scrambled to his feet, holding the gun in his hand. We had not exactly left things on good terms last we met.

"You! You did this. You killed him!" he said, enraged. He held the gun up to my head, preparing to finish off my brother's job. Tears streamed down the boy's cheek as he mourned the loss of his father. He cocked the gun about to shoot when another door swung open.

Moments later, police and security erupted into the room, surrounding the two of us and the dead body. An officer took the gun off Frank and all the security pointed their guns at me, ready to fire. From amongst the soldiers, one emerged, took one look at the dead body and paused for a moment in disbelief. He had let the Prime Minister die on his watch. He then glanced at me and pointed.

"Jason, you are under arrest for the murder of Mr Theodore Clifford. This is the end for you. Enjoy the rest of your life rotting in prison." There was no point resisting as my arms were seized, before being cuffed in a most forceful manner.

"I will make sure you suffer for what you did" Frank screamed at me as I was escorted out of the room and into the streets which were now heaving with guards and policemen. The shouting and the crying were all overwhelming. No matter how bad the next few days were going to be, I had to remember that I saved this country. It was me. Julian was now no longer a threat. But I had killed my own brother. My parents died years ago so I had just killed my only remaining family. That was impossible. Julian had brought this on himself. I was at no fault here. But anyway, this whole situation was an utter mess and I was at the centre of it.

Epilogue: 14 Days Later

"Alright, time is up, hand in your essays now." Huge sighs of relief filled the room. "Boris, stop writing." The boy begrudgingly put his pen down and glanced at his page of barely legible scribbles.

"I've had an absolute stinker, sir," Boris said, handing Mr Griffin the piece of paper. The teacher adjusted his glasses and continued moving. One by one, the class members all handed in their work. As usual, Raj had written out the entire Bible and Wilfred tried to email his work. Mr Griffin walked past the empty desk next to me and reached out his hand. I gently passed him my work, which was complete and absolute waffle. What do you expect from someone who had missed huge chunks of school? I would be lucky to get any marks at all.

"Thank you, Jason," The old man smiled. "It is good to have you back". And at that moment Haresh slapped my back, sending tingles up my spine, aggravating old wounds.

"Ready for the game tonight" he whispered to me. "With Frank gone, we need our next star player". I smiled back, hoping to get out of the situation. I had endured more than enough violence for one lifetime.

After glancing at his watch, Mr Griffin looked at the class and said,

"You can go 5 minutes early considering you have worked so hard." After a huge gasp of excitement, the class flocked out within seconds, leaving the teacher to his devices. As everyone was leaving, he quickly added, "Consider this a one off". Upon exiting, the classroom, I noticed that Raj was walking by himself, looking glum.

"Hey buddy" I said. "I just wanted to apologise over what has happened between us over the last few months. I guess I wanted to be cool like Frank but that got me nowhere. Hopefully you can forgive me.

"Of course," Raj cried. "Just don't use some weird story about being possessed by your dead brother as your excuse." I smiled. Raj had no idea what was possible. The idea of me getting powers still perplexed me. The entire theoretical field of science had completely changed and it would definitely take time to get used to. And that reminded me.

Free period time.

This was my first Free period in what felt like years. Hopefully nobody would disturb me. I briefly checked my emails, hoping to see nothing from Mr Grove about some meeting and so was pleased to see an empty schedule.

In the Sixth Form Centre, the general noise slowly dissipated as I walked in. The eyes everywhere felt like daggers staring at me. When I initially returned to school, the stares were much more prevalent, and tons of people asked me questions. Fortunately for me, today everyone simply returned to their conversations and their phones, ignoring my presence. After Christmas everyone would have forgotten about me again. Hopefully.

At the other end of the room, I could see Wilfred who was playing on his iPhone, sitting alone. So I decided to head over. Hopefully he did not hate me for getting him sent to prison.

"Hi, erm, I just wanted to say that I am er- sorry for getting you arrested. It was totally my fault and I dragged you into it."

"Don't worry Jason," he said reassuringly. "You were desperate. Anyways, do you know how cool it was in the secret Government facility. I got to witness all sorts of epic gadgets. That would not have happened if not for you and 'The Big Red Dog'."

"Thank you," I laughed nervously. "I erm assume you have not heard anything from Frank."

"Sadly not. Ever since the incident with his father, nobody has seen or heard from him". I gulped to myself. Even though Frank had lost somebody close, so had I. The loss of Julian was more than I was expecting. It hurt more than it should have. Much more.

"Without Clifford, you guys are toast!" bellowed the St Pete's School Team Captain. He stood in front of his army with his arms spread out. "Show me what you have got." I glanced around at the rest of our team. There should have been no way that we could win. Especially without our star player.

When the game started, I seized hold of the ball. Members of the opposition bombarded me one by one. The first guy came from the right and smacked me clean onto the ground before yanking the ball off of me.

One time loop later, the first guy came at me from the right and I slid out my leg. He hurtled over me and rolled across the field. While watching him fail, another member grabbed me around the waist and easily disposed of me.

This time, I sidestepped to the right. Three people all approached me at once, and with great precision, I dodged all of them and passed through before scoring a try. I repeated the same formula for every round and in the end Queen's came out victorious.

"Excellent work!" said Wilfred as we carried home the trophy that day.

Later that day, on the bus home, I glanced at my phone to check the news, a new habit of mine.

'Special Agent Achilles Pronounced Dead after 2 weeks in Intensive Care'

I was not sure what to make of that. It took me a while to comprehend as I just stared out the bus window for the next few minutes.

Upon arriving at home, Mum asked me "How was school?"

"It was good". Even though I knew she was not my real Mum, it was best just to play along with it. Mum and Dad had tried so hard to be my real parents that they might as well have been. The only difference between them and my real parents were just genetics, something that hardly bothered me. I would keep the fact that I knew away from them. Maybe they never intended to tell me, but there must have been something about it on my Birth Certificate.

My house felt the exact same as before, furniture was barely moved. I was told that the house was ransacked by the Police to find evidence against me but they were unsuccessful. Drawers had been emptied and even plates had been smashed. The other day, Mum showed me pictures of the house after the search and it was horrifying but luckily her and Dad had put the place exactly as it was. A few things felt different in the house, notably that one of my posters had been ripped. Did the Police really expect to find some sort of nuclear codes written on the back? Mum had put a long piece of Sellotape across the poster but the tear was still obvious. My computer was also missing, probably taken in for evidence. They probably had a look at my search history, YouTube recommendations, the whole lot.

Furthermore, my favourite Teddy Bear had been decapitated. The police had ripped the head off of him, hoping to find some sort of illegal drugs or weapons. Now the bear had been stapled back together, but he looked more like Frankenstein now than anything.

At Dinner, we sat around the table, discussing the day.

"So how did that timed Economics essay go?" Mum asked.

"Erm well it was pretty bad. I have missed so much work that it was hard to write on the relevant topic." I said, cutting a piece of broccoli.

"How was the Rugby game against St Pete's?" Dad said, getting excited.

"Oh, well we won" I said bluntly in the most unenthusiastic way. At that moment he stood up and did a mini victory dance before giving me a high-five.

"See, I told you Sarah. One of our boys would become a Rugby Champion." Finally, something that I outshone Julian in.

"That reminds me," Mum said, "These two letters came for you in the post". She handed over the letters with my name written.

"It's probably the BBC asking him to do another interview" Dad added. Regardless, I still got that childish excitement whenever I received a new letter. After finishing my meal, I went to my bedroom, closed the door and opened the first letter.

Dear Jason,

We, at the BBC want to make a documentary called 'The Madness of Minister Ted'. The programme will discuss the death of Ted Clifford's wife and how it drove him to insanity to the point where he eventually took his own life. We want to interview you for this programme to find out first hand what it was like to be framed for murder by the Prime Minister. It was utterly unfair what happened to you, so we want to shed light on some of the finer details.

Yours Sincerely

Gregory Scott

Director of Media

So that was a no. The more I got interviewed, the more likely it would be for me to reveal the truth, which was a no-no. Mine and Julian's powers needed to be kept hidden from the general public. The only people that knew of Julian's powers were me, and the handful of Government officials that saw the recording of me fighting Julian. They watched my phone recording in full, and witnessed the footage of me lying down while blood appeared on my face. For me, I was fighting Julian in the 'Mind Emporium' but all my phone saw was me on the floor down magically getting more and more injured over time.

In fact, they were surprisingly understanding of my story. They decided that this should be kept away from the public so they created a cover-up story. It went as follows.

After the death of Ted's wife, he went insane. To the fact that he started to abuse his power. He looked at his son and picked one of his friends to do a social experiment on. (Me). Using deepfake and photoshop, he was able to create photos of me killing my brother and me planting a bomb in my school. Ted then put a million-pound bounty on my head just for the sake of it. Eventually after some mishaps, Ted went full psycho and took his own life with a bullet.

It was a very strange cover up story but at least it kept the public calm for the most part. The more interviews that I would partake in, the more likely that people would be able to see past the cover-up story. Very few people knew the truth.

It was a lot to take in. In fact the last 2 months were a hell of a lot to take in. And don't get me started on how much catch-up I still had to do for school. Raj had agreed to help me with some of it, but even that might not have been enough.

Eventually I put the first letter down and glanced at the second one. Either it would be about another interview or about some overdue eye-appointment. This particular envelope was quite thick with papers and heavier than the other one, which intrigued me. Upon opening it, I was greeted by several pages of beautifully handwritten writing. Without thinking, I raced into the letter.

Dear Jason,

Things did not go end well for us during our last encounter. And I wanted to say that I wish that fate had a different plan. But the truth is, I am dead and you are most probably the cause of my death. If you are feeling guilty about it, then do not. Guilt is just a chemical reaction in the human brain. Nothing that cannot be overcome. I have written this letter to you in order to give my final goodbyes.

It was never personal with you. You were always a good brother. A bit lazy, but still a decent person. When I was in my final year at Queen's, as head boy, I felt as if I was the most powerful person in the world. All of a sudden, hundreds of pupils were forced to look up to me and I could ensure rules across the school to reduce suffering. Because that was the purpose of all my actions, to stop suffering. Every day at school I would hear the thoughts of boys who were in pain, whether it be abusive parents or mourning the loss of family. And do not get me started on how many stressful thoughts I read. Tests after tests after tests.

So as Head Boy, I took it upon myself to request to Mr Ford that the school should hire some new counsellors. That way, people could work on their mental health and therefore be happier. But soon I would realise that this made little to no difference. The counsellor could not make the dark thoughts go away, only supress them. And supressing emotions is not the same as removing them. Rather than help the school some more, I decided to focus more on my life, my academia, my upcoming Oxford interview. At the end of the year, I unsurprisingly achieved 4A*s but that did not change anything about the suffering around me.

There is a philosophical question asking whether or not we are born evil and I know for sure that we are all born good. We only become bad from the exposure to the suffering around us. If I could somehow remove that exposure from children then there would be no bad men. A school bully bullies the short kids at school. But that bully only bullies to release his built up anger from home because he probably has an abusive father who beats him and his mother every day. And that father only abuses his family because he is overstressed at work from long hours and little pay from his boss. The chain of evil keeps on going and going. So I decided that something needed to be done about this. There was no point living in a society that was built upon the suffering of others.

Upon leaving Queen's I discovered that joining the Year 7 would be none other than Frank Clifford, the son of the unpopular Prime Minister Ted Clifford. Now here is the thing about politics. Politicians are very disconnected from the general public. They pledge to build houses and help the youth but do they really go through with that? For the most part, politicians are corrupt men who are only where they are because of their rich parents. They are not hard workers, they do not care about the public, only themselves. There needed to be someone righteous who could rule this country and I knew exactly who.

When Frank was admitted to the school, I quickly discovered that you were the same age as him hence I paid for you to go to his school. I am aware that it was a sleezy move on my behalf but it was necessary. One of my powers is the ability to take over somebody's body. But here is the catch, I can only possess someone if they have a deep connection with me. So after a few years of planning, I came up with a plan. First I would buy you the latest phone and then take you to the cinema. By that point you would like me enough that it would be easy to take your body. Then I would spend as long as it would take to make Frank my friend using your body. Luckily that took 30 days for him to trust me enough to take his body. And from there I possessed his father. Phase 1 of my plan was now complete.

I am sure that you know the rest. While using your body I stabbed my original body to frame you for murder. I also planted a bomb in your school to kill both Frank and you. You two would be the only ones that could figure out my plan. Frank would see that his father would be acting funny and so would very quickly catch on. I spent some time studying Ted Clifford, so that I could eventually mimic his behaviour, the way he walks, eats, et cetera. However, it is incredibly difficult and requires immense discipline to fit into someone else's life entirely. By killing you and Frank, my chances of being caught out would be minimal considering Ted had no other family. After killing the two of you, I would work bit by bit to reduce suffering in this country. You know the rest.

Nevertheless, there is another matter we must discuss. The two of us are different from everyone else. We have dark matter in our blood. Untraceable, but still present. At the time of me writing this letter you still have not developed your powers but I would say you will have if you have defeated me. So if I am dead then you must have developed your abilities to overthrow me.

Before I go, I must warn you. You need to make sure that you never ever use your gifts in public. Trust me. If the general public sees you shooting lasers or something then they will go insane. The entire world would be full of superstition and horror. You would be most likely hunted down and executed for being a freak. You need to keep a low profile. The human brain cannot comprehend what you and I possess. And that brings me to my next point. I have been doing some extensive research behind our powers and I have reason to believe that there may be more like us. There is no evidence to suggest this, but there may as well be hundreds if not thousands like us who have kept a very low profile. Just be careful what you do out there.

And that bring me to my final point, dear brother. If you are reading this, then you are the most clever, strong willed and caring person I know. If our real parents could see you now, they would be so proud of their little Jason. It pained me deeply to have to use you to get what I wanted. If you are reading this, then you won. Fair and square. It is for that reason that I am giving you a parting gift.

I know much you hate school and you probably have a ton of work to catch up on. School is a waste of time, it does not teach you any important life skills. You could easily teach yourself half the stuff. So I decided that it is time for the next phase of your life. You do not have to follow in my footsteps. In fact you get to decide your own future. No school, no parents, no older brother, just you. I need you to become the greatest person to have ever lived on this planet. And for that, you need a little head start. Which is why I have put my entire inheritance under your name. It is a lot of money and it will help you to decide what you want in life. I know that whatever you do, it will involve saving the lives of millions, helping the needy, whatever. I want you to pursue your dreams. Do whatever you want in life.

The exact amount of money is written overleaf.

Your Sincerely,

Julian

A tear splashed onto the page, smudging the ink and before I could react any further, a vast urge pulled me to the next page and here it was. My entire future depended on this next number.

Holy sh-

Printed in Great Britain
by Amazon